TO GUARD A SOUL

Dani Avelle

CONTENTS

DEDICATION

For David, who believes in my dreams even when I get lost along the way.

NOTE TO READERS

Specific scenes may be triggering for some readers:

A character tells a short story that includes a brief mention of rape. Brief mention of a character in the past dying from suicide. One scene that readers with emetophobia may find uncomfortable.

GLOSSARY

Celestia: planet in the Realm of Lights

Channels: angelic term for the path travelled between realms and between the Retreats and Zircon

Gehenna: planet in the Realm of Shadows

Realm of Bones: home of the humans

Realm of Hallows: home of the three Fates and the realm where souls are created before being distributed to the other realms

Realm of Lights: home of the angels

Realm of Shadows: home of the devils

Retreats: located in the Realm of Bones but not visible to humans, where angels choose and prepare for Assignments

Zircon: planet in the Realm of Bones; the angelic/devil term for "earth"

1

LUCIE

I have been alive for one-hundred-and-eleven years. But August 1st will be my first day on Earth—or, as we angels call it, Zircon.

"Assignments begin in 90 days," I moan, curling my head into my hands. Surrounding me are anatomy designs and sketches and textbooks, the table a landscape of meticulously organized chaos. I'm working on my final project before Dekucation graduation—which is an even closer 59 days away. My head is filled with numbers and the imaginary sounds of clocks ticking the time away, dooming me to failure. I've never managed stress well, and these last months prior to graduation have been the most stressful few months of my entire life thus far.

Someone yanks on my long blonde ponytail, lifting my head from my hands, and my blue eyes meet familiar green ones.

"You said that wrong," chides Dayva, my best friend for nearly all 111 years of my life. She was Cast four months after me, and our parents lived next door to each other, so we grew up practically attached at the wing bones. "It's supposed to be said with excitement! exclamation! joy! Not like you're preparing for a funeral."

Of course she would say that. Although we are best friends in every sense of the term, we are not at all similar. She is fiery and daring, the antithesis of my calculated, studious self. We are the embodiment of the classic "opposites attract" cliche, and graduation prep is highlighting our personality differences more than ever.

Dayva plops herself down on the cushioned bench beside me and surveys the full table. "You are way further ahead on your grad project than I am, so I don't know why you're stressing so much—the Magisters are going to pass you with flying colours. Plus, you've always been top of your class—you're going to be an ace Guardian angel."

I sigh, not ready to give up my dramatics just yet. "I need another century before I'll feel ready," I argue.

Dayva crosses her arms and rolls her eyes at me for what is probably the ten billionth time in our lives. "The best way to learn is by doing. We prepare as much as we can here on Celestia, and then we keep learning when we go to Zircon. There's only so much you can learn from reading texts or peeking through Channels before we have to just experience it for ourselves."

I narrow my eyes at her, my heart hurting a little knowing that I only have 90 more days to see her as she is now, the way I've known her my whole life. She has beautiful red hair that is smooth and glossy, perfect for flipping behind her shoulder with the attitude she always carries. Like all angels, her skin is flawless, a perfect canvas for the dramatic freckles laid upon her skin like the constellations of our ancestors. She's beautiful, but that generality is hardly worth mentioning; I'm not bragging when I say that we all are. As angelic beings, we are always Cast as perfection in body, so there's not an angel in existence that wouldn't bring any human to their knees in awe of their beauty—which is why we can't show up on Zircon in these heavenly bodies.

Instead, we Guardian angels spend time during our final years of Dekucation in the Realm of Lights creating Forms that our souls can inhabit on Zircon, which is in the human realm—also known as the Realm of Bones. We learn to mold Zircon components and create a library of 70 Forms, from which we can choose to transfer our souls into for each human Assignment we take on as a Guardian angel. These Forms must run the gamut of race, size, and age—and be the perfect culmination of forgettable and ordinary.

Dayva might say she's further behind on the project than me, but she's only saying that in an attempt to lift my spirits. I've seen Dayva work as hard on her collection of Forms as I have. I'm proud of both of our efforts, though it's emotional to know that the version of Dayva I've loved for so long will never exist again. Next time she inhabits her Cast body, she'll have the same features as now, but aged 777 years from now. She'll find herself both familiar and unfamiliar with the heavenly body she returns to, having Departed as a young adult of 111 years old and Returned a middle-aged 888. Of course, the same goes for me, but a part of me fears I'm going to fail as a Guardian angel of Zircon, and that I'll get pulled after my first few Assignments so I'll Return without having changed much. That doesn't occur often—one or two Guardians every graduating class of thousands—but still. It could happen.

I tilt my head back and stare at the ceiling to avoid looking at her anymore, too saddened by the thought of all the change I have no control over. I have worked so hard to succeed, limiting distractions and spending all of my time preparing for my Departure to Zircon, thriving in this environment that has no surprises. Every morning, I wake up and I know what the day will look like down to the minute, and though I've spent my life preparing for the many varied lives I will experience in a new realm, I can't help but wonder if I'm incapable of success anywhere but here. Where everything is always the same.

"Come on, Lucie," says Dayva, pushing up from her chair. "Let's go get some food. You've been working on this all day, and you need to fuel for productivity. Like you said, we only have 90 days left, and then we won't see most of our friends for, potentially, centuries. Part of preparing to graduate isn't just getting ready for Assignments—it's being present in your life here and preparing to say goodbye."

She's standing over me again now, her serious face blocking my view of the ceiling. "That sounded awfully philosophical for your lackadaisical brand," I say, raising an eyebrow.

Her serious expression breaks into a mischievous one, and she leans past me to grab one of the open textbooks from the table. "That's 'cause they aren't my words—they're Mikah's," she says with a smirk. I look down to see the text in her hand and sure enough—not her words, but Mikah's, the original father of angels who had set the foundation for all the work that angels do to this day.

I grab the book from her and slide it back on the table as I rise. "Right. I should know by now that if you ever wax poetic like that, something is wrong."

She winks before spinning and taking off in a sprint, running for the ledge of The Compository. There are no outer walls on any of the public buildings, giving us unfettered access to fly in to any place at any time. Plus, we don't have weather like on Zircon; the days are always perfect and clear, the skies always painted in vivid blue and purple hues, the air always warm.

"Last one to The Pearl!" It is an intentionally unfinished colloquialism, a compromise between us as children—I am a perfectionist, but I hate competition, and I would throw a fit every time she would say "last one's a rotten unicorn!" or any variation of the insult, since I always lost and never wanted to be a rotten anything. (Okay, it's possible I am competitive and just a sore loser. Regardless, I've made it a point to only ever compete with myself to do better, be better.) So instead, Dayva started finishing the sentence before it ended, a kind of truce that satisfied both our souls.

I watch her disappear over the ledge as I follow in a more restrained fashion behind her, stepping out into the sky as she swoops and swirls below me, her burnished red wings sparkling in the sharp sunlight. I pull my wings from my back as I fall and relish the rush of wind that combs through their golden feathers as I join her, my heart once again saddened, this time by the reminder of my wings' confinement to the Realm of Lights—which means only a very short 60 days of flight remain.

***

We land together on The Pearl's encircling patio, the gleaming white stone warm beneath our bare feet. I look down at my toes, at the jewelry adorning them, and try not to deflate from the knowledge I'll have to wear shoes pretty much all the time when I'm in the Realm of Bones. I'll have to wear all kinds of things I won't want to, and I feel claustrophobic thinking about the undergarments and layers that will be required. In the Realm of Lights, we wear very little, for while we have the same outward structure as humans, our Cast bodies are definitively not human in how they experience a physical world. For one thing, our heavenly bodies experience pain to a much lesser degree than our Forms will on Zircon. We also don't know what it means to be cold—there's no such thing as any temperature that isn't on a scale from warm to hot here. As such, we don't use blankets, which humans seemed to be obsessed with. Simple silk rompers are all that anyone wears—when they choose to. Some angels, usually the older ones, prefer to forgo all garments as they near Luminescence, wanting to be as free as possible before they give up their souls and their energies become Luminaries—the stars that shine and guide above all the realms. We also don't put hats on our heads or tinted glasses on our eyes to shade our vision from the two burning suns, as we are always surrounded by light, even exuding a shimmering light ourselves.

"Hey! How are your final projects coming along?"

The question pulls me from my toe adornment mourning, and I looked up to see Crescent and Saffi strolling toward us, both of them with shimmering silver wings stretching from their backs. Some angels like to keep their wings out at all times, and since everything in our realm is built for angelic beings, they rarely get in the way. Dayva and I have always preferred to tuck ours back into ourselves when not flying, because both of us love the rush of falling before pulling them out. Plus, it's always magical to watch the transformation from beautiful to ethereal that happens when an angel unfurls their wings.

I tuck mine away now, shrugging in response to Saffi's question. "It's coming, I guess. I'm struggling with the older Forms, though," I admit. "I don't think I'll ever want to start out at 80 human years old, you know?"

Saffi shudders, her white-blonde hair shining in waves over her collarbones. "Right? I'm spending most of my time perfecting the details on my 16 to 50 Forms and accepting a lowered grade for mediocre elders—if I'm not going to use them, why bother investing time into them?"

I frown, seeing her point but not able to reconcile the idea for myself, needing to always give perfection in any project I take on. Dayva sees my face and laughs, a knowing glint in her eye, then tugs on my hand to lead me into The Pearl. "You guys eating?" she asks over her shoulder to the pair as we step closer to the heavenly scent of carbs.

"We just did," replies Crescent. Her hair is close to the same colour as Saffi's, but cut into a chic chin-length bob that she tucks behind her ears. "We're off to play some wingball now. Catch you guys later!"

With a wave goodbye, they gracefully lift their wings, their silver feathers shimmering as they step off the ledge we'd just landed on. I return the wave before lurching after Dayva as she drags me toward the centre of The Pearl, where dozens of buffets await. My mouth waters at the scent—tonight's theme is red, and everything on offer smells or tastes or looks of the colour. Much of our food is reminiscent of what's available on Zircon, but like everything on Celestia, it's more vibrant, flavourful, and aesthetic than in the Realm of Bones.

"Let's go sit with Ellis and Lysander," Dayva suggests as we fill our plates, nodding her head to a table situated beside the Eternal Falls on one side of the university dining hall. I grab two—okay, three—chocolate-covered strawberries to finish filling my plate before following her through the maze of tables to Ellis and Lysander, whose plates hold only traces of sauce from their own meals.

They look up as we approach, their chiselled features softening in smiles.

"I can see the headlines now: 'Lucie Emerges from The Compository.' We were beginning to suspect someone glued you to the chair in there. We haven't seen you anywhere else in days," comments Ellis, scooching down the bench to make room for Dayva. She snuggles up beside him and gives him a peck on his high cheekbone, and I can't miss the sparkle that lights up in his eyes.

I barely stop myself from sighing. Dayva knows I don't approve of her leading the poor boy on for the past thirty-plus years. He's convinced they're falling in love, but she's kept him on the ropes, leaning into his affection and then breaking away from it to find her entertainment elsewhere, before circling back again. She says she loves living a wandering existence, and that Ellis knows this—but to me, it's evident his soul doesn't quite agree with hers on this matter.

Lysander and I, though, have never been more than passing friends—mostly in each other's orbit because of Ellis and Dayva's on-again, off-again relationship. So when he moves over to let me slide in beside him, I smile in thanks but keep my lips to myself. He's nice, and I've no reason to believe he thinks any differently of me, but there are certainly no sparks. And even if there had been, I wouldn't have allowed those sparks to catch fire. I can't afford distractions to my studies or my pursuit of a position on the High Council one day.

The angels appointed as High Magisters are the most knowledgeable teachers in the realm, the ones who make governing decisions and help maintain the balance of the realms.

Mikah, the founding father Dayva quoted to me at The Compository earlier, had been one of the original High Magisters, which shows how esteemed the positions are. Very few angels ever reach that status, but I've dreamt about it since I was old enough to understand the various angelic positions.

I turn my attention to Ellis and his quip about my work ethic. "I just want to make sure my Forms are perfect."

Lysander chuckles beside me. "Did you forget how the point is literally to make sure they aren't?"

I elbow him. "You know what I mean. Perfectly imperfect, then."

"Are you guys almost done creating your Forms?" Dayva asks around a mouthful of lasagna.

Ellis swings a toned arm across the seat behind her. "I finished weeks ago. Zander, however...dude hasn't even started."

I choke on a strawberry, requiring a few pats on the back from Lysander. When I can breathe again, I turn to him in astonishment. "What does he mean, you haven't even started?" I demand.

Lysander shrugs, pulling his long caramel hair into a ponytail, and I duck to avoid being hit with his elbow as he wraps a ribbon around it. "I've got the bases, obviously, from building over the last few decades, and I've got a bunch of components, but I haven't gotten around to the actual Form assembly yet."

"You do realize we begin Zircon Assignments in 90 days? Which means we graduate in 59 and Depart Celestia in 60. And your Forms have to be submitted for grading in 39. How are you not panicking?" My stress builds at the thought of being in his situation. It has happened before, where an unprepared or lazy Guardian went to Zircon with only a handful of Forms. It wasn't such a big deal in the Ancient Days before they developed cameras. But in the last few centamillenium, with digital images as prolific as they are, we can't get away with recycling the same Forms. Humans are simply too likely to identify us as our own doppelgangers across both centuries and geography. In fact, the High Council won't permit Departures for Guardians with less than two dozen Forms, and it's rumoured that number could rise to a minimum 40. Each Guardian should, ideally, have the maximum number allowed: 70. The overachiever I am, I'm working on 100, even though I'll have to leave so many behind. I realize I'm adding more stress than required, but I want to choose my best ones and not settle with some "good enough" Forms.

Lysander worries his bottom lip. "When you point out the numbers like that—59, 39—it does sound close, doesn't it?"

Dayva, Ellis, and I just look at him pointedly. "Do you want to end up repeating the last decade?" The question comes from Dayva, mumbled around another mouthful of lasagna, and I switch my gaze to roll my eyes at her. "Gross."

Lysander looks a little green around the edges, if such a thing can happen to angels.

"Remember the last cad we learned about who had to re-do Dek 10?" Dayva continues, finally swallowing before obnoxiously opening her mouth in my direction to show me it's empty. "That guy was so ashamed, he ended up jumping a Channel two years in. RIP." She puts a hand to her forehead in mock salute, but I shiver. If you jump a Channel without your halo, which you only receive when you graduate Dek, you could end up lost in the haze between realms or find yourself in the Realm of Bones as a mortal, with no way to ever return to the Realm of Lights. You would live and die a human, in a human lifespan. It hasn't happened in any recent millennium, but it sounds horrible.

Ellis mirrors my shiver and pulls Dayva in a little closer. Lysander betrays his growing nervousness by squirming beside me. "39 days? You're sure?" he asks, turning to me.

I nod, and Dayva, mouth full once again, backs me up. "This is Lucie we're talking about—she always knows her deadlines."

"I think I'm going to go work on a few things..."

I stand to allow the suddenly stressed Lysander to slide past me, the trio of us remaining exchanging smirks at his hustled beeline to The Compository where us Dek 10s have spent most of the past few years with our heads in books and digital platforms learning the final lessons of our century-long education. As far as Dekucation goes, Dek 10, despite being stressful, has been one of my favourites. Building Forms for sure surpasses Dek 3, where we learn about the history of all four Realms of Almega—of Hallows, Lights, Bones, and Shadows, and how the universe requires a balance of opposites to exist, light to shadow being one of them. From the oldest realm, the Realm of Hallows, the three Fates create souls and appoint them to humans, angels, or devils, the latter of whom bring chaos to the human realm that angels strive to counteract.

I slide back into the booth as Ellis says, "Before you guys showed up, we were talking about what the chances are of finding siblings on Zircon. Lysander knows a Guardian who Returned last year who found her sister during her first Assignment. They even took on a few parallel Assignments together. So it is possible."

Dayva sighs, slumping back into the soft booth. "You're so lucky that your brother is an Intermediary at the same Retreat you're going to," she says to Ellis. "You'll get to see him all the time."

I take a long sip of warm, sweet pomegranate juice, distracted for a moment by wondering what it will feel like to drink something cold on Zircon before registering what Dayva said. "Your brother's an Intermediary?" I ask Ellis, setting the now-empty glass back on the table. "I knew he was stationed at our Retreat, but not that he was an Intermediary." Intermediaries work closely with Guardians to set up identities and integrate Guardians into their new life in the month before each Assignment begins. They also escort the Guardians through the Channels to and from the Retreat for each Assignment. Each Intermediary has around 100 Guardians under their watch, usually centred around specific geographic areas for efficiency, although they continue to Overlook Guardians when they move as necessitated by their Assignment's geographical movements.

He nods, an eager smile stretching across his youthful features. He's always looked younger than the rest of us, something we often tease him for, but which he says will benefit him when we Return. (Annoyingly, he's probably right.) "Yep. He's been there, oh, 75 or so years now? It's going to be such a trip to see him there."

"That's cool. You should take an Assignment where he Overlooks you," I say.

"It's dumb that the High Magisters make it difficult to find or connect with other Guardians when on Zircon," interrupts Dayva, a sour tone lacing her words. "At least for family. I miss Cato so much. It's only been 25 years, but it's so sad to think about the possibility I won't see him again until we Return."

My soul does a funny little dance at the mention of Cato, and I hasten to school my features and ensure my face remains neutral, unwilling to reveal the ridiculous torch I've carried for my best friend's brother for nearly a century.

Being 25 years Dayva's senior, Cato had already moved out of his parents' place by the time Dayva and I were Cast. Despite the age difference, he had fostered a close relationship with his little sister, which meant he'd had to put up with her best friend, too, since Dayva and I were rarely found without the other within wings' length.

I haven't seen him since he Departed, of course, and for the most part, I've managed to tuck my thoughts of him away, filing him as a distraction that I not only don't want but would also never amount to anything. I will always be firmly planted in his "little sister's best friend" category, which is why I've never breathed a word of my crush to anyone. Not even Dayva, who knows everything else about me—likely even better than I do. It's the only thing I've ever hidden from her, and I swallow the wave of guilt that always washes through me when I think about it.

Ellis nods, the movement yanking me back from my futile pining over Dayva's brother. "It seems arbitrary to me, too," he says. "In my opinion, it could be very helpful to be informed on where our close friends or family members are situated. We could choose Assignments nearby and have them mentor us in the beginning. But, like I said—there's always a chance you find Cato."

"Lucky your only 'sibling' is me," Dayva jokes, her attention back to me, "and we can at least choose our first Assignments together. But if I were in charge around here, this is the kind of change I'd make. Lucie, make a note of that for when you become a High Magister, will you?" She pushes back her plate and crosses her arms over her chest. "We're going to call up the Fates and demand they hear all these amazing ideas of mine when we Return."

I smirk. "I like how you think you'll get to have any power by me becoming a High Magister, when I expect I'll be too busy to even take any appointments with you." Tossing my ponytail over my shoulder, I tease her with a haughty expression.

She responds by flipping her middle finger at me—a gesture that crosses all realms. "Your soul can't live without mine, dear sister, so good luck with that." She winks, and I wave her off, though my soul tightens in panic at the thought of losing her. While technically my soul can exist in the absence of hers, it would break me if either of us ever tried to sever our friendship. Every soul has multiple soulmates with varying levels of connection, and our two souls connect on one of the deepest attachment levels. I will do anything for Dayva, and I know it's a reciprocated devotion.

Ellis pulls her in close. I'm certain they're also soulmates by how they're always drawn back together, though I can't quite discern to what level. "I'm sure you'll both be an appropriate menace to the High Council and the Fates and shake things up around here," he says, kissing her cheek. As Dayva's body begins to melt into his embrace, I decide it's my cue to exit. I slide out of the booth and grab my plate. "Well, I should get back to work. Those Forms won't build themselves."

"No, Lucie—" Dayva moves to grab my arm as I retreat but I dodge her grip and wave goodbye instead, leaving the two of them behind, along with the stems of my strawberries and the inappropriate thoughts of my best friend's brother. Tracing the same path to The Compository as Lysander, I return to the safety of my Dek 10 table, where the success or failure of my future dreams and goals will in part be determined by the perfection (or imperfection) of the Forms that are due in a mere 39 days.

2

LUCIE

59 DAYS LATER

I can't breathe. My body feels stifled under the floor-length silk gown, and in this moment, I would swear to the Fates that I must absorb oxygen not through my lungs but directly through my skin, causing me to suffocate to an early Luminescence from the silk wrapped around me.

"Sit still," Dayva hisses in my ear. Her face is steeled in a practiced expression of calm, belying the annoyance in her whisper. "You're going to get us in trouble."

Despite myself, I huff—as if I'd ever been the instigator of trouble. That title belongs solely to Dayva. "I can't breathe," I whisper back. "If we don't wear this much fabric normally, why do they force us into these cloth abominations for graduation?" I swallow, the high-neck style of the ice-blue gown tightening around my neck like a noose with every breath. I make a mental note to avoid all choker styles on Zircon, where

I'll experience physical discomfort and pain to a much higher degree. Just the thought of having to wear shirts and bras every day makes my soul squirm.

If I'm being honest, though, I know I can't blame all of this panic on the silk of my dress. I'm panicking because of what this ceremony represents—the end of Dekucation and the beginning of my pursuit of a future seat on the High Council. Every action and reaction on Zircon will be weighed against my bid to become a High Magister. One wrong decision could destroy my chances, so every move I make has to be considered against those consequences.

Dayva pinches my hip as a warning just before the High Council walk by us on their way to the centre of the stage, where they will crown us with the halos of graduates. I muster every ounce of willpower I can find to stand statuesque with my wings at attention as the ceremony begins and the High Magisters recognize the names of the graduates. I should pay attention, respect the work of my fellow graduates, but all I can do is envision myself in the esteemed position of High Magister, anointing halos to graduates some thousand years in the future.

I shiver, not from a cold I've never known, but from a tangled mix of excitement and trepidation.

***

Hours later, the graduating class tosses their halos into the air amidst ear-splitting whistles and cheers. The sparkling silver crowns sound like the chimes humans hang in the wind as they clash in the air, each size ringing a distinctive melodious note.

Despite the chaos of them all being tossed up at once, they each descend in a direct line back to their graduate. Each halo is tied eternally to one angel, created from our Casts and then stored for over a century as the minerals grow to form our halos. Once bestowed upon us, they become an inseparable part of us in every realm. They grant us access to travel the Channels, but they also bind us to each human we Assign ourselves to Guard until their expirations. Usually, Guardians wear them as tattoos on their Realm of Bones Forms, but prior to humanity's obsession with tattoos, Guardians bore them on their Forms through what the humans call "birth marks." In Celestia, angels wear them as crowns or keep them in a display case when in their homes, as they can withstand being placed a few metres from their angel when in the Realm of Lights.

I'm caught up in the celebration as the halos tumble around us, each gently falling back to their angel. Not one angel in our class failed to graduate as a Guardian or Intermediary—not even Lysander, who had taken heed of my reality check two months prior and had spent every spare moment since grinding out an acceptable portfolio of Forms.

Dayva snags her halo from its descent toward her and places it reverently atop her intricate red braids, then leans forward to envelop me in a hug.

"We've got this, Lucie," she says, her voice strong and encouraging in my ear. I squeeze her, appreciating that she knows the emotions of my soul so well without my having to say a word. "Tomorrow, we start the greatest adventure of our lives: we'll jump the Channels and be the best Guardians Zircon has ever seen. This is not scary—this is liberating!" By the end of her speech, she is crowing, leaning back and tossing her halo into the sky again. Her green eyes glitter with fierce determination, and I let her confidence wash through me, gripping to her words and her hand as I nod.

"Let's par-tay!" The holler comes from Ellis, who's elbowing his way toward us through the crowd of thousands of similarly blue-frocked graduates. Various neckline styles accommodate each angel's style preferences, and I berate myself for not choosing something more open and less choking. I never wear clothing with high necks, and I can't remember why I thought graduation was the time to start. Likely some flimsy, waxy poetic reason such as "a new style to represent starting a new chapter of life."

Ellis reaches us and wraps his arms around Dayva's waist before lifting and spinning her, the circumference of the swing causing her to accidentally kick a few others, but no one seems to care. He smashes his face into hers, and she cups his cheeks as she responds in earnest to his kiss. Clearly, one last night of Celestial bliss awaits them. I'm glad, at least, that she is "on" with Ellis for our last night here. He'd sworn to find an Assignment near her, despite her warnings that all bets will be off when we reach the Realm of Bones. She says she wants to be free to write her stories there with no remaining romantic strings to encumber her. But for tonight, the pain of the future is tomorrow's problem, the joy of the present the only thing that matters. I look around and see couples, throuples, others grabbing for each other, winging away to the skies, and know the night will be full of sex and drink, final hurrahs in perfect bodies with perfect wings.

No one reaches out for me in that way. I've had various entanglements over the past century, though nothing ever amounted to more than a fun romp on a bed a time or few. I've remained focussed on my goals, and my studious nature had me curled up at home with textbooks on nights when

Dayva collided with the "night" life and enjoyed the varied flavours of angelic anatomy. (That's another thing I am curious about—the dark. It's never dark here, only shades of light and lighter, and I wonder what it will be like to experience complete darkness for the first time on Zircon).

Tonight won't differ from most nights. I'll go home to my quiet hideaway one more time, a now nearly empty room that will soon house a young Dek 1 student for the duration of their century-long studies. I'll stare at the ceiling alone until finally sleep takes me—if it takes me—and tomorrow, I'll say goodbye to my parents and join the rest of my graduating class of Guardians and Intermediaries as we jump the Channels to our new lives. I won't Return to the Realm of Lights or my home planet of Celestia until I've completed my 777-year chapter on Zircon.

"Are you coming to Evermore?" I break from my reverie and find Crescent touching my elbow as she inquires about whether I'll be attending the graduating party being held in the city's fanciest club.

"I might head home instead," I hedge. "I think it will make me more sad to go out and partake in an extended goodbye with everyone. Not saying goodbye is just easier."

Crescent nods, understanding in her eyes. She and I are not dissimilar in our studious, independent natures. She pulls me in for a quick hug, and I embrace her in return, careful to avoid touching her wings—it's an erotic place for most angels, which is another reason I like to keep mine tucked away unless in use, as I hate accidental brushes. I've never actually had them out during sex, either, as it's part of how I've kept things casual with sexual partners. According to Dayva (or almost any other angel), I am missing out "big-time," but I figure it's just one more thing to miss when I take my wingless Zircon Forms. I have enough to be stressed about without adding the loss of a sexual pleasure I can't recreate outside the Realm of Lights.

"I'll see you in 777 years, then," Crescent says when she lets me go, and I nod, giving her a sad smile. As new grads, we'll spend our first month in the Realm of Bones at one of sixty Retreats, where we'll pick our first Assignments and get situated. Dayva and I are assigned to the same one, along with Saffi and Ellis. Lysander and Crescent are headed to a different one. Sometimes angels can be transferred between Retreats, either by request or as human population densities vary between regions, but it's not common. So in all likelihood, I won't run into Crescent until we Return.

"May the Fates be kind," I say as she turns away, and then I push off my toes skyward, releasing my gold wings as I do.

Usually, flying makes me feel light as a feather—yes, pun intended—but my wings weigh on my back tonight, as though burdened by the knowledge they're about to be left behind. But I force them to move, to push me higher and higher, until I'm taking in the striking view of Celestia that sparkles with life below me. I memorize the sight and let myself sink into the depth of complicated emotions tumbling around me. Then I flip over so I'm flying wing-side down, relishing the heat of Celestia's two suns across my chest and the caress of the warm wind against my skin. I take in the stars that sparkle through the bright blue-and-purple-hued sky, comforted with knowing that at least in the realms of both Lights and Bones, the star-stricken skies reflect the same constellations, angelic ancestors offering guidance to those who seek it.

Someday, I'll become a Luminary too, joining my energy to theirs for eternity. But first, I have a lot of lives to live.

3

LUCIE

I squeeze Dayva's hand, my heart hammering in my throat as I stare at the enormous opaque doorway of the Channel before us. Having said my goodbyes to my parents that morning, I don't search for them in the sea of thousands of angels come to watch our graduating class make their jumps to Zircon, though they are somewhere in the stands around or the skies above. I'm looking ahead now, and only ahead, I remind myself as I take a deep breath of my home realm's pure air.

This is what I've been preparing for my whole life, and the thrum of excitement is finally louder than the drum of stress.

Transparent Sighting Channels exist throughout the Realm of Lights, where angels can catch glimpses into the Realm of Bones. Parents use it to keep updated on their children, Magisters of all levels use it to demonstrate lessons, and sometimes we use them purely for entertainment. But these Channels are strictly for viewing purposes, incapable of transporting angels between realms. And they are small—no larger than an average textbook.

But the six Channels that loom before us in each corner of the hexagonal Amphitheatre allow travel between the angelic realm and the human one. We'll spend our first month situated at a Retreat, picking our Assignments and making arrangements for it with our Intermediaries. We'll also Return to our designated Retreat after completion or closure of an Assignment, where we will have another month to arrange another Assignment. It's a cycle we will repeat until we reached our 777th year on Zircon, at which time we'll go through another Channel ceremony just like this—but in reverse, when we'll come home to Celestia to celebrations that vibrate through our entire realm. Even home-body me can't resist the parties that ensue when a class Returns each year—they are that epic.

Each Amphitheatre Channel is a dozen feet wide and twice as high, and angels step through in groups of five, grasping each other's hands as anchors, not wanting to get lost in between. Each group has either a Magister who goes back and forth throughout the ceremony to escort Guardians through the Channels, or an Intermediary graduate who has practiced navigating simulation Channels that replicate the environment of the haze between realms (as they can't jump actual Channels until they have their halos). And although I trust the Intermediary graduate in our line to get us to Zircon, a pinprick of fear sparks in my soul that he'll lose his way and we'll spend eternity in the haze. With only a half-dozen historical instances of angels getting lost in the haze, it's not likely to happen, but still. No one knows what became of them, since they have never Arrived or Returned, and the mystery of it makes my soul uneasy.

Saffi grabs my other hand; Ellis attaches to Dayva's free hand, and Saffi also clutches the hand of the Intermediary graduate, an angel I'm not very familiar with and, in the moment of adrenaline, can't recall a name for. We all exchange looks of excitement with each step that brings us closer to our Channel, not daring to breathe a word and break the intense silence that cloaks the Amphitheatre—not by rule or regulation, but as a natural result of nervous anticipation from graduates and reverent observation by everyone else.

Six lines remain in front of us.

Five.

Four.

I attempt to steady my breathing as I watch the number of heads before us dwindle. Familiar heads, of friends and acquaintances I've spent a century with, all of them vanishing into the milky white haze of the Channel as if they've never been.

Three.

Two.

We step up on the cerulean blue carpet as one and turn our heads to the Channelkeeper. We wait with bated breath for their signal.

And then we jump.

Or rather, we step forward, the "jumping" part of crossing a Channel a bit of a misnomer.

I watch my leg disappear into the pearlescent, swirling mist as I take a step. But as soon as my face enters the haze, I'm disoriented. Consumed by the white mist, I'm unsure if my eyes are seeing the colour or if they simply aren't working, as I can see nothing—not Dayva, not Saffi, though I know they're with me, as they're squeezing my hands as fiercely as I'm squeezing theirs.

The very air around me seems to breathe as it moves against my skin. I suppose it's like we're falling, but not in the chaotic way of stepping off a building before you unfurl your wings. No, this is a strange, syrupy-slow fall of control. There's no pressure against my feet or any other part of my body to orient me to directions, so I can't distinguish up from down, anchored only to the angels beside me.

I try not to think of what it would be like to get lost for eternity in the white nothingness and attempt to find appreciation in the experience, of being present during my first jump—though I send a thought of thankfulness to the Fates for Casting me as a Guardian and not an Intermediary destined to spend so much more time travelling the Channels.

The haze is utterly silent, which adds to the unsettling aura of blindness—and yet at the edges of consciousness, it's almost as if I'm can hear the echo of voices, like a distant memory. I strain to hear more, to pull a thread of sound from the periphery, but the silence between is too thick and heavy to grasp anything more than the faint awareness. It's hard to describe how it is both silent and yet not, and I begin to panic at not being in control of a situation I can't understand.

A gentle pressure rises against our feet, landing us from the fall, and the distraction of the sensation pulls me from the chaos tumbling around in my soul before the panic can grow roots.

Then, together, we enter the Realm of Bones.

***

I mentioned how Return Ceremonies are a party, right? It seems in a century of Dekucation, no one had bothered to inform us about Arrival Ceremony parties.

The moment we enter the Realm of Bones, we are assaulted by unfamiliar sounds and colours and scents. It's enough to give a body whiplash after the intense silence of the Departure Ceremony and utter stillness of the jump. We've travelled right into the thick of a boisterous celebration dedicated to our welcome.

But I don't have time to comprehend or adjust to my new surroundings before a woman with glossy dark skin appears in front of us in a bright yellow dress. "Line 87, you're with me!" she shouts over the cacophony with a giant smile that pushes up apple cheeks and reveals quaint lines around her eyes. I don't react, can't react, finding myself struck still as I assess her. While I'd built Forms, this was the first one I'd seen inhabited by a soul that wasn't through the distance of a Sighting Channel, and I am mesmerized by the details that make the Form so wholly human. She waves her arm through the air. "Follow me!"

Still holding hands, the five of us turn to follow and I startle at the sight of light strawberry hair in front of me. Gone is Dayva's fiery red hair; in its place, a pale version beginning to frizz, bearing none of the sleek gloss her hair had shone with only seconds ago. And she is short—a good six inches shorter than her angelic body.

We all seem to realize and remember simultaneously that we all now look different, having jumped into our first Forms—our Retreat Forms, the ones we will always take the moment we enter Retreat premises. Dayva yanks on Ellis' arm to turn him and then whirls to me, and Saffi pulls the Intermediary up as we all gape at each other.

"Come on, come on," the yellow-dress woman calls from an open door a few metres away.

We stumble after her, our heads turning on fascinated swivels as we seek our classmates, for familiar faces we know we won't find. Leaving behind the chaos of the main Channel room to another grand, open room where the sound of music is muted, we find various other angels gathered in the space. It seems each line of graduates that travelled through the Channel together has a specific angel from the Retreat assigned to them, as each of the groups of five has a person dressed in yellow in some fashion talking to them.

"Welcome to Zircon!" The woman who had dragged us here beams again. We instinctively form a semi-circle around her, but none of us drop each other's hands yet, still seeking the comfort of familiar souls through our touch. "I'm Idele," she says by way of introduction. "I'm an Intermediary, and it's my job to get you situated with the basics. Then you can head back to the party or do some exploring—whatever you want! The party will go all night, so there's no rush to hurry back—though you can, of course, I certainly want to get back as soon as possible—there's no party like an Arrival party!—except, of course, a Return party—" the words tumble out of Idele's rosy lips (from lipstick, I note, not naturally that flush like they would have been in Celestia), and I blink hard at her, trying to focus on everything she is saying and not on the strange Zircon scents that reach me even inside the building—damp, earthen, green (known by the sample kits we'd studied), or the strange faces of everyone I'd known mere moments before.

"Every line is assigned a wing; you five will bunk with lines 80 to 89. We'll head to your wing now and grab your entry kits, then you can choose your rooms. So let's hurry before lines 88 and 89 get here so you still have some decent rooms to pick from!"

She takes off at a light jog down a wide hallway to our right, her tight curls bouncing against her shoulders as she hurries toward another door. Ellis, Dayva, Saffi, what's-his-name, and I hurry to follow, still glancing at each other in awe.

We finally let go of each other's hands as we inspect our own Forms. While we quick-step behind her, I bring my arms up to scrutinize some of the details come to life in the Retreat Form I'd worked so painstakingly on. I had created and placed each freckle on my arm; I'd wanted more than the scant few present on this Form, but after six months of making freckles for all my various Forms, I sacrificed a few in the name of sanity.

We are all wearing the silk rompers of different styles from our realm, but I notice how they hang a little more limply on our Zircon Forms than our perfect Celestial ones. We don't have the perfect curves and muscles the garments were designed for; they are tight in some places and hanging drab in others. I become conscious of the weight of my breasts, of the jiggle of my hips, of the tastebud bumps on my tongue, as I begin to mentally explore this new body.

After a minute or two of hustling to keep up with Idele (she is small but speedy!), we reach a large curved entrance that has the word "OCTO" painted in decorative script above it. A young man and an older woman sit a table to the side, chatting amicably as they watch the recent graduates mingle with other angels in the common area of the Octo wing. They look up when we approach and offer warm smiles to us much in the same way Idele had.

"Hi! Welcome to Octo." The greeting comes from the man, who has curly brown hair that tumbles down his wide forehead. A piercing curves around the centre of his bottom lip, which is much plumper than its thinner counterpart above. His yellow t-shirt stretches across his chest, and I wonder if he lost marks on this Form's grade for how perfectly muscular he looks. Thick black-rimmed glasses frame his deep brown eyes, giving him a sexy, nerdy visage. He catches my gaze and grins a little wider, as if noticing my assessing look, and I can feel my skin warming.

Dayva glances at me and her eyes widen, before she chokes on a chuckle she tries too hard to suppress. I don't know what she finds funny, but I glare at her, my skin cooling. I haven't looked in a reflection yet—

"Welcome to your new Retreat home," echoes the woman behind the table, interrupting my anxious spiral. I estimate her human Form age around 40. "I'm Chessa, and this is Arden."

"Arden?"

The question comes from Ellis. We all look at him, and I note that his Retreat Form looks far more mature than his Celestial body. I guess he didn't want to be teased about looking so young in this Realm, too.

Dayva grabs my arm and squeezes my bicep, and I realize why when Ellis steps forward and draws a startled Arden into a long hug. "Brother, it's so good to see you!"

"Ellis! No shit, it's really you?" He pushes him back, an arm's length from him, to survey his Form.

Ellis' face beams in delight. If we'd have been in the Realm of Lights, it literally would have been glowing. "Yeah, it's me," Ellis chokes out, not embarrassed that tears have risen to his eyes. Arden looks emotional too as he pulls him in to another bear hug.

I glance down at Dayva, a wide smile on her face as she watches the reunion, clearly happy for Ellis to be reunited with his brother. But I know the emotion she's hiding for his sake, a sadness in missing her own brother, and I remove my arm from her grip and wrap it around her shoulders to squeeze her to me instead. She knows that I know her soul in this moment. That familiar pang of guilt eats at me, knowing she isn't aware that I also feel some type of way about her brother, but I shove it down to refocus on the present.

Idele's clapping, the cheery smile having never wavered from her face. "How exciting is this? I'm so happy for you two! You'll have lots of time to catch up, I promise, but for now," she turns away from the reunion to face all of us, "we'll pass on your entry kits, which have a few basics to get you started, like hygienic products and simple clothing items based on your Retreat Form measurements. The shirts have your names on the front and back because, as I'm sure you've figured out by now, it gets pretty confusing when you suddenly can't recognize anyone. You'll also get a name plaque—go ahead and pick any of the rooms with empty plaque slots and slide yours in to claim your room. Each kit has a Tone as well, which you'll take with you when you head out on Assignments, updated with the most modern smart tech Zircon has to offer. Uploaded to the first screen are shortcuts to the Retreat app, where you can message any angel currently at the Retreat. Plus, it has schedules and general FAQ information and Retreat maps, because this place is a bit maze-like and it can take a minute to get your bearings."

"I'll fetch your kits so you can get settled and then head to the party," says Arden. "What are your names?" He backs up to an open doorway behind him as he asks, and Chessa leans forward from her chair at the table to mark our names on a transparent Tone screen in front of her.

"Dayva."

"Saffi."

"Oswin."

Right—Oswin! That's his name.

"Lucie," I say when Arden's gaze turns to me.

"Ellis, Dayva, Saffi, Oswin, Lucie," he repeats. "Nice to meet you all. I'll be right back." Then he turns and disappears into the room behind him.

"I've gotta go collect another line," says Idele as she jogs backward from our little group with a wave. "I have a few more to corral and then I'm drinking my weight in tequila! See you guys!"

We wave her off and then turn to see Arden emerging with five bright blue duffel bags slung over his arms, each with our names embroidered on them. He rounds the table to pass each one to us, though I avoid looking at him when he reaches me. But his hand brushes my forearm as he hands me my bag, and my body temperature rises again. Dayva giggles beside me. I turn to glare at her, but she ignores me as she nudges Saffi, who looks at me and starts smirking as well. I realize this time that it must have something to do with the warm flush I'm experiencing, and I rack my brain as I try to puzzle out what flaw I made in this Zircon Form.

"I'll find you guys at the party later," Arden says, mostly to Ellis as he claps him on the back once more.

We walk through the Octo archway, and as soon as we are out of earshot of Arden and Chessa, Saffi and Dayva burst into the giggles they'd barely contained earlier. Oswin and Ellis startle, looking between them, confused.

"What in the Fates are you giggling about?" I put my free hand on my hip, frowning. "Did I do something wrong with this Form? I haven't seen it yet, and you're scaring me."

Saffi grins wider, exposing two differently sized dimples. "Oh, no, not at all. You're great, the perfect girl-next-door simple in this Form. No errors to be found."

My eyes widen, and Dayva hurries to shake her head. "She means perfectly imperfect, very human. There's nothing overtly wrong."

I narrow my eyes at her, noting how her new strawberry curls are getting frizzier with every minute. "Those smiles threatening to break your new faces in half say otherwise."

"Hey, we should get rooms before the next line gets in," Ellis interrupts, motioning to the entrance we'd just left where Arden is already handing out another round of blue bags.

"We're coming back to this later," I warn the girls, just as Oswin darts away, saying, "There's one!" He slides his name into the placeholder of a door a few metres from us before opening it and disappearing inside. Saffi soon finds one as well, and then we discover two next to each other. Dayva denies Ellis' request to be neighbours, sliding her name plate into one of them and then grabbing mine and claiming the door beside it for me. He sighs, his long arms falling to his side in defeat as he leaves us to the pair of rooms in search of another close by.

"Didn't you have your last hurrah with him and then end things once and for all this morning?" I ask.

Dayva nods. "Yeah, and he said he would respect it, but that 'he'll be around for when I need some heavenly sex.'" She brings up her hands to form quotation marks in the air as she says the last part and rolls her eyes.

I snort. "Someone thinks highly of themselves."

She turns and watches his progress as he walks further down the hall, her face scrunching in thought. "I mean, the man does know how to use his tools..."

"Okay, okay, don't backslide day one, Dayva. That's not fair to him." I give her arm a light smack, and she turns her new hazel eyes back to me. "Says the one who kept turning into a chili pepper every time Arden looked at her," she challenges with a mischievous smirk.

I feel my skin become warm again. "Ok, what in the world keeps happening?" I push open the door of my bedroom, spy the mirror over the dresser and dart to it, tossing my bag on the bed as I pass it. Stopping short, I take in the first look of my first Zircon Form.

Her face is decidedly more red than I had made it, but the tint dissipates as I stare at her/me, and I realize that's what the warm feeling was. Dayva leans against the doorjamb to my room, not leaving to enter hers yet. "Yep. You turn red when you find someone attractive. That's going to be fun for everyone."

She laughs as I groan. "Everyone but me. How did this happen? I didn't program it to do that. And I sure as anything would have removed that option if I'd seen it."

Dayva shrugs, adjusting the duffel bag from where it's sliding down her shoulder. "Don't you remember that little section on Soul Peculiars? Some things about our personalities are just innate to our souls, and sometimes they are expressed in Zircon Forms in ways we can't adjust for. The veil between our souls and our bodies is thinner here."

I sigh. "Right. We both know how much I love surprises, so this is will be super fun for me, for sure. So I guess I'm going to turn red any time I find someone attractive? I'm not interested in Arden, by the way. He's just cute," I add in protest at her raised eyebrows. She laughs again at my dismay, disappearing around the doorframe as she heads to her own room.

It's going to be a long 777 years.

I close the door and turn back to the mirror, dropping my romper to reveal my naked Form. Running my hands over it, I judge its texture against how I envisioned it when I made it, mostly satisfied with the outcome, noting the cute little bellybutton piercing sparkling on my stomach that I forgot I'd added as a last touch. I cup my smooth breasts, curious at the way the nipples seem more sensitive than my Celestial ones, before I turn my back to the mirror and peer at my rounded ass, which also features a few freckles.

The tattoo across my shoulder blade draws my gaze up. I'm aware of my halo in the tattoo, almost like a soft heartbeat pulsing parallel to mine, and I wrap one arm across my chest and over my shoulder to touch my fingers to it. It feels no different from the skin—maybe just a degree warmer, but it's somehow comforting to see the dark ink depicting a stack of books. It assures me that despite the strange adjustment of settling into a new body, I am still Lucie, a Guardian angel from the Realm of Lights.

A knock at my door startles me. "Lucie, Dayva, you ready yet? Let's check this place out!" It's Saffi, and I call out "One minute!" as I turn to the duffel bag I'd slung on the bed. I zip it open and yank out the first t-shirt I see, along with a pair of jeans. I eye the bra, trying to decide if I can skip wearing it before deciding the jeans will be enough to get used to without adding the constriction of a bra. Besides—my cup size is small on my Retreat Form, so I figure I can get away with it.

I pull on the denim, grimacing at the snug pull around my hips but thankful for the wide-leg style, then pull the shirt over my head. I tie it in a knot under my breasts to make it a crop-top and add a little support for my boobs, then flip my head upside down and arrange my long brown hair into a messy topknot. After surveying the result in the mirror, I nod at my reflection, deeming it good enough. Eager to check out my new home base, I leave the makeup for another time, not interested in diving into anything more than these basics right now.

We soon discover that even with shirts that display our names emblazoned across the chest and back, it's a mental drain to keep memorizing new faces and trying to reconcile them with the people we'd known just hours prior. Speaking of mental drain—I've never felt mental fatigue like I'm feeling now, just an hour after arriving on Zircon. Magisters and Returnees had warned us that the weight of our bodies would take some getting used to with the added gravity of the realm and that our human brains would take time to adjust to the stimulation of connecting with our angelic souls, but learning about it isn't the same as experiencing it. I'm thankful to note that I'm not the only one feeling addled; even without our identifying shirts, it would have been easy to identify all the new arrivals by the dazed expressions we all share.

Saffi, Dayva, Ellis, and I (we didn't know where Oswin had gone, but none of us had been close with him in Celestia anyway), spend an hour wandering around, opting to find things through experience rather than by using the maps of the Retreat on our Tones. We use similar technology on Celestia, so it won't take long to become comfortable with the tech here, either. Dekamillenium ago, after technology began racing at breakneck speed on Zircon with artificial intelligence, the Fates had put the brakes on tech advancements, allowing very few improvements or upgrades to move forward since.

I tug at my jean waistband and resist every urge I have to throw off the pants—my legs have never felt so strangled. The collar of my t-shirt itches, and I squirm at the uncomfortable seams under my arms.

"You get used to the clothes, I promise."

I turn from where the four of us are standing at the entrance to a dining hall. We've seen this one three times and yet still haven't found our way back to the main Arrival party and are almost ready to admit defeat and pull up our maps.

Arden stands behind us, his hands in his pockets, looking comfortable (okay, looking hot) in his own jeans. I fight my soul's instinct to blush this time and win—just barely.

"I hope that happens sooner than later, because I'm ready to strip these clothes off right now," I say. I realize too late how that sounded, and I swear my soul crows in triumph as heat blazes across my face. Arden's widening grin at my discomfort doesn't help as I stammer, "I mean, I won't, obviously, but I could—but I wouldn't..."

Dayva has mercy on me and jumps in. "The clothes suck, but what really sucks is how we can't find our way around this maze without having to refer to the map. I can hear the party—why can't I get to it?" She crosses her arms in frustration, then frowns down at them; her Retreat Form has a far less ample bosom than her usual one. On Celestia, when she crossed her arms, they would push her already impressive breasts up to create cleavage that was difficult to tear your eyes from. In this body, her forearms didn't even touch her chest. She turns to me, hiss-whispering, "I think I made a grave mistake."

Her comments dampen my embarrassment, and I smirk as Arden says, "I was heading to the party myself; I'll take you guys there."

"Thanks," says Ellis, the only one of us to respond—Dayva distracted by her lack of cleavage, me too embarrassed to even try speaking again. Ellis moves forward to walk with him, but not before he leans in to whisper in Dayva's ear. It must be something flirty, I'm guessing to do with her boobs, because she rolls her eyes and gives him a little smack on the ass as he steps by. Saffi and I both shake our heads at her, and she raises her hands in mock defence before spinning to follow the brothers.

"So how do you like being an Intermediary?" Ellis asks Arden as we head back in the direction we'd just come from.

"It's pretty much what I expected," Arden says. "Dek prepares us well, so there aren't many surprises. I think the Guardians have a harder time starting out their roles, but as Intermediaries we're plug-and-play most of the time," he explains. "I've had a lot of fun diving more deeply into the tech side of things here, though, and working with the advanced security teams."

"Diving into tech how?"

Arden shrugs, his answer vague as he says something about finding and developing codes, and it's cute to see Ellis enamoured with his older brother. Despite the gentle laugh lines Ellis added to his Retreat Form, the youthful exuberance of his soul still somehow makes him seem younger than he is. His soul must carry that kind of energy regardless of the body it lives within.

Arden leads us into a large gathering area, and I recognize it as the place we'd crossed right out of the Arrival Ceremony hall. The music heightens as we walk through it, and Guardians and Intermediaries of all sizes, shapes, age, and inebriation levels mingle around us in small groups, hanging out just outside the loud party central we're approaching.

Arden catches the door to the Arrival room as two angels push through it, holding it open and beckoning us through. He raises his voice raised to compete with the pumping music. "Bar's that way—" he calls out, motioning to his right, "games are that way—" to his left, "and dancing over there," straight ahead of us.

Ellis claps him on the shoulder. "Let's get a drink!" Arden grins in agreement as he throws an arm around his brother and steers him to the bar.

My admiration of Arden's departing rear end doesn't go unnoticed, and Dayva grabs my elbow and presses her face close to the side of my head, tickling the hairs around my face as her hot breath hits my ear. "Lucie! An hour in the Realm of Bones and you're ready to bone Ellis' brother? I mean, I'm all for it—"

I interrupt her by pulling away from her wicked smile and grab Saffi's hand to steer us to the bar, shooting Dayva an annoyed grimace over my shoulder as she laughs. In the moments it takes us to wind through the crowd and reach the bar, I right my head. Arden may be attractive, but I'm not here to have momentary crushes. I'm here to get my first Assignment and start my new life. Plus, I realize as I survey the gyrating, laughing crowd around me, there are plenty of handsome Forms around here I could crush on, if I wanted to—ones that wouldn't potentially complicate matters by being Ellis' brother.

I bite my lip as we step up to the bar platform, and I lean back against it to get a better view over the dance floor. I realize Cato could be out there, dancing beneath the strobe lights. We don't know what his Retreat Form looks like, so he could be anyone...

Saffi pushes a shot glass into my hands and my friends gather in a small circle, their Form faces lighting up in the vibrant colours of the flashing lights.

"To us—may the Fates be kind!" Saffi cries out, all of us lifting our glasses to clink them between us before throwing the pink liquid down our throats. For once, I don't fight it when Dayva grabs Saffi's and my hands and pulls us toward the dance floor. Their twin expressions of glee make me laugh, a deep, heart-happy laugh they soon join me in, and moments later, we lose ourselves to the thrumming sounds, movements, and alcohol of our Arrival party.

4

LUCIE

"Fuck."

I groan, the word woefully inadequate to describe the pain I'm in. I get it now, pain—how much more deeply humans experience it than angels. Every joint and muscle are screaming at me. And my head—it feels swollen, and there must be someone banging on my skull. My eyes are still closed and I think maybe I'll never open them again, maybe this is what it feels like to Luminesce.

"Fuck is right," a voice mumbles from somewhere above me.

I use all the strength I can muster to roll from my front onto my back and immediately regret the sudden movement, my stomach clenching in protest. "Okay, I'm SO not into this," I grouse.

A retching sound comes from elsewhere in the room, making my throat turn inside out and I gag in response. My eyelids drag open and I look in desperation for somewhere

I can also empty my stomach contents. Through my fog of consciousness, I realize I'm laying on the floor of someone's room, a blanket twisted up around my legs. In the brightening morning light, I spy Dayva sprawled out beside me, still unconscious; Saffi sitting on the edge of the bed, the owner of the voice from above me; and Ellis kneeling over the bottom dresser drawer—the vomit culprit.

I gag again as he throws up and I feel something rise in my chest. Clapping a hand over my mouth, I fight my way out of the blanket prison I'm tangled in, my limbs moving like molasses in response to the hangover and Zircon gravity.

I make it to the bathroom with no time to spare, projectile vomiting into the sink, kicking the door shut behind me. Panic leaves me fumbling for the bathroom light as the closed door leaves me stuck in the darkness, and I sag in relief when my fingers find it and bright light fills the space. I haven't yet experienced true darkness, having partied in the club full of bright strobe lights last night, and I'm not about to introduce myself to it while hungover.

The Form reflecting me in the mirror is a spectacle: her hair sticks out at all angles from a poorly woven braid, her eyes are puffy and cheeks swollen and her shirt—I drop my gaze from the mirror to my body, where I find the bottom of my shirt cut off into a cropped style. I vaguely recall being annoyed that the knot I'd tied wouldn't stay and convincing the angel bartender to cut it off. I raise my hands above my head and cringe when I see how the shirt lifts above my braless breasts and wonder how many times I'd done that last night. Not that I'd have been the only one—we were angels, after all, comfortable with nudity, and I saw plenty of breasts jiggling in on the dance floor last night. It just hadn't been my intention to add my two to the melee, but evidently I'd cracked through my studious introvert shell more than usual.

The sparkling bellybutton piercing is twisted backward above my underwear—and only my underwear, which makes me wonder where my jeans are. Wonder, but not miss them, just the memory of their scratchy constriction making me shiver.

I splash my face with warm water from the tap and pull my hair the rest of the way from its braid, grimacing at the greasiness of it. Our hair, our bodies—nothing ever got dirty in the Realm of Lights. We bathed and showered to change our scent from one pretty smell to another, and because it just felt nice to, but most of us only did so a few times a year. Having to constantly clean ourselves is one of the most difficult adjustments we'll have to make in the Realm of Bones, according to textbooks and Returnees. I'm inclined to agree already, one day in.

The bathroom door shoves open, narrowly missing my hip as Saffi stumbles in, her attire similar to mine. She hisses against the bright light. "These eyes suck. Why are they so sensitive?" she grouses as she leans past me and turns on the shower. "Also, why is everyone in my room?"

"Fuckers, this is my room," Dayva's groggy voice counters, signalling that she's also awake—sort of. Then, "Ellis, tell me you did not just throw up in my dresser." Saffi's eyes widen at her threatening tone and she slams the bathroom door closed as Dayva's voice turns into a screech as she threatens to kill Ellis, chop him up into pieces and mail them individually to various devils in the Realm of Shadows with instructions to eat them. Despite my roiling stomach and the agony in my veins, I smirk at her creative threats, thankful to not be on the receiving end.

"Yeah, I'm not going out there for a while," Saffi says, shimmying her underwear off and pulling her shirt over her head as she steps into the shower. "Dibs on the shower—good luck out there."

I rinse my mouth before peeking out the door to assess the situation. The room's empty, flooded further with light from the hall through the open door, the bottom drawer of Dayva's dresser missing. I make a dash for the door, but just as I turn into the hallway to make the ten-foot scramble to where my room awaits, I look up and freeze.

Arden freezes, too. He looks at me, and then he *really* looks at me, dropping his gaze to my feet and taking his time to peruse his way up my body until his gaze reaches my eyes again. Every nerve tingles under his assessment. I'm proud of this Form, don't get me wrong, but there's a heat in his eyes that makes me wonder if I should have added another imperfection or two.

"Um, hey," I squeak. I know my body is blushing and I can't do a thing about it. But was my brain blushing too? Why else would I lose the ability to come up with any semblance of intelligent conversation?

He swallows. I think I detect a faint pinking of his own skin as he fiddles with his glasses and says with a slight grin, "Hey. Looks like I ducked out of the party too early, because everyone was fully dressed when I left."

I scrunch up my nose. "Last night's all a little...blurry. As in, that's an understatement and I remember literally nothing after we took that first shot." I hear another person vomiting in a room down the hall, and it reminds my body of its perilous state. I clap a hand over my mouth again, eyes widening as my body threatens to betray me right in front of this handsome Form. But Arden just smiles a little wider and reaches out to open my door before stepping back and gesturing at me enter. I try to swallow my embarrassment, but this is not a situation where anything is going down—only up. For the second time that morning, I barely get to the bathroom before I vomit, but I flick on the light this time as I kick the bathroom door closed to shield Arden from the regrettable view.

His laughter follows me anyway. "Your soul's a sympathetic puker, huh? That's an unfortunate Peculiar."

I groan, glaring at myself in the mirror and hoping my soul knows I'm aiming my frustration at her. "I swear my soul's out to get me at this point."

"Hey, have you seen Ellis this morning?" he asks, his voice muffled from behind the door. "I was coming to see if he wanted to grab lunch together, but if he's at all in a similar state as you, I'm guessing food might not be the highest note on his priority list right now."

"Based on how he filled Dayva's bottom dresser drawer with his stomach's contents about five minutes ago, I'm going to say your assumption is probably correct." I lean against the counter, refusing to re-open the door to him in my current condition. At least I'd taken my hair out of its wild braid; it hung stringy by my face but less chaotic. "Also, he might be dead, because Dayva was threatening to murder him in a pretty brutal fashion because of that."

He chuckles. "Got it. Right then, I'll go see if I can save him before that happens. I'll see you later." The sound of a door closing follows, and I breathe a sigh of relief before eyeing the tub beside me. Never before had a shower seemed so appealing, and so I turn on the spray and step right in, clothes and all. The powerful water pressure strips my skin of sweat and alcohol and brings blessed refreshment to my foggy brain as I prepare to win the battle against my new nemesis, the human hangover.

***

"There are so many options."

Dayva's voice holds a hint of distress, and I can't blame her—I feel the same sense of overwhelm. We're in the Assignment Room, which is littered with luxurious seats and shiny desks, and have curled into two recliners that we dragged beside each other to a corner by the large windows overlooking the mountain vista beyond the Retreat. We each hold our Tones, their transparent screens expanded to full size as we navigate the Assignment app.

We have a week to assign ourselves to the humans we want to bind our halos to. Then we'll have three weeks to work with Intermediaries, preparing to enter lives on Zircon to keep our humans from dying before their pre-designated expiration dates.

I wince as a wave of nausea rolls through me, my stomach still not recovered from the previous night's escapades. After I'd showered, I'd fallen into bed to take a nap, where I'd slept until mid-afternoon. When I woke, I rallied, throwing on another name-emblazoned t-shirt and a pair of loose cotton shorts. I'm still not sure where my jeans ended up, but I'm not eager to hunt for them. I wonder if I can avoid wearing them in all 777 years on Zircon.

"Remember, this is just one of many Assignments," I say, trying to be the voice of reason. "Every Assignment will help inform us of what we like and don't, but we have to start somewhere. And we need to get back to our original plan—why did we start scrolling through Assignments in Brazil when we decided thirty years ago that we wanted to take our first ones in Canada?"

Dayva blinks, then resets the app on her Tone. "You're right. Beautiful, nature-filled Canada—we made that decision for a reason. But Lucie," she whines, "there are not enough years to go all the places I want to go! What if my Assignment hates travelling so I don't get to go anywhere? I'll die. I'll simply Luminesce right here on Zircon."

I rest my head back against the soft leather as I laugh. "That's not possible, but anyway, I think you're forgetting how many Assignments we can take in 777 years. There's plenty of time to travel. Take one medium-length Assignment with me to start, and then you can take as many short-term ones as you want and travel the world."

She scowls. "I don't think it's fair that when we come back to the Retreat after an Assignment that our memories immediately dim by 50 years. I want to remember every experience, otherwise, what's the point? Might as well take the longest Assignments with humans born to nomadic families and take a chance on travelling the world with them, so at least you remember things more clearly for a longer period."

I shake my head. "Not me. I don't want to feel fresh grief every time I fail an Assignment—or fall in love, or break someone's heart. I want to move on so I can give my next Assignment my full energy." All the memories from our Assignments will fade once we pass through a Channel, floating through our minds in the way dreams do—hazy, some things just out of reach. Memories concerning other identified Guardians would remain the strongest. But since memories are linked to each Form, if we ever choose an Assignment that keeps us in the same Form to continue in its life, the memories will return to full vibrancy when we travel back through the Channels to resume our same life with the new Assignment.

She shrugs. "Different strokes, I guess. Doesn't matter what my opinion is about it—it's the way it always has been, so it's the way it always will be." Her voice holds an edge to it, ever the angel pushing boundaries and questioning regulations. "Make note that I think we should have the option. I want this brought up as an issue when you're a High Magister." She sighs, then refocuses on her Tone. "Ok, let's set the filter to Vancouver, 20 to 40 year Assignments."

I follow her lead and input the filter. We compare and contrast available profiles, trying to find two humans whose lives we can insert ourselves into with the best chance of remaining in each other's lives for the duration of the Assignments.

***

After spending the afternoon flipping through Assignments, we wander off to find some dinner. We find ourselves sitting at a table with Idele, the Intermediary who had first welcomed us to Zircon. I listen to the stories being swapped among the angels and smile and nod as I poke around the potatoes on my plate—they are fine, I guess; nothing like the creamy texture of my realm, and the gravy falls a little bland. Everything in the Realm of Bones falls flat compared to the Realm of Lights, which I knew would be the case, but it's still a disappointment, especially regarding food. I'm sure the nerves knotting in my stomach don't help matters, either, as the food is sitting heavier than it should. I'm feeling the pressure of sorting through Assignment options to pick my first one. Dayva is bending under the stress too, not her usual effervescent self at the table, happier to listen than to talk or engage. She perks up, though, when Idele begins reminiscing on her own Arrival 25 years earlier.

"25 years ago?" Dayva interrupts, leaning across me to get Idele's attention. She's never been one for decorum. "Did you graduate with my brother Cato?"

She purses her lips, causing wrinkles to crease across her chin. "Cato? I don't remember him, but it doesn't mean I didn't. You know how impossible it is to be familiar with every person in your graduating class." She waves her hand as if to prove her point by motioning to the hundreds of other recent graduates we Arrived with, and I'm momentarily distracted by her manicured fingernails that sparkle with blue polish. I glance at my own bare nails, wondering if there will be a time when I will want to put colourful covers on them as well—something I find hard to consider based on the hours I spent crafting each one. "But maybe Mellonia does—I think I saw her in here a few minutes ago..." She trails off as she half-stands from the bench and surveys the massive dining hall.

I wonder how in the Fates she's going to find who she's looking for in a room with so many angels, but it's only a moment before she spots her target. "Mello!" she hollers above the din of conversation to a woman just about to exit the dining room. Her voice carries, belying the small stature it originates from. Despite the distance, Mello must hear her, as she pauses mid-stride and looks around. Idele waves and calls out her name again. "Mello! Come here for a second."

Mello lifts her chin to acknowledge her and weaves through the tables until she reaches us. She doesn't have time to say anything before Idele immediately grills her. "Do you know a guy named Cato? Graduated with us? That's—" she points at Dayva, "his sister. I don't remember him, but maybe you do?"

Mello swings her legs across the bench to sit as she looks at Dayva, a large smile breaking over her face, contrasting against the other finer features of her visage. "Cato! Good guy." Her skin tints a little, and I can't help but lean forward in interest. Is that how I look when I blush? And why, exactly, is she blushing?

A glance at Dayva and her narrowed eyes and I'm sure she's wondering the same thing—but unlike me, Dayva doesn't have a filter, so she blurts out, "Did you date?"

Mello chuckles, tucking her short blonde bob behind both ears as her creamy pallor returns. "No, but not for lack of my trying. We had a bit of fun our first month after Arriving as our rooms are in the same wing and we found some common ground working out at the gym together every morning."

For some stupid reason, I begin to blush at the idea of Cato with someone. I hurriedly shove a bite of now-cold potatoes in my mouth to distract myself from the thought—a little too hastily, as it turns out, causing me to almost choke on them.

"Girl, you good?" Dayva looks at me, a strange expression on her face, and I chug my water, waving her off and nodding as I pull myself back together.

Idele returns her attention to Mello once she sees that I'm done sputtering, and cocks her head. "I do not recall you having a little Retreat fling when we Arrived! Mello, you sexy piece, you."

Mello rolls her eyes, then pushes against the table as if to stand. "Like I said, it was nothing serious, but he's a nice guy for sure. Who knows though, if things were different..."

All four of us nod, knowing she is referring to the difficulty of connecting with angels beyond the Retreat and how the system is set up to keep us from forming meaningful attachments to each other while on Zircon.

"Anyway," Mello says, standing, "It was nice to meet you, Cato's sister, but I've got to finish packing—I'm out of here tomorrow." She lifts a hand in a departing wave. "May the Fates be kind!"

From the way Dayva slumps beside me, I know she's both happy and sad to have met someone who knew Cato here, even if it was momentary. Idele turns back to us as I finally join the conversation. "Isn't it hard to say goodbye so casually when you might not see an angel again until your Return?" I ask her.

She shrugs, her pink sweater slipping down the inward curve of one of her shoulders. "Honestly, yes and no—it's just par for the course, so you get used to it after an Assignment or two."

I nod, as if I understand, though I don't think I will until I experience it myself.

"Do you think we should take a long or short first Assignment?" I ask. We've been told the pros and cons of each, and it's ultimately our decision, but it's interesting to hear other angels' perspectives. Of course, we've only heard from Returnees, whose memories of their first Assignments are long blurred, a mere flicker of recollections after centuries. This would be the first time we'd hear from someone still early in their time in the human realm, whose memory would be more fresh. She's an Intermediary, but she'd have listened to the experiences of hundreds of Guardians, so I'm interested in her perspective.

But Idele shrugs, the movement pulling her sweater farther down her shoulder before she grabs at it and pulls it back up. I note that she's not wearing a bra, so I decide if she's been at the Retreat for the past quarter century and still is choosing to forgo them here, then I don't need to be in a hurry to wear those constricting boob jails when at the Retreat, either. "Honestly, everyone's different. You'll figure out what you like. Some Guardians prefer Assignments shorter than five years, while others only take the multi-decade long ones. A lot of first-timers take ones in the 20-year range so they can get the hang of things on Zircon before having to switch lives too quickly."

"Lucie and I want to take our first Assignments together," Dayva pipes up, leaning slightly across me again. "Have any of the Guardians you've Overlooked done that?"

The other angels at the table begin to stack their trays. "No, but I've heard it can be fun," she says as she follows suit and adds her tray to the pile. "Sorry, we gotta go; we're going to play some tennis. Good luck picking your first Assignments!"

"Hey, thanks," I say as she slides off the bench, and Dayva adds, "We appreciate hearing about Cato!"

"May the Fates be kind," Idele says in parting.

Dayva and I look each at each other, communicating without words that we are both done eating and ready to return to the Assignment Room. We spend the evening there, finding and comparing profiles, making notes. After a couple hours, I lay the Tone on my lap and arch my back to stretch, taking a moment to enjoy the beautiful sunset through the floor-to-ceiling windows in front of us.

"What if we fail?"

I look over at Dayva, surprised by her whisper. Her focus is still on the tablet in front of her, but her mind is clearly elsewhere.

"What if I fail?" she repeats, this time turning the focus to herself.

"Lots of Guardians fail Assignments," I assure her, though the knot in my stomach cinches tighter at the thought. While it is true, it's certainly not something I want for either of us.

As Guardians, it's our job to keep the humans we bind ourselves to alive until their predestined expiration date. The Tones on our laps have that information: the day their souls are bound to bodies on Zircon, and the day their souls will exit the realm. It's how we know whether an Assignment will be long or short.

We take on Assignments in advance of a human's 17th birthday—the equivalent of 444 fortnights. On their birthday, we bind to them through our halos as their Guardian angel, our job to ensure they don't die before their expiration date. However, the devils from the Realm of Shadows are working as hard as we are to do exactly the opposite—to ensure that humans do die prior to their predestined date of death.

But things work a little differently for devils. They spend 666 years on Zircon and don't sign on to individual humans like we do. Instead, they are agents of general chaos, running amok, trying to kill off as many humans as they can. They aren't aware of the expiration dates like we are, so everything they do has a little more panic infused into it, generally speaking. Before humans turn 17, devils can't interfere, so we don't need to guard the humans younger than that. This doesn't mean they can't die, it just means they're only susceptible to the dangers of natural Zircon, be it disease, accident, or otherwise.

"I know, but I really hate failing, Lucie." Dayva turns to me, her face pensive. She knows I understand—the perfectionist in me feels the same as the competitive side in her that hates to lose at anything, work or play. Failing an Assignment would be devastating to both of us. And while Dayva may rail against the idea of having our memories dim out after each Assignment, I'm sure that at least part of the reason that system is in place is for angels like us, who need distance from the immediate emotions and burden of failure to move on. I don't say that, though.

Instead, I say, "You're going to be fine. You've prepared better for this than so many others. And hey," I nudge her arm with my elbow, our bodies parallel in the same recliners we'd been in earlier that day, "Definitely you will not fail your first Assignment because you've got me, and we've got each other's backs."

She swallows. I know it's a temporary emotion for her, but I'm always honoured when she shows vulnerability around me. I'm the only one she's comfortable enough to do so with, and I treasure the responsibility.

"I'm sick to my stomach when I think about failing—about failing Celestia, the Realm of Lights, and my human's soul. I'm going to get attached to them, and of course I want their souls to rest, not wander alone in agony for eternity."

The burden of duty weighs in the air between us as we fall silent, each losing ourselves to our own thoughts. Souls being kept from finding their ultimate peace if we don't do our jobs is a difficult failure to imagine, and it will only be that much worse once we bind ourselves to a human. I glance down at the Tone in my lap, where it's opened to a sweet 16-year-old's face, and my heart lurches at the thought of it. Nevermind the fact that the Realm of Lights exists on the power of souls who reach their expiration dates and thus can rest in peace. This contrasts with the Realm of Shadows, which is powered by the souls the devils bring to early expirations who will wander hopelessly for eternity. Rumour has it that sometimes, if you listen carefully on Zircon, you can hear their cries of agony drifting by on the wind. It's why angels and devils hate each other so fiercely—our very existences depend on the other's failures.

I don't have any words of comfort for Dayva, and I doubt scrolling any more Assignments will help tonight.

"Come on." I close my Tone and uncurl from the recliner. "I think we need to sleep. Everything will look better in the morning, when we aren't battling hangovers and have at least a full day of life in this realm under our belts."

I reach for her hand and gently tug her to her feet. I'm eager to sleep in my bed tonight, and not on the floor of someone else's room. The nap I took this morning was a tease to a blissful night's sleep, and by the way my body is dragging, it's clear that human bodies take a lot longer to recover from a night of drinking than angelic ones—something I'm noting for future reference.

5

LUCIE

The next morning, I awaken with a brighter outlook on life. I feel a lightness in my soul as I roll over on my bed to look out the window. The sun is just beginning to rise, but my room is already bright; I'm still not ready to embrace darkness yet, and so I kept the lights on all night. While I know from Sighting Channels that the night has a beauty of its own, my angelic nature will always be drawn to light, and I already miss the eternal light of Celestia. Light is safe and comfortable. In this new world, I'll hold on to the things of home that I can for as long as possible, which might mean sleeping with a light on for a long time yet.

Some of the angels I Arrived with had gone outside the first night to experience darkness in this new realm, to look upon the Luminaries glowing dully against the black velvet sky. It's pretty enough, I suppose, having only glanced out the window in the middle of the night when I'd gone to the bathroom, but not in the same vibrant way the stars sparkle against the blue heavens in the Realm of Lights.

I watch the morning come to life through the window as the navy mountains lighten to pink and the ashen greens of the woods deepen under the strengthening rays of the Realm of Bones' one sun. When the sun finally crests a ridge and fully banishes the night, I head to the shower, not needing to pause to remove any clothing before stepping into the stream—I slept naked, refusing to be confined yet by the clothing of this realm while I sleep.

I've just finished pulling on another name-branded t-shirt with a pair of pastel blue shorts when Dayva and Ellis knock on my door. I walk with them to find breakfast, though we're waylaid halfway there when a crowd draws our attention to the Channel room. We slip in and note the bags, the hugs, and realize the space doubles as an exit room for Assignments.

A shrill whistle cuts through the din of chatter, and everyone quiets, their attentions drawn to the large man standing on a small stage. He has a Tone in his hands, open to its largest screen size. The lights in the room reflect off his bald head, though the massive beard he wears on his face makes up for the lack of hair on his head, his lips barely visible as he speaks.

"Good morning, angels!" His voice booms through the room. "It looks like we have 3,084 Guardians heading out today. Some of you I'll see again within a few days, and some of you I'll greet again in a few decades. Whatever the Assignment length, from me and every angel past, present, and future, we wish you all success on your Assignments. May the Fates be kind!"

A cheer goes up from around us and everyone returns to their goodbyes, and a moment later, the first Guardian steps through the Channel holding his Intermediary's hand. The pearlescent mist swirls around their shapes; a few seconds later, another pair of angels follow, and soon a line of Guardians forms, waiting to be led to their new lives by their Intermediary.

We stand and observe for a few minutes, and then Dayva points partway down the line where a woman stands with a duffel over her shoulder, patiently waiting for her turn. "Oh look, there's Mello."

As though our attention on her draws her focus, her gaze turns to ours. She gives us a bright and cheerful wave, which we happily return—including the friendly but confused Ellis, so we quickly fill him on our cafe conversation yesterday. We watch as she links arms with her Intermediary, a giant of a man that looks like the humans' fairytale of Hercules, before they disappear together into the Channel.

No sooner have their ankles disappeared into the haze than Ellis pipes up. "My stomach is grumpy—it needs food." My belly grumbles in assent and we make our way to the dining room to fuel up on pancakes and bacon before spending another day in the Assignment Room.

***

Dayva and I pick our Assignments on our fifth day at the Retreat: two best friends living in Vancouver. They've been friends since they were toddlers, so we figure there's a decent chance they'll remain close long-term, especially if we're in their lives as friends to each other.

It's strange to feel so much adrenaline coursing through me as I clutch Dayva's hand, our free hands both hovering over our Tones. All we have to do is click "Assign," and then there's no going back.

"I've never felt my heart race like this," Dayva says, her eyes glued to the display of the human girl in front of her. "It kind of hurts, to be honest," she admits.

I let out a nervous laugh. "Everything about these Zircon Forms 'kind of hurts' if you think about it for too long."

"Ready?" She lowers a finger to an inch above the screen, and I do the same.

"On three." We count down and then, together, press the green bars. A message pops up on each of our screens, congratulating us, and I skim mine:

CONGRATULATIONS ON CHOOSING YOUR FIRST AS-
SIGNMENT, LUCIE!
TERRA WILL REACH THE AGE OF GUARDIANSHIP IN:
25D 4H 15M 32S

I notice the countdown also appears at the top of the Tone's screen, each second ticking down, which does nothing to calm my adrenaline.

YOUR INTERMEDIARY FOR THIS ASSIGNMENT IS
RUEL.
THEY WILL MEET YOU TOMORROW AT 09:00 IN CON-
FERENCE ROOM 42.

"Oh, we have the same Intermediary," Dayva comments as she looks over at my screen.

"Makes sense based on them being assigned Guardians to specific regions," I note. They follow us throughout the duration of our Assignments, which means we won't change Intermediaries even if it's necessary that we move elsewhere on

Zircon during an Assignment. Each Intermediary has one specific region within which they will always begin Overlooking Guardians.

"My meeting's at 11 with them, but I wonder if I should just come with you at 9, since we're planning to do our Assignments in tandem anyway."

I nod in agreement, then look back to my Tone, exiting the welcome screen and revealing the Assignment page once again. Terra's smiling face stares back at me, the button beneath her no longer green but pink, the word "Assigned" written across it in bold font. I take a deep breath.

I'm ready.

6

LUCIE

My palms are sweating, and I almost drop my Tone as I hide the countdown by turning off the screen and slipping it into my pocket. We're in the 24-hour window in which we can leave the Retreat to begin our Assignments—representing the divine number 1212 to embody 12 hours of day and 12 hours of night, the balance of lights and shadows.

I rub my hands down the front of my linen dress to wipe away the damp clamminess of my skin, the murmur of good-byes washing around me. Everything about being here in this moment feels surreal. It seems like only yesterday I stood against the wall with Ellis and Dayva and watched Mello step through the Channel to her next Assignment, but it's somehow already our turn.

"Hey, yo!" Saffi reaches me and Ellis with a cry before letting her five massive bags fall to the ground. "I was worried I was going to miss the beginning and that you'd leave without saying goodbye!"

Ellis raises a brow at her five bags. "Do you think you packed enough?"

Saffi puts her hands on her hips and sticks her tongue out at him. "My Assignment is a rich kid, so it's important I start with an impressive closet. I have a bunch of stuff being delivered to the apartment later today as well." She surveys his single duffel bag with suspicion. "However, I don't think you're bringing enough. You do know you should change underwear more than once a week, right?"

Dayva gags, approaching us just in time to hear Saffi's comment. She'd run off to the bathroom, though the glazed donuts in each hand give away her apparent pit stop at the refreshments table. Ellis reaches for one but she snags it back and hastily bites both of them before grumbling through a full mouth, "Get your own! I need these."

A whistle breaks through the clamour, and we fall silent to listen to the same speech we'd heard a month before—and a few times since when we'd stopped by to watch on the way to breakfast. A thrill runs up my spine as angels begin jumping the Channel, and the four of us join the line, Saffi kicking three of her bags along, slinging two over her shoulder. Dayva and I each have a duffel and a rolling case, filled with items we purchased over the last month to fit the needs of our Assignments.

Saffi's Assignment is on the opposite side of the continent in New York—she wanted somewhere with high fashion connections, with plans to work in the fashion industry. Ellis chose an Assignment in Calgary, a compromise to Dayva; he wanted to come to Vancouver with us but Dayva told him in no uncertain terms was he allowed to follow us there. She'd meant it when she said she wanted space, and I'm proud and surprised that she's maintained her friendship boundary with him ever since we Arrived. He'd relented with another western Canadian city, finding an Assignment that would finish within two days of hers. Dayva said that after a year, he could try to track her down, and maybe then they could keep in touch—otherwise, she'd see him at the Retreat in 31 years, if they were both successful with their Assignments. Though she won't admit it, I know it's hard for her to say goodbye to him—romantic benefits aside, he is one of her closest friends. The way she finally relents and gives him a donut as we shuffle up in line so she has a hand free to tuck into his sends a pang of sadness through my heart. While Ellis respects her need for independence, I'm sure it hurts him more than he'll ever admit. I harbour a secret hope that one day they'll allow themselves to fall in love, though I'll never tell Dayva that—she'd do even more to keep him at arms length as a way of further proving her independent soul, the stubborn angel that she is.

Ellis is chatting with his Intermediary, and I look around for ours and spot Ruel walking our way. Their hair is cropped close to their head, their face sporting the serious, no-nonsense expression Dayva and I have come to know over the past three weeks as we've worked with them to set up our backgrounds and create space for us to pop into lives without causing ripples. They give Dayva and me a quick once-over, noting our outfits and bags. "You two ready?"

I swallow, but nod as Dayva answers with an enthusiastic, "Fates, yes!" She's nervous too, but she hides it under a bravado I wish I had.

The Hercules of a man who had escorted Mello through the Channel is also Saffi's Intermediary. He finds us as our turn to jump approaches, and I smirk when Saffi's skin pinks up in his presence. She's spent a couple nights with him this week that resulted in, apparently, "the most mind-blowing sex" she's ever had, though she refuses to impart any details further than saying sex in a human Form rivals that of angelic sex when wings are involved. But in the same breath, she also insists there's nothing more than a physical attraction between them. ("He's honestly got a pretty dull personality, unfortunately. But Fates, if he doesn't know how to use his tongue...")

We near the front of the line, and Saffi turns to give each of us a quick hug. "May the Fates be kind," she says, her voice thick with emotion as she says goodbye. Reed slings two of Saffi's bags over his shoulder as if they weigh nothing and grabs a wheeled suitcase with his other hand. Saffi hauls a bag up across her chest and clutches the handle of her other rolling bag, and then, lacing her fingers with his, she steps through the swirling white wall at the Channelkeeper's signal.

Just like that, she's gone, as if she never were, the mist resettling to its slow swirl.

Ellis suddenly spins from his place in front of us and clutches Dayva by the shoulders. He plants a smacking kiss on her startled lips without a word, then grabs his Intermediary's hand and follows Saffi and Reed into the Channel.

Dayva blinks, standing there in momentary shock. I grab her hand to refocus her attention—we'll talk about that later, but right now, we've got more important things to focus on. Ruel grabs my other hand and a moment later, the Channelkeeper nods at us.

And with that, we step into the haze en route to our first lives on Zircon.

***

The silence is once again so loud it hurts my ears, every nerve in my body firing in a desperation to understand the impossible physics of falling without gravity. My heart hammers in my throat and I wonder how many times I'll have to go through the haze before I get used to it, or if I ever will.

Once again, the edges of the silence seem frayed with the promise of sound. I try to push through the muted quiet to get to it, but this jump takes far less time than the one between realms, and in what must have been just seconds, our feet solidify against earth. I squeeze Dayva's hand as she squeezes mine, and then we step forward.

Ruel and two women greet us, standing stock still before us. The women are both wholly familiar and yet utterly not.

Dayva gasps, dropping my hand so that both of hers are free to reach up and clutch her boobs, the woman in the mirror mimicking the movement. "That's more like it," she says with a wide grin, her once-again ample bosom on display under a low-cut black t-shirt. "I already feel more like myself."

I laugh, feeling my heart rate settle now that my feet are on solid ground and I'm no longer floating in the haze. "Really? Even though your hair looks like that?" I'm referring to her chic black bob, cut to her collarbones, the hair shiny and pin-straight—a far cry from her Celestia style.

"Definitely," she says with confidence, moving her hands from her chest to run them through her hair. Her eyes feature a slight tilt, her small mouth complementing the other delicate features of her face. From a human point of view, she's stunning—almost to where I bet she got a low grade on it for not having enough imperfections.

Turning to my reflection, I study my much lower-key body. This Form is tall, with wide hips and shoulders. I'm a dark blonde, with thick straight hair reaching to my waist and blunt bangs framing my face. Curious eyes stare back at me from behind long, lush eyelashes. Perhaps the best way to describe my face is "muted." It's pretty enough, but not any more so than the next person's, easily passed over in a crowd.

I sense Dayva assessing me as well, so I do a little spin-turn. My linen dress is a bit shorter on this Form, the silhouette accentuating the length of my legs and making my waist appear small compared to my hips. She gives me two thumbs up. "You look perfect, Lucie. Classic beauty, excellent craftsmanship, five stars."

"Right, you two good?" Ruel finally interrupts from where they've stood to the side, arms crossed as they allowed us a moment to acclimate to our new Forms.

"We're good," Dayva and I say together. I smile, and she smiles, and then we laugh, the sound filling the small bathroom as we let the release of laughter wash through us. Even Ruel lets slip a rare smile before a Channel appears behind them. They give us a nod before stepping backward through the haze, the white rectangle disappearing the moment they're through.

Left to ourselves, we take one last look in the mirror and check out our halos. In this Form, mine is an armband-style tattoo just below my elbow. Filled-in and negative-spaced lines loop my forearm, with floral details woven in an intricate design around the bands. Dayva had opted to decorate this Form with a patchwork of tattoos scattered on various locations across the entire right side of her body, her halo taking the space of a bejeweled sword running the length of her forearm, blood dripping from its tip to encircle her wrist.

"Pretty badass Form you got there," I compliment her as she hooks an arm through mine.

"I know. It almost failed," she says, sporting a proud smirk, and I gently bump my hip against hers in mock exasperation. Together, we push through the bathroom doors into the humming Vancouver airport terminal. She shoots me a devious smile, one that is not at all similar to the smiles of her Celestia body or Retreat Form, and yet somehow is still an exact representation of her beautiful, mischievous soul.

We follow the signs to the exit and hop in a self-driving taxi, inputting the address of the apartment set to become our new home. We're quiet as it zips along the streets, our faces pressed against the car windows as we take in the first close-up sights of a Zircon city. It's almost too much to process, but before long, we reach our destination.

Our apartment looms over us as we stand on the sidewalk before it, our brains scrambling to match reality to the images we'd seen on our Tones at the Retreat. It's quite an old building; Vancouver is an expensive place to live, so our backstory is based on living on an inheritance from our "grandmothers." We've been given credit cards with access to endless funds, but we're only to spend within the parameters of what makes sense for the lives we create. When we get jobs, we will do our best to live using just those Zircon-earned dollars.

We've decided to Guard our Assignments as their friends and grow up with them. So we're entering in 18-year-old Forms, eager to begin university in the fall, where our humans have talked about attending themselves for years. While we can't guarantee their life choices and will live our lives in connection to them throughout their lives regardless of where they choose to do so, Dayva and I have done everything we can to increase our chances of staying close to each other by finding two lifelong best friends who plan to continue education in Vancouver together. To keep things simple, we are also entering as best friends with each other.

Sharing the same birthday is a convenient bonus that allows Dayva and I to truly begin our Assignments in tandem. As they've done every year since they were six years old, the girls are hosting a joint birthday party at Terra's house—she has the more laid-back parents, who are planning to enjoy cocktails next door during the party, checking in once in a while. Everyone from the school is invited, and we've inserted ourselves as friends of another classmate.

In the meantime, we plan to have a restful night's sleep and finish preparing as much as we can for the life that awaits us. Grabbing my best friend's hand, we pull open the apartment lobby door together, eager to get started.

7

LUCIE

"**F**uck sakes," I mutter, yanking my hand back from the stream of water. I'd gotten eyeliner on my fingers and wanted to rinse it off but forgot that I'd need to turn the hot water on, that not all taps automatically pour warm or hot. Instead, as I'd discovered the first time I'd turned on the shower, the default seemed ice-cold, and I hated it, regretting having ever wondered what cold felt like. Dayva and I had spent too long last night putting our arms under the icy stream, pulling the temp from not-quite-warm to blistering cold, marvelling and hissing at the novel sensation. But it's only day two and already the excitement of the new temperature phenomenon is wearing thin. "We might have made a mistake moving to Canada," I grumble to myself as I switch the tap to encourage the water to warm. "I might die when winter comes."

"Is it too pink? I think it's too pink."

Dayva interrupts me as she enters the bathroom, elbowing me out of the way so she can get closer to the small circle of mirror hung above the sink.

"Ugh, we need to figure out a new mirror situation," I complain, making a mental note to purchase a full-length mirror or two as soon as possible.

She ignores me, pursing her lips and studying her lipstick. "It's definitely too pink."

I pick up my mascara and use my ample hips to maneuver back into prime mirror position and floss my lashes with the dark gunk. We experimented with makeup at the Retreat a bit, but with new skin tones and face arrangements, we've spent the past hour re-learning how to apply it in a way that complements the different features. "It's fine. You look great. Actually—maybe a little too great," I say on second thought as glance at her again. "You're right. Lose the lipstick and go natural."

Dayva nods and grabs a glob of toilet paper to wipe her lips clean, then glances at her Tone—the same one as at the Retreat, minus the Retreat-specific software. "We gotta go. You ready?"

I'm about to answer her when I gasp, my forearm tattoo suddenly burning hot on my skin. I drop the mascara in the sink and scramble for my Tone on the counter, pulling up the holographic display.

TERRA HAS REACHED THE AGE OF GUARDIANSHIP.
oD oH oM oS

YOUR HALO HAS BEEN BOUND TO HER SOUL UNTIL THE CONCLUSION OF THE ASSIGNMENT.
MAY THE FATES BE KIND!

Dayva grabs my arm, and I realize the tattoo is not only burning, but glowing with ethereal silver light. "What's happening? Is *it* happening right now? Does it feel different? Lucie!" The questions are rapid fire and end in exasperation, despite her not having given me a breath of time in which to respond.

I touch my tattoo, but it's not hot against my fingers. "It's burning hot," I say.

She touches a tentative finger to it and frowns. "Doesn't feel like it is."

"I know, it doesn't feel like it to touch, but trust me, it's—"

Just as quickly as the burn and shimmer had appeared, it falls away, leaving behind the very ordinary tattoo, though we both agree it looks more crisp, more freshly inked than the two-to-three years I'd pre-dated it when creating the Form.

"How long until Ainsley reaches the age?"

She flips open her Tone, where the screen informs her that there's an hour remaining. "I better monitor this so I can duck away when my halo binds," she notes wryly. "The last thing I need is to be the weird kid who shows up with a fucking glow-stick tattoo."

"Yes, please pay attention to that," I say before I turn to her and give her a once-over. "Anyway, are we ready to go now?"

Dayva steps back to survey my outfit. My black cargo pants are a light linen, and I opted not to feel strangled by choosing a cropped shirt with a wide neck, happy to forgo a bra in place of a more comfortable bikini in anticipation of the backyard pool at Terra's house. I have three piercings in each earlobe, little studs sparkling against the bathroom light thanks to my long hair being pulled up into a dramatic ponytail that keeps falling over my shoulder. Just like my Retreat Form, I've also got a belly-button piercing, which peeks above the top band of my pants.

"Nailed it. I think we look perfect." Her ripped jean shorts reveal a hint of cheek, and a baggy black rock band t-shirt tucked in the front gives her a sweet-but-edgy vibe. I slip on sandals while she ties up sneakers, and then we're off, my heartrate thrilling as we step into the fading light of evening. I'd been too chicken at the Retreat to go outside at night, opting for the baptism-by-fire version of my first night as an official Guardian.

Our pre-ordered self-driving taxi is waiting outside the apartment, and ten minutes later, it's depositing us on a busy suburban street where people are coming and going from a well-kept maroon house.

I run my fingers across my tattoo, where my halo rests dull and dormant once again, still unassuming in appearance but now binding me to my pledge of keeping a human's soul in her body for the next 29 years. But I've no more time to stress about the responsibility I now bear as Dayva struts forward toward the house, and I do my best to emulate her confidence. I keep my head on a swivel as I look for the classmate—Clementine—that we're using as our invitation in. Ruel had manipulated some photographs and worked other Intermediary angles to make it seem like we'd gone to a summer camp with her a few years prior, and then Dayva and I had reached out under the guise of reconnecting. Turns out, it's surprisingly easy to manipulate humans into creating memories that don't exist through the power of suggestion.

"Dayva, Lucie!" Clementine spots us first, and I look over to see her jogging toward us in the front yard, a red solo cup in one hand splashing its contents over the side as it bounces with the swinging of her arms. She's sporting a neon orange bikini top, a pair of unbuttoned, faded jean shorts and black flip-flops, and wears her damp hair pulled back in a chaotic bun. "I'm so glad you guys made it." Her eyes have a slight glaze to them, alcohol clearly at work. "Can you believe it's been three years since we met at summer camp? I'm so excited you've moved here!" She stumbles a bit as she moves to hug us, the sharp frames of her red glasses digging into my cheek. "Come on inside—you have to meet the birthday girls!"

Dayva waggles her eyebrows at me, her eyes sparkling in anticipation. My stomach flutters and I figure my soul won't be able to hide its excitement, so I don't even bother to try, smiling broadly back at her as we follow the drunken Clementine through the propped-open front door. I briefly wonder if anyone I know will take Clementine on as an Assignment, her birthday three months from now.

"Terrrrrra!" Clementine squeals, the high pitch stark against the deep thrum of music. A girl turns from the kitchen bar and frowns.

"Clemmy—are you drunk?" She grabs the cup from her hand and brings it to her nose. "Fuck. Clem, we gotta keep this low-key or my parents are gonna shut us down before things even get started. Here," she says, dumping the offending liquid into the sink and turning on the tap to fill it with water, "drink this right now."

Clementine, unbothered, takes the cup but motions to us. "This is Dayva and Lucie, the friends I told you about from camp."

Terra looks at us finally, her face softening as she smiles. My entire universe shrinks to her in that moment as I see the photos and videos of my Assignment come to physical life in front of me. She's tall, like I am, but doesn't have the curves of my Form; she's lean and willowy, her face bare of makeup but for some mascara, her cheeks naturally pink with a slight blush of rosacea. Her hair is thin, though tonight she's curled it and pinned it half-up to make it look thicker, but it suits the rest of her narrow features—a slim nose, small lips, eyes that nearly disappear when she smiles and her cheeks push up into them, not dissimilar to how Dayva's do now, too.

"Hi, I'm Terra," she says, her voice young and sweet. "Nice to meet you—glad you could make it. Drinks are here, pool's out back, and snacks are everywhere."

I can't stop grinning like an idiot, but I try to tone it down a bit and lean against the counter, hoping to portray the picture of chill. "Thanks for letting us crash your party."

"And happy birthday!" adds Dayva, though it comes out muffled around a bite she's already taken of some kind of custard and chocolate bar. I give her a look, and she covers her mouth in apology and hurries to swallow before she tacks on, "One more year of high school and then freedom!"

Terra pushes her hair back behind her neck, exposing sharp shoulders that emerge from a tight tank top. She's wearing baggy high-waisted jeans, a pale blue. "Trust me, I'm counting the days. Clem says you guys are at UBC?"

"Well, two weeks from now we will be," I say, referring to the semester start at the University of British Columbia.

"I can't wait. I'm going to major in journalism," Terra says, reaching for one of the bars on the platter beside Dayva. "Ainsley wants to go into law, so she's starting with a criminology degree."

"Did I hear my name?"

A curvy blonde materializes beside Terra, and Clementine again gushes, "This is Dayva and Lucie, my friends from camp! They just moved here from Seattle."

"Clem. Drink your water," Terra admonishes, pushing Clementine's arm and cup up to her mouth.

"Yes, Mom," Clem manages, her words dripping with sarcasm. But to her credit, she does gulp down the water, though the cup clunks against her her teeth when she first raises it to her mouth.

"Hey," Ainsley says to us, her voice soft and eyes kind. She's between Dayva and me in height, her hair falling in a Hollywood-style wave from a high ponytail. I glance at Dayva to see how she's reacting to meeting her Assignment, and I'm impressed by how nonchalant she looks. It's only the white knuckles holding the countertop tight that give off anything but a relaxed vibe. I, for one, feel myself relaxing now that we've met our Assignments in true flesh and bone.

Dayva and I both echo greetings, then Ainsley says, "I was coming over 'cause I need a partner in beer pong. Birthday girl team?"

She directs her question to Terra, but Terra scrunches up her nose. "You know I suck at that game. Plus, I promised my brother I'd pop into the pool for a bit."

"I'm a fierce beer pong athlete," Dayva proclaims, pushing away from the counter. "If you want a winning partner, I'm in for it."

Ainsley raises her brow, assessing Dayva's small but mighty presence. "Okay girl, go off," she says approvingly. "Show me what you've got." She grabs Dayva's arm and leads her down a hallway and out of sight, Dayva turning at the last minute to send me a wink—target acquired. I grin, then turn back to Terra. "So, about this pool?" I say.

"You got a suit?"

I pull my t-shirt up to reveal the sparkling blue bikini beneath it.

"I love a girl who comes prepared for a pool party. Right, come on—I'll introduce you to the other mermaids out there," she says with a laugh.

I turn to Clementine to see if she wants to come as well, but she's disappeared, so I shrug and follow Terra out to the backyard.

A glistening pool with underwater lights is the feature of the backyard, the water glowing in the encroaching darkness of night. We step out just in time to be splashed by someone doing a cannonball from the diving board. It's louder out here, kids having a good time, and a small thrill runs through my soul—I get to be a part of this life.

"Terra! We're doing a diving competition!" A girl in a tiny yellow bikini top and low-slung board shorts sits on the edge of the pool across from us, legs dangling in the water. She squeezes her braid in her fists, rivulets of pool water running down her wrists. "Show 'em how it's done!"

Terra tosses the girl a grin, steps out of her jeans and wiggles out of her tank top. "That's Hailey, Ainsley's girlfriend," she says to me as she strips down. "They've been together since, like, grade eight. Also, I'm a competitive diver," she adds before she steps up to the diving board.

I knew that, of course, but I don't have to feign being impressed when she flips off the low diving board in a perfect tuck and arch. Her head breaks through the water to whistles and shouts of "ten out of ten!" and a couple of sarcastic "not your best works."

I strip my clothes off as well and move to slide into the pool in a much less audience-forward way when I hear Terra call to me from where she's treading water in the middle of the pool. "No, no, show us what you've got! Everyone, this is Lucie. Lucie, everyone!"

The dozen other people in various states of pool immersion call out hellos. I notice many of them, guys and girls alike, shooting appreciative glances over my Form in its skimpy swimsuit. Thankfully, I like this Form, I'm proud of this Form, and though I feel my soul leading the charge for a blush under their assessments, I don't let it stop me from stepping with confidence onto the diving board.

I'm an excellent diver; most angels are. We get our wings on our 17th birthday, but we start diving as soon as we can swim as young children. We practice flipping and spinning off pool diving boards and waterfalls, so when we do get our wings, we can more readily accept the idea of leaping off structures in Celestia before spreading our wings to catch us. I miss bearing the weight of those wings between my shoulder blades and, not for the first time, wonder why we're not allowed them in this realm—even if only for rare emergency Assignment purposes.

Shrugging off the thought and refocusing on the situation I do have control over, I turn on the board's edge and inch my heels over until I'm balancing on my tiptoes. I've figured diving will be an easy way I can relate to Terra, so I've positioned myself on the UBC dive team, which she also has plans to join. This dive is an opportunity to begin connecting with her, and I hope she sees me as a friendly diving peer and not her competition.

I bounce a couple of test bounces before I jump. I spin, I pivot, the world blurring before me, and I enter the water almost perfectly—intentionally flexing a foot ever-so-slightly to create a small splash.

The water is just on the cool side of warm, thankfully, so not too shocking to my new human senses. I break the surface of the water and smooth my bangs back before I realize everyone's gone quiet, the only sound the music. I freeze, my gaze shooting to Terra, who has pulled herself up to sit beside Hailey. And then everyone erupts.

"10 out of 10!"

"Holy shit, that was good!"

"Who is this chick, exactly?"

"Terra, you've got competition!"

The way Terra's kicking the water with her feet and grinning at me with that massive smile? I let out a relieved exhale, knowing I'm ok, she's ok, we'll be ok—she's the kind of person who encourages the success of others and isn't intimidated by them.

"Lucie, what the hell! You're a diver, too!" I breaststroke over to her and grab pool's edge. "Are you on the UBC dive team?" she asks.

I nod, and she squeals, kicking her feet again, but this time not raising them to splash above the water because of my position in the pool beside her. "I knew I liked you! We like her," she says to Hailey before introducing the two of us.

Hailey smiles, leaning back on her hands. "Terra, you like everyone. Of course we like her."

Terra laughs, then looks past me to the diving board. "Beat that, Cato!"

For the second time in as many minutes, I freeze.

Cato isn't a popular human name.

With a rush of adrenaline, I turn, my fingers gripping the edge of the pool like my life depends on it, and I stare up at the man striding across the diving board. His eight-pack gleams in the reflective light of the pool, his shaggy dark hair dripping across his face. He stands at the edge of the diving board, his short board shorts showing off chiseled quad muscles and an impressive bulge. I'm aware of my skin heating as I raise my eyes to his, and my soul stutters as his crystal blue eyes meet my assessing gaze—though there's no hint of recognition from him. Of course, there wouldn't be; even if he is Dayva's brother, he doesn't know my Forms, and I don't know his. My name wouldn't trigger anything for him—unlike his name, mine isn't an uncommon one here.

He smirks in my direction, a man who knows what he's working with and that women admire it, and I sink lower into the water, all the way to my chin, willing the water to temper the heat of my skin as I internally scream at my soul to listen to reason. This isn't my—Dayva's—Cato. The chances are ridiculously slim. I'm at war with myself about whether I even want him to be; if not, I can justify my attraction and who knows, maybe kindle something there, because what woman wouldn't want to run her tongue along those abs? But if it is him, I'll have to get myself in check quick, because a) I will not distract myself with anyone, human or angel, beyond the call of duty or casual sexual release and b) he doesn't see me as anything more than his little sister's best friend, anyway. There's no point in me spending any more of my time having a useless crush on him. Plus, there's no way I can involve myself with Dayva's brother, even if points a) and b) didn't exist. It would be too weird. Right?

As Cato raises his hands above his head, the movement accentuating the strong V lines leading into his shorts, I clench my legs together and remind myself of my final point—even if it is "our" Cato, he'll never be interested in his little sister's bestie, so any attraction in any realm from my side is irrelevant.

He dives—a perfect swan dive, free of flips or tricks but leaving not a hint of splash when he enters the water. Everyone whistles and cheers as Terra leans toward me and says, "He's on UBC's senior dive team with my brother, so you'll get to know them both too."

I nod, forcing my focus from the man in question and back to her. "Oh, that's awesome," I manage. "Is your brother here?"

Terra points to another guy across the pool and down from us. "That's him there."

Cato's swimming over to him now, the two laughing at something I can't make out over the music. Cato shakes his head as he reaches his friend, sending droplets flying from his wavy hair, and my pace quickens at the way the movement highlights his sharp jawline.

I have to find out, either way.

Hailey's standing and Terra's pulling herself out of the pool and I move to push myself up out of the water to follow them when I hear a man's voice say, "You've got some skills."

I've already pulled halfway out of the pool, so I spin to sit instead of continuing to a stand, my heart in my throat. Cato's swum up behind me. He puts a hand on the ledge, his pinky finger mere inches from my thighs and the dangling strings of my bottoms. One swift movement and he could untie—

"I could say the same for you," I hear myself saying, my voice coming out more sure than I expected. He looks at me, his gaze dropping for a second to my chest, and I feel my nipples pebble—due to the air against my wet bikini or his stare, I won't say, though I can guess. But when his eyes meet mine again, there's a heat in them I don't know how to deal with. So, like a dummy, I don't do or say anything. I just look at him.

A voice from the house hollers at Hailey to come see her girlfriend kicking ass at beer pong. Hailey and Terra grab towels from the grass behind us. "See you inside?" Terra asks me, hesitating to leave me. I shoot her a smile and nod, the two scurrying off as I turn back to the man in the water.

"I'm Cato."

"Lucie."

"I haven't seen you around before, Lucie."

"I'm an old friend of Clementine's and just moved here. She invited us out to meet some of her friends."

In an effortless movement, he slides up and sits beside me, close enough for me to feel the heat from his body. "Us?" he asks.

Angling my head to look at his face, I bite my lip, stressed, and I don't miss how it draws his gaze. I pop my lip out from between my teeth, internally cursing at the inadvertent flirting I'm engaging in. I need to get it together. This is my chance—the moment I say Dayva's name, I'll know if he's angel Cato or simply a human with the same name. Dayva is also not a common human name, and there's no way he won't react to hearing it if he's her brother. "Yeah," I say, studying him, "me and my roommate, Dayva."

The heat in his gaze extinguishes like water doused over a flame, and the muscles from his jaw all the way through his core visibly tense. I feel equally extinguished, the tiny spark of hope my soul had been protecting that maybe he'd keep look-ing at me that way even if he knew who I was, drenched with reality's disappointment. He stares at me, and in the heartbeats that pass between us, I realign my priorities and focus on how much it will mean to Dayva when she realizes she won the lottery with the one-in-a-crazy-high-number chance that we would stumble upon her brother during our first full day on Zircon. "Yep. Dayva," I repeat, still trying to be subtle.

"Lucie?" His voice comes out raspy, and he's blinking at me too many times, as if trying to clear me from his vision. "You're here...with Dayva?"

I keep nodding. Then, even though I'm confident it's him, I say carefully, "We Arrived 30 days ago. Terra and Ainsley's 17th

birthday was the perfect opportunity to…assign ourselves new friends." Any human could take the sentence at face value. To a Guardian, it would mean so much more.

A slow grin splits his face. Before I can register what's happening, he's scrambling to his feet and yanking me to mine. And then, to my shock, I'm in his arms and he's hugging me. My skin slides against his, water against water, heartbeat to heartbeat, and yet all I do is stand there with my arms stuck to my sides like an idiot.

"Cato," I hiss. He can't hug me like this—we aren't supposed to know each other.

He releases me and glances around, but it seems like everyone left to witness Ainsley's beer pong domination, leaving us momentarily alone on the pool deck. Thanks to the darkened night, or maybe out of the kindness of his heart, he doesn't notice or draw attention to the fact I'm crimson from the contact. "Damn, Lucie, what are the chances? And you're with Dayva? She's here?" He looks toward the house, eager Golden Retriever energy trapped in a sinfully sexy man's body. It's a heady combination, and I swallow hard.

"She's playing beer pong with Ainsley," I answer, the words no sooner out of my mouth than he's tossing me a folded towel from a chair behind him. He wraps one around his waist; I mimic his movements by curling the towel around my own hips.

"She's going to be stunned," he says, his grin wide enough to split his face as he motions for me to lead the way into the house. I acquiesce, leading us through the halls to my best friend and his little sister, battling with the knowledge that this is the best thing ever for Dayva—and might just be the worst thing ever for me.

8

CATO

I follow Lucie into the house, though I'm having a hard time believing it's really her, and that my sister is here, too. As we often keep our Cast names for simplicity, it's easy enough for Guardians to look each other up during Assignments and try to connect with Celestia friends. But sometimes it's necessary for us to take another name, like if the Assignment we take on is of a same or similar name, has someone close to them it would be confusing for, or if the culture requires it. In these cases, it's not always possible to find the Guardian you seek. And while Guardians make up a large percentage of the Zircon population, most of the time, we have no idea who is or isn't a Guardian unless the familiarity of a name triggers a realization.

If Lucie had come on her own, I mightn't have thought twice about it; she's the third Lucie I've met on this Assignment alone. But Dayva is not a common name here, so of course that made me wonder. Right now, I'm beyond thankful Dayva and I both kept our names for our current Assignments.

I'm also currently trying not to stare at Lucie's impressive ass, which is wrapped snugly in a towel in front of me, swaying with each step as she leads me to my sister.

I had noticed her the moment she'd stripped down to her bathing suit, before I'd known she was my little sister's best friend—but so had everyone else. Her Form is that deadly combination of thick and thin in all the right places, her height and long blonde hair completing the perfect package. But of course, if I'd have known who she was, I never would have flirted with her—because, I'll say it again: she's been my little sister's best friend for, literally, ever. Lucie has been hanging around since she was Cast, practically becoming an extension of my family, and I hadn't ever thought of her in a sexual way before. I certainly didn't mean for that to start now. Sure, I'd noticed how she'd turned into an attractive angel over the years, but she'd always just been...studious, head-in-the-books Lucie.

I have to hand it to her, though; her Form is beautiful. Not in a dramatic way, but in a classic, simple manner. The generous curve of her hips is accentuated further by the strings of her bikini bottom that draw up to her waist, and the triangles of blue fabric against her chest reveal the softest glimpse of what I recently learned is called "side boob," and I am definitely a fan of said side boob. My fingers want to brush against it, to slip under the thin fabric and feel the weight of each breast in my palms—

"Who's winning?"

Lucie's voice cuts through my daydream, and I swallow hard, trying to regain focus. *My little sister's best friend,* I chastise myself for the third time in as many minutes, trying to calm the semi I feel beginning to push against the towel. Thank goodness for the towel and that I'm not just waltzing around right now in the flimsy material of my trunks. Sexy Form or not, that's Lucie, and that's the end of the story.

"Dayva's my secret weapon!" Ainsley looks over at us with a smug grin on her face. "I hereby claim her as my beer pong partner from now to forevermore. Olympics, here we come!"

A small, dark-haired woman steps up to the table beside her, and I glance sideways at Lucie, who gives me a nod and an accompanying smile that lights up her face, excitement shimmering in her eyes at the prospect of re-uniting brother and sister.

Dayva and I grew up pretty close in Celestia. I was 25 when she was Cast, but I loved having a little sister to dote on. As she got older and wilder, I became the one to pull her out of trouble or cover her tracks before our parents got involved, but I never minded. She was bold and funny, unafraid and competitive, and I never backed down from a challenge from her—whether racing through the skies, shoving as many strawberries into our mouths as we could, or any other number of competitions Dayva dreamt up.

I can't help the smile that breaks over my own face as Dayva bounces the ball in a perfect arc across the table and it lands with a satisfying "plop" in the final cup of the opposing team's—a stark difference to Dayva and Ainsley's side, where the blunted triangle formation shows that only one cup took a hit.

"Gold medal, motherfuckers!" Dayva jumps up and down, grabbing Ainsley's hand to hold it high in the air in triumph, and I know for sure that this spirited woman is my sister.

Chants of "Drink! Drink! Drink!" rise from all the other partygoers gathered around the room. Hailey pours two shots from the bar behind her and hands them each to Dayva and Ainsley, planting a solid kiss on her girlfriend's lips as she does.

"To new friends and new beer pong champions!" Ainsley calls out amidst cheers. The pair tosses the shots back and then Lucie beelines it around the couch we're standing behind toward my sister as four new players step up to arrange the table.

Dayva lifts her hand to high-five Lucie and me as she says, "Congratulations on high-fiving beer pong royalty." I laugh, but Lucie doesn't give her time to continue grandstanding before she's grabbing her hand and dragging her back out the way we came—to the darker backyard, I realize, where the music and space will allow us a modicum of privacy to tell Dayva who I am. "What? What's going on?" Dayva asks, stumbling after her, confused.

I follow, thankful to have Dayva between me and Lucie, making it far easier to keep my eyes away from Lucie's perfect ass.

Lucie drags Dayva outside and then across the lawn to the corner of the yard, where an empty picnic table is dimly lit by a string of red patio lights overhead. She sits down and yanks Dayva to the bench beside her. I sit down across from them, my grin wide and mischievous—a twin to Lucie's, I note.

"Okay, what the fuck, Lucie? I needed to celebrate with my new fans." Dayva crosses her arms over her chest, scowling. "Also, who the hell is this guy, and why do you both look like you know something I don't? I hate not being part of secrets and schemes. I am the schemer—I am the scheme embodied!"

I lean forward, chuckling. "Yep, that's Dayva all right. The Form might be different, the voice might be minimally less annoying, but the sour personality? That's all Dayva."

Dayva's head tilts to the side, her face suddenly less annoyed and more intrigued. "The Form?" she asks, a note of caution laced through her words. She looks over to Lucie, who's sitting sideways on the bench, giving me the perfect view of that tantalizing side boob that I'm struggling to avert my gaze from.

Lucie nods, her eyes sparkling. "Say hello to a fellow Guardian."

Dayva raises her eyebrows but uncrosses her arms as she leans forward to study me, as if there's any clue about who I might have been in Celestia lingering in this Form. She repeats her question from earlier. "A fellow Guardian, hey? Okay, well, who are you? Do we know you?"

I note the way she uses "we," showing how interlocked she is with Lucie, and I'm happy to see their relationship hasn't changed in the 25 years since I departed. I'm about to open my mouth to tease her more, to draw up her frustration again before giving her the answer—it's what siblings do, after all, and I'd missed riling up my sister. But Lucie is bouncing up and down, and before I can say anything else, she blurts out in the loudest whisper known to humans—"It's Cato!"

Dayva freezes. For a second, ten, twenty. Until Lucie's smile falters and she pokes her best friend in the ribs. "Dayva?"

And then Dayva's rounding the picnic table and I barely have the time to stand and untangle my legs from the picnic bench before she's choking me in a fierce hug, her arms locking so tightly around my neck I can barely breathe. I wrap my arms around the unfamiliar Form housing my sister's soul and squeeze her back just as tight. Over her shoulder, I see Lucie, her elbows on the table, chin rested in her hands as she watches our reunion, quiet tears of happiness for her best friend sliding down each cheek. Despite myself, my soul stutters, certain I've never seen anything quite so breathtaking.

9

LUCIE

ONE WEEK LATER

Standing in the middle of the apartment, hands on my hips, I turn in a slow, full circle and survey our living space. I've spent the last week trying to add some personality to the blank canvas of the apartment and am pretty satisfied with the result. I've painted the walls a midnight blue and hung spray-painted gold frames from the thrift store of various sizes and shapes across the walls. Patterned cushions spruce up grey couches, and a fluorescent pink carpet keeps the dented wood coffee table from sliding around in the middle of the living room.

I grab my Tone and note the time as I turn up the volume on the playlist a little more. We're having some of our new friends over for a small "apartment-warming" party in a couple of hours. The fridge and counter are full of snacks, but otherwise, the place is clean and tidy. It isn't a large space, though, so we've limited our invite list to Clementine, Ainsley, Hailey,

Cato, Terra, and Terra's brother—who, Dayva had learned via text from Cato since the birthday party, is his Assignment. Which means Cato and I are going to be in each other's orbits a lot. Even more than Dayva and I might overlap. The thought makes my stomach do strange, uncomfortable flips.

We haven't had an opportunity to chat much with Cato, as moments after revealing his identity to Dayva, the birthday girls had rounded everyone up for cake and a few group games. Cato had left soon after to go to another friend's place with Forest, but he'd tapped Tones with us to exchange contact info before leaving.

Dayva's halo had bound to Ainsley a few minutes later—thankfully, she'd paid close attention to the time and slipped off to hide in the bathroom just before it happened. She'd sent him a message to let him know, and they'd been texting ever since. Although I had his number and he had mine, neither of us had reached out. It felt weird to do; we hadn't really been friends in Celestia, just friend*ly*, so I don't think we would have even had anything to talk about. Dayva relays info to me from their conversations, and I try to put the image of his perfect tan skin glistening with water out of my mind. I need to focus on connecting with Terra and settling into the rhythm of this new life on Zircon before starting university.

Dayva is out grabbing drinks and ice, so with one last satisfied glance at the living room, I head into the bathroom to shower and get ready for the party, bringing my Tone and its music with me.

It hasn't taken me long to realize how intensely I dislike the human hair we are required to incorporate on most of our Forms—and I'm not talking about head hair. I mean leg hair, armpit hair, etc. Not only must humans shower frequently to avoid smelling like rotting flesh, but at least as women, the current social standard is to shave the majority off, which just seems like a waste of time to me. But of course, in my typical bid for perfection, I bow to the responsibility of upholding social norms and keep every part of me shaved smooth, from my toes to my armpits. I even razor bare my entire pubic region, unable to handle the itchiness that the growth of hair gives me. I may have sliced myself open once or twice in the most sensitive regions, but I'm sure I'll get better at it.

Once I've washed, shampooed, scrubbed, exfoliated, and shaved, I step out to blow-dry and curl my hair and put on makeup. I decide to keep the makeup minimal and soft; a little pink for my cheeks and mascara for my lashes, and then I try a natural, dusty-rose shade of lip gloss. It contrasts well against my blonde hair, I decide as I purse my lips. I tame my bangs as the final touch and then step back from the small mirror above the sink and turn to the full-length one we bought that's now hanging on the back of the bathroom door.

I'm naked, having let myself air dry while I primped, the light romper I'd worn into the bathroom shoved into the washing machine behind me. I take in my Form, still getting used to the strange way gravity pulls on human skin even in youth. But standing there nude, clothed only with my armband tattoo, a bellybutton piercing, six ear piercings, and long hair draped over one shoulder, I admit I feel nearly as confident in this Form as I did in my Celestia body.

Another glance at my Tone tells me I still have a half hour until everyone arrives, so I grab it and open the door to the living room, not caring if Dayva is home to see me naked. We may not be in Celestia anymore, but we'd grown up around nakedness and didn't care to wear constraining clothes all the time around the apartment.

I step out and press "stop" on my Tone to pause the music from playing, only bothering to look up when Dayva erupts into a coughing fit—and find myself staring straight into the icy blues of the man I'd been trying all week to get out of my system.

10

CATO

I try.

I swear, I try so hard to keep my eyes locked on hers, but they stage a mutiny against my willpower and traitorously disobey.

My gaze falls first to her lips, glossy and full, slightly agape in surprise. The world around me disappears, becoming nothing more than hollow background noise as I follow the lean curve of her neck to the gentle edges of her collarbones. I wonder briefly who body-snatched me, because never before have I found collarbones so enticing. I take a full look across her breasts, her rosy nipples pebbling under my stare or from the cooler temperature of the living room, I don't know, and at the moment I don't care, turned on from their peaks regardless.

Lower, my eyes sweep across the smooth expanse of her stomach, catching on the sparkly blue gem pierced through her bellybutton, and then I admire the perfect V where her thighs meet. She's completely bare, freshly shaven, and soft. My throat feels thick, but I continue all the way down her long legs to her narrow feet, where I notice how her second toes are just longer than her big toes, a common Zircon Form component.

She doesn't move during my assessment until Dayva leans across the kitchen counter and whacks me up the backside of my skull. I wince and tear my gaze away from the angel (and I use the word in both the literal sense and the human sense of perfection) in front of me to glare at my sister. "Cato, gross," Dayva chides, wrinkling her nose up at me. "That's Lucie you just eye-fucked, you absolute moron. You can perv on anyone you want but not her, never her, no matter what Form she's in. She's practically your sister."

I don't dare say it, but I disagree—Lucie may be familiar to me, but she's far from family, according to my traitorous eyes and their best friend, my dick, which is now pummelling the fly of my jeans. I flash my eyes back over to Lucie, but she's gone, the door next to the bathroom slamming shut on my view of her backside. Swivelling on the stool to turn back to Dayva, I attempt to act casual as I resume pouring bags of chips into waiting bowls.

Apparently satisfied that she's reigned in her dumb brother and thankfully clueless to the raging hard-on I'm sporting beneath the counter, Dayva proceeds to jabber on about something Ainsley told her earlier in the week. But while I'm listening to her, I don't register anything she says. I hear myself responding with the right conversational encouragements of "mhmm" and "oh yeah?" but my consciousness is absent from reality. My mind is otherwise occupied with replaying the image of the sexy blonde with bangs that dip into her eyelashes and molten lava-ringed brown eyes that tell me I'm in big, big trouble.

What's more worrying, though, is that I seem to be perfectly okay with that.

11

LUCIE

I hear Dayva prattling on as she gets the snacks ready, Cato laughing at something she says. The sound brings heat to my cheeks—I'd been too stunned before for even my soul to register a blush as I'd waltzed out naked, practically right into my childhood crush's arms.

I scurry across the bedroom to push open the window, looking for a breeze to cool the belated flush of my skin. The way he'd looked so surprised when I'd stepped out, which I'm sure had been a mirror image of my own face...but then his gaze had roamed down, over every inch of me, pausing at the apex of my thighs, where I'm almost certain he could see my vulva pulse in hopeful anticipation.

The entire interaction had probably lasted only a second or two, as Dayva had quickly clocked him on the head when she'd seen me come out of the bathroom naked and I had run—literally run—for the safety of my bedroom. Yes, we'd grown up around nakedness, and I feel no shame in this Form, but things are different here than in the Realm of Lights. Cato and I, we are both so...human here, and the rules aren't the same, and his gaze had been so heavy, so heated...my pussy pulses again, begging for attention—preferably in the form of Cato's tongue, fingers, or dick (really, she won't be picky, my soul insists, playing wing woman for my vulva)—but I sit on my bed and cross my legs as tightly as I can instead.

It would seem my childhood crush had only dimmed in the time since his Departure, laying dormant but awoken the minute we reconnected. Yes, his Form is exceedingly hand-some, but I'm beginning to think it doesn't matter what Form he appears in. It's the soul behind his eyes in any realm that draws me like a hypnotized moth to a burning flame.

I sigh, standing again to rummage through my dresser, which I've already filled to overflowing with clothes. Although I don't enjoy wearing them, they are admittedly addicting to buy, with their endlessly fun colours and patterns and styles. I pull out a bra and underwear along with a baggy high-neck t-shirt, knowing I'll hate the constriction of fabric across my chest, and a pair of white canvas shorts. It's a modest look, an intentional choice to guard myself from any more of Cato's lingering gazes. I know well enough that he reacted as any male would to being abruptly confronted with a naked woman's body. It meant nothing more than momentary lust, and there is no point in allowing myself to think otherwise; as much as my soul might protest, I'm aware that only heartbreak, guilt, and compromise await down any path leading me to Cato, or any relationship. I'd promised myself a long, long time ago that I would never jeopardize my identity or my goals for someone else. Not even the man I'd loved in secret for a century.

I hear the front door open and new voices enter the apartment, which is my cue that it's safe to exit. More body buffers will keep me from having to feel awkward around Cato and an oblivious Dayva. With a final glance in the full-length mirror I'd also purchased for my bedroom, I split my long hair down my back and bring it forward over my shoulders as an extra shield over my chest and open the door to greet the rest of our houseguests with a casual smile.

***

We're sitting around the living room, some of us on the L-shaped couch or kitchen stools, some of us sprawling on the ground. I'm on the floor, and in an unfortunate unfolding of events, Cato is too, reclined next to me with his back against the couch and legs extended half under the coffee table. I clutch one of my pretty throw pillows on my lap and comb my fingers repetitively through one of the corner tassels in distraction.

"So, how did you two meet?" The question comes from Dayva as she motions between Cato and Forest, who's idly swivelling back and forth on a stool with a beer dangling between his fingers. He's got short-cropped blond hair and the typical toned body of a diver. His frame is the same lean, rectangular build as Terra's, and it's obvious they're related in the similar mannerisms they share. They also must share the same line of souls, both of them having extended warm and gracious welcomes to Dayva and me ever since the birthday party. Ainsley has also been quick to accept us into the friend group. Altogether, we have felt immense relief. More often are the stories of Guardians struggling in their chosen roles, or needing to change the relationship of their roles to their Assignments, or disliking their human entirely. It seems we have lucked out in a big way with our first Assignments.

"It's not an exciting story—we met the first day of UBC team practice three years ago," says Forest, his voice a soft, deep tone.

All four of the human women laugh, but Dayva and I aren't sure why until Cato jumps in to expand on the tale, a wry grin creasing his face as he looks at Forest. "That's the boring version of the story. The actual story is that he was so nervous, he had one of the most epic bellyflops I've ever seen on his very first dive. The fucker actually knocked himself out on impact. I realized it right away and dove in to grab him and swim him to the edge. But not before he came to in a panic and nearly drowned me as he tried to get his bearings."

I look to Forest for confirmation, and he rolls his eyes, a small smile tipping the edges of his lips up. He tilts his beer back and finishes it with a long swig before placing it on the counter behind him, content to let Cato continue the story.

"Ambulance was called and everything," Cato goes on. I sip my canned Bellini, enjoying watching him in this new environment. Looking at him and knowing who he is makes me feel both homesick and somehow also like I am home, a dichotomy of emotions I'll sort out later. "Coach said he hadn't seen anyone fail so epically in a decade, and wondered if his file got mixed up with someone else's and he'd made the team by mistake, because clearly he was a shit diver who couldn't even handle the pressure of one day of practice." We all giggle except for Forest, who just shrugs. "Turns out, it wasn't just Forest being a Nervous Nelly; they realized when the next person went to dive an hour later that the diving board had a loose bolt in it and on his takeoff, it ripped through and shifted the board sideways by a couple inches, which obviously threw everything off. Anyway, when the docs cleared him to get back to the pool a couple weeks later, we all out went out as a team and he bought me a beer to thank me for saving his life—"

Forest interrupts now, amusement playing across his laid-back features. "Which has somehow turned into what, 500? All I know is this man has swindled his way into never having to buy another beer again as long as I'm around." He flicks the bottle cap of a fresh beer Cato's direction.

Cato deftly catches it with one hand. "Again, you're welcome for saving your life," he retorts.

"Pretty sure other people jumped in to help right away," Hailey supplies. "I think he'd have been just fine without you acting as a Guardian angel."

Everyone laughs, but I inhale a sharp breath at those words right as I go to take another sip of my drink, which causes me to breathe the liquid into my lungs instead. I cough and sputter, my eyes darting to Dayva, who flashes me an amused, knowing look. While the term "guardian angel" is used loosely by humans and I'm certain none of the human souls in this room will ever realize how accurate Hailey's comment is, it still caught me off guard to hear it vocalized in the Realm of Bones like that for the first time.

I lean forward as I try to regain my composure. A hand taps a gentle rhythm against my back, and a low chuckle sounds by my ear as Cato, the person nearest me, attempts to help. "You good?"

My coughs dwindle and conversation moves on around us as I finally nod, refusing to look him in the eye, his handsome face far too close to my flushing one. "Am good," I squeak.

His hand falls from my back, and I miss its weight as we both lean back into our spots. Cato adds to another story that Terra's telling, but I'm distracted by Clementine, who's sitting on the couch behind Cato, her legs now uncurled and draped down beside him. One of them shifts as she leans forward to grab a brownie from the table, her calf pressing against his arm. I can't help but pay more attention to their interactions and note how she gazes at Cato when he speaks, laughs a little louder at his jokes, offers to fetch him water when she stands to go to the kitchen.

I can't blame her for having the same crush I do, but I also can't stop the spark of uninvited jealousy that flickers in my soul.

12

LUCIE

FIRST DAY OF CLASSES

I feel a thrill course through me, and I shiver. Dayva gives me a weird look from her desk next to me, but I just shrug.

I can't help it if I'm delighted to be attending a real-life Zircon university as a real-life student. While my job as a Guardian takes precedence over everything else, the fact is that most of the time, Guardians are just living their own version of a human life. I am determined to make it a good life, every single time, which includes being an A+ student. I love learning, and while we cover the basics of human education throughout our Deks, I don't care if it's mostly review—I'll still give my best human work and be engaged with my classes, because that's the role I've set for myself in pursuit of my long-term goals.

Papers rustle and I glance at the time on my Tone to see class is almost over. I only have one class today, but I have dive practice this afternoon.

Although Terra isn't in university yet, the college partners with high school teams to promote the sport and hone the skills of up-and-coming divers. Terra's on an elite school team, so they join the junior university dive team (the one I'm on for now) for three practices a week. As the first day of the semester, today is one of those days.

As we pocket our Tones and stand, Dayva prods my side with a gentle nudge. "Guy down the row in the green shirt? He's been checking you out all class. Keep an eye on him, maybe say hi sometime."

I look, and sure enough, I find him looking back at me. He shoots me a quick smile and then exits the row, and I wait for the inevitable blush. But it doesn't come, and I'm both surprised and disappointed. He was cute, with those two dimples, and I wouldn't mind a little casual fling. A girl has needs, after all, and just because I plan to stay away from commitments until it makes sense to for this Assignment, doesn't mean I plan to stay celibate. But I guess he's not my soul's type, so I shrug half-heartedly. "Yeah, maybe. But it's class number one—I gotta keep my options open," I hedge.

I don't need to be looking at my best friend to know she's rolling her eyes as I follow her into the busy hallway. "I'm not saying you gotta marry the guy," she huffs. "You've had hook-ups before—all I'm suggesting is a little human-to-human interaction. You know, take this Form out for a test ride." We're walking side-by-side now and she smacks my ass to emphasize her words.

"And what about you, little miss head-turner?" I tease back. "Congrats to me for turning one head—but we literally walk down the hall and there's not one person who doesn't drool over you."

Dayva dusts off her shoulders, confidence radiating from her. "What can I say? I build damn good Forms."

We exit to the green in the middle of the campus, the sun a welcoming sight to our angelic souls. "I'm kind of nervous about it, to be honest," Dayva admits as we stroll to a spot on the lawn. We don't need to communicate to know where we are going—that's what happens when you've been best friends for over a century.

"About having sex?" We plop our bags down and then lie on our stomachs, letting the sun warm our air-conditioned bodies. "It's not like it's your first time."

We both fold our arms beneath our heads and lay a cheek on them, looking at each other. She purses her lips. "Yeah, but it kind of is. It's my first time in this body. And it's also been a decade—or two," she amends begrudgingly at my raised eyebrow, "since I've done it with anyone other than Ellis."

I'm silent for a moment before I pose my sensitive question. "Do you miss him?"

She shifts, pulling an arm free, and begins picking at the grass with one hand as she considers my question. "Yes, and no? I don't regret telling him I need this space, because I need to be on my own without him to fall back on. I've got you and that's all I truly want or need. And we've been on and off for decades—he needs the space as much or more than I do. We can see how and where we stand when we Return." She pauses, and I let the silence sit comfortably between us. "But of course I miss him. Next to you, he was my best friend. How could I not?"

I reach over and tuck her hair behind her ears, my heart sad for her, and sad for me too, as I think about all the friends and family we have scattered across both realms. "I'm so glad you have Cato, at least," I whisper, hoping the mention of her beloved brother brings her partway back to happy.

She blinks up at me, and I stare into the eyes I barely know and the soul I know so well as she grabs my hand and twines her fingers with mine. "Yes, at least we have Cato," she whispers, and I try to ignore how my heart twitches at the way she adds me into the equation. I roll onto my back and close my eyes against the sun as it glows against my face, hiding the tangle of emotions lying in my soul beneath it.

***

"Lucie! Come here!"

I turn to the familiar voice echoing across the pool and spot Terra waving at me from within a small group of other swimsuit-clad humans. I let out an internal sigh of relief at seeing her friendly face. Although I'll befriend the rest of my junior team given a bit of time, it's always intimidating to walk into a group of people you don't know, especially when many of them have known each other for years.

I round the pool to join the group, and Terra introduces me to five other girls and four guys. A few of them are on the high school team, and the rest are on my junior team. Each team has about 20 divers, so after exchanging polite greetings, I look around to try to assess who else is on the team. I don't have to wonder long, though, as a sharp whistle sounds and a woman's voice calls our teams to meet at the bleachers—which I realize is where I already am.

The cue must also be for the team in the time block before us to finish, and when I spot Forest climbing out of the water, I realize belatedly that it's the senior team—the best of the best, which also happens to be the team Cato's on. He appears with a couple of girls from behind the diving towers, all of them laughing, and my heart squeezes at the display of cut muscles that make up every inch of Cato's body. Again, I question how such a perfect Form didn't get a failing grade, but at another glance at the surrounding divers, I realize he's not alone in his muscle definition—it's kind of the standard with these divers. I bite my lip, wondering if I made a mistake with the Form I chose. While strong, I'm not as slender and lithe as many of the girls, and my height places me well above most of them and at eye-level with many of the boys. Cato's got me beat by a couple of inches, but as he gets closer, flanked by two very small, Dayva-esque bodies, I feel bulky and unattractive, for the first time questioning my Form choice.

"Juniors, we're going out tonight!" one of the guys calls out as he wraps a towel around his waist.

"Team bonding," adds a girl pushing out of the water a few feet from me—who stands to my height. She smiles at me, a tall girl acknowledging a tall girl. "You all are required to come," she says with mock seriousness.

"We're meeting at 11 at Bar Furthermore," the first boy says as he walks by. "See ya'll there!" I cock my head at the name, amused at the private joke I hold between me, myself, and I as I acknowledge the humorous opposite symmetry it holds to the Evermore club in Celestia.

The rest of the seniors amble past, greeting and joking with the juniors they know, despite one of our coaches, a stunning woman with a head full of waist-length braids, trying to shoo them on and get us organized.

"See you there." A hand slips across my back. Before I can turn to look for my best friend's brother, the only person who could make me tense up with three such innocuous words, I'm distracted by a scream and a splash.

"Forest, you're DEAD!" The declaration comes from a scowling Terra as she swims to the edge of the pool, her attention laser focussed on Forest, who strides away with his hands in the air, making it clear that brother pranked sister.

The hand slips from my back as Cato leaves to follow his friend. A moment later, Coach divvies us into groups, and I have no further time to think about anyone or anything beyond my role as a competitive university team diver.

13

CATO

I had volunteered as the designated driver tonight, so the drink I'm nursing is a diet soda and nothing else, but I'm not one to let a lack of alcohol keep me from enjoying myself. As the music of Bar Furthermore, the popular bar adjacent to campus, pulses through the crowds of people on the dance floor, I lean over the second-floor railing with Hailey as we watch the dive team members ebb and flow throughout the throng of bodies below.

Hailey, on the other hand, is not at all sober. Last year, the province had lowered its drinking age to that of its Alberta neighbour, and she'd been making the most of it since her 18th birthday a few months earlier. I'd picked up Forest at his house and then her from the restaurant she worked at on my way, though we'd been inside the bar two minutes before we'd lost Forest.

I glimpse him now—double fisting his favourite local IPA and dancing suggestively with a pretty blonde (or is it two, maybe three? pretty blondes). He happens to look up and spot me, and he shouts something I can't discern over the deafening club music, raising his beers in a "cheers"-ing motion at me, clanking them together. I smile, lifting my soda in response.

"Some...somebody's getting lucky tonight." Hailey leans against me to yell in my ear, her words slurred and her breath almost strong enough to get me drunk by proximity. "Bets on how many?"

I sip my soda and pretend to study Forest intently before making my decision. "My money's on two, but he's gonna try for all three. I don't think the one with the ponytail is as into it, though."

She turns back to the dance floor and nods, grabbing my elbow for support as the movement inadvertently makes her wobble. "A tenner—you're on."

"Let's get you some water." I'm about to lead her to the bar when arms drape over us both, accompanied by the faint scent of chlorine.

"My loves!" Terra squeals, her cheeks flushed pink. "Found you guys! Having fun?"

I turn my head and raise my brows—Terra's 17, but it's easy to get into bars underage if you have half a mind to. And with how she's done her make-up and taped up her boobs under her skin-tight purple top, I can't imagine it had been difficult for her to gain access. There's always a back door and a bouncer willing to be bribed. She smirks at me, as if reading my thoughts.

Ainsley, always somewhere close by her lifelong best friend, pushes up under Terra's arm to wrap Hailey in a hug. Hailey plants a fat, clumsy kiss on her cheek, and Ainsley cringes, far from being on the same sloppy-drunk level as her girlfriend. I laugh, and dip my head to shout in her ear, "I was just taking her to get some water—she needs it."

Terra and Ainsley grab Hailey's hands and pull her over to the bar. I turn back to look over the balcony, trying to convince myself I haven't been waiting for, and am certainly not looking for, one tall, curvaceous woman in particular. But of course, as soon as I spot her, it becomes difficult to even pretend to lie to myself.

Lucie's dressed in a glittering black romper, the V of the neck reaching past her sternum. Her hair's tied up in a ponytail, the waves falling from it still long enough to reach her lower back. She's braided her bangs back, leaving her face open and making her expressive eyes seem even larger. She's sipping a pink drink and laughing with a few of the dive team around the bar below. Or rather—flirting with them, all of them guys who I know are feeling some type of way about her exposed cleavage.

I frown. She's my little sister's best friend, and it's her first Assignment. It's only natural that I keep an eye out for her, my mind tries to convince my soul. No nefarious reasons present.

I go to push away from the railing when I pause, noticing Lucie's body language abruptly shifting from relaxed to tense. She sets her glass down on the bar and turns from the boys, waving them off as they ask her something. One hand goes to the delicate flower armband tattoo circling her arm, and she rubs it—and then I know what's wrong. Her bound halo is burning against her skin, alerting her that her Assignment is in danger.

My stomach drops as I turn and scan the mezzanine area for Terra, knowing that if she went to the balcony bar, I'm closer to her than Lucie. I move in that direction even though I can't see her, driven by my angelic need to help a fellow Guardian, to help save a human soul from any number of dangers.

The stronger the halo burns, the more serious the threat. But I remember my own first alerts without a baseline for what was a mild irritation to an agonizing burn, and the panic that it caused me. I'm at least thankful to realize that the dragon encircling my bicep isn't burning, so I'm confident Forest isn't in danger.

Forest is my second Assignment. I was surprised when my halo alerted me on my first day as his Guardian, before I'd even introduced myself, but I was ready—I was always ready. The halo had warmed with a mild heat an hour before the event and not increased with time. The moment I saw his dive go sideways, I knew it was the trigger for the alert. I dived in a split second after he hit the water—too fast for anyone to comprehend what was happening. The heat disappeared from the tattoo as soon as I touched him, the warning mild because there were so many other people around that he probably would have been okay without my interference—probably, but no guarantee.

That's the other thing with the halo alert system—while helpful and essential, it's also incredibly vague. The danger could be imminent, or it could be up to six hours away. We always take risks as Guardians when we choose to live apart from our Assignments, but the average warning gives us 30 minutes or more, and for the lifetimes we lead, it's something we decide to gamble on for most of our Assignments. My apartment building is just two blocks from Forest's house, though, so I can get there even on foot within two minutes if necessary.

As I scan for Terra, I see Lucie winding her way up the staircase on the other side of the balcony, her sparkling romper reflecting the spinning lights of the dance floor. She ignores everyone in her path, rubbing furiously at her arm, and I grow more concerned. While she might not have a baseline, surely she wouldn't be clutching at it with that much distress if the threat were menial.

I push past people to get to the bar, and then spot Hailey's backward cap. I shove closer but can't find Terra, and I feel genuine fear coil at the base of my spine. For Terra, who Dayva told me is a 29-year Assignment, and for Lucie, who would be devastated to not only fail her first Assignment so early but have to leave Dayva. And, truthfully, I'm also scared for myself. I'm not ready to lose Lucie for 777 years—though I don't know why, because I haven't so much as given her a second thought since I Departed. But I don't have time to think about that now.

"Hailey, where'd Terra go?" I yell in Hailey's ear when I get to her and Ainsley at the bar. She turns to me, her eyes a little less glazed than ten minutes ago. "Bathroom," she shouts back, pointing behind her. I aim that way without further explanation when I hear my name being called from behind me.

"Cato!" Lucie's just a few feet from me, barging through the crowd. Her eyes are wild, and my eyes drop to her arm where she's clawing at her tattoo, the skin red and raw already. I don't stop to quiz her about the situation. I just grab her hand and start running.

We're just steps from the bathroom doors when I see it—a flash of purple behind the door closing to our right. I make an instinctive decision to follow it. I've never chased down someone else's Assignment, but I've learned to lean in to my Guardian instincts, and even though Terra isn't my Assignment, I hope they'll lead me right in this case, too.

I pivot and Lucie doesn't question me, just grips my hand harder as we rush to the black door that blends into the wall, the only evidence of it being a door denoted by the red exit sign glowing above it. I push through and we spill outside in the alley, empty but for a tall figure and a stumbling woman in a purple shirt heading to a car sitting a block away.

Without stopping to assess the situation further, I yank my hand from Lucie's and take off down the alley, cursing the Fates for not allowing us our wings for moments like these, my footsteps sounding too loud in the alley. My heart hammers as I focus in on the man, who turns to see where the running steps are coming from.

As he turns, Terra's knees give out, and by the way she catches the man off-guard, I think she's gone unconscious. While she's slight and would be easy to pick up and carry, the sudden onset of her weight combined with the immediate threat of me running full tilt toward him has him stumble, and I can see him doing the math in his head. He takes only a second to come to a conclusion, and he drops my Assignment's sister and makes a run to the waiting car.

I let him go. He's not my job. Technically, neither is she, but in helping Lucie protect her, I've also protected Forest from a world of pain, and ensured a soul wasn't taken prematurely for the Realm of Shadows. I skid to a stop at Terra's side and ignore the car as it races away.

Lucie is only a split second behind me, and she slides baseball-style to Terra's other side. She reaches out to cup her Assignment's face. I know with certainty that Terra's out of danger when Lucie uses her free hand to gingerly touch her tattoo, where she's clawed right through the design and drawn blood. She winces, the halo's burn gone, replaced by the tender pain of human injury.

Relief courses through me—it's been years since I have experienced that level of adrenaline, and I shoot her a shaky, but hopefully reassuring, smile. "Welcome to the Guardian life."

14

LUCIE

"**I**s she safe now?" I hate the tremble in my voice, the panic still coursing through my body.

"Your halo's not burning anymore, is it?" Cato asks, his voice gentle, as though he knows I'm still perched precariously on a ridge of anxiety.

I shake my head, more vigorously than is necessary.

"Then she's safe," he assures me. "Come on; I'll carry her to my car. You can use my Tone to call Forest." He shifts from his position on his knees to reach into his jeans pocket to grab his Tone. When I reach across Terra to take it from him, he wraps his hand around mine and squeezes it first. "Lucie, it's ok. You did good, sweetheart. You did so good."

I hear his words, but I don't believe him—if I'd done well, Terra wouldn't be unconscious in a back alley. But now's not the time to argue over my Guardian skills, so I nod and take the Tone from him.

I get ahold of Forest, whose lighthearted demeanour shifts the moment he registers the words "Terra" and "hospital." He says he'll find Ainsley and a ride to the hospital, and call their parents.

I hang up as we climb into Cato's car. Taking care not to jostle her more than needed, Cato lays Terra across the backseat and I climb in the back to be with her, placing her head on my lap. She stirs, moaning, and I soothe her with calming words as I stroke her hair.

Terra's parents are already there when we arrive, their house much closer to the hospital than the university bar is. I let Cato give them the rundown, paying careful attention to how he phrases the story. According to him, he'd been heading to the bathrooms when he saw her through the closing outside door, and figured she was slipping out with a few friends for a smoke or some fresh air and decided to join them. Of course, when he pushed the door open and saw her being dragged down the alley, he jumped into action.

"Lucie saw me leave and followed me out," he explains as a way of introducing me. They glance at me but turn back to Cato, and I can't blame them—their daughter is lying in a hospital bed, and a random girl is the least of their concerns right now. "Forest is on his way, too," I add, a small part of me hoping to be helpful after having failed so miserably at my first true test of Guardianship.

Hailey and Ainsley show up a few minutes later, and we all hang around for another hour and give statements to the police. Terra regains consciousness and though the hospital staff won't permit us all to visit her, Forest comes out to inform us she's going to be fine, telling us she'd been heavily dosed with a quick-acting drug to make her an easy target, likely ingested through a drink. He gives Cato a long, long hug, and

Cato reciprocates. The picture of them embracing is finally what breaks through my survival mode, and tears slip down my cheek. Forest sees when he releases Cato and engulfs me in a fierce hug where I cry into his shoulder. I've known him for two short weeks and I'm beyond touched that he already shares his care with me. "She's okay, I promise," he whispers in my ear, his voice cracking. "Thank you for taking care of her tonight."

"I should have done more," I say, my words muffled into his shirt. "If she'd gotten in that car..."

A third hand touches my back, and I know it's Cato. "But she didn't," he says firmly. "And you did everything you could have."

"Text me," Cato says to Forest by way of goodbye after I hug Ainsley and Hailey too. His arm wraps around my waist, and I'm too tired to feel anything but thankful that he's here as he leads me out of the hospital and toward his car.

He opens the passenger door and guides me in before rounding to enter the driver's seat. He doesn't say anything, just starts the car and heads in the direction of my apartment. We drive in heavy silence, each of us in our own heads, my right hand tenderly pressing against the raw skin of my left arm's tattoo.

We pull into my apartment's parking lot, but he doesn't drive up to the door, manoeuvring into a parking space instead.

"Is Dayva home?" he asks as he turns off the car. I'm too tired even to stress at how much time I've spent in semi-darkness this evening, barely registering the dimly lit parking lot filled with shadows and deep night that would normally have my heart racing. Can Forms run out of adrenaline? Because I think I'm empty.

I nod. "I think so. I invited her out tonight, but she wanted me to have my own time with the dive teams."

He raises his eyebrows. "I know I haven't seen her in 25 years, but that's impressive—the Dayva I left behind never would have turned up an opportunity to party."

I attempt a weak smile. "Maybe, but she has always had my best interests at heart."

Cato reaches over and gently lifts the hand that's scratching at the scabs forming on my tattoo. "Lucie."

The way he says my name cuts through the fog of my mind.

"Look at me." It's a demand, but it's not; it's an invitation to connect, to share my vulnerability with him. And though I'll debrief everything with Dayva, it won't be the same, because Cato was there. He knew—

"How did you know?" I say suddenly, the events of the night playing rapid-fire through my mind's eye. "You pulled me outside, not the other way around. How did you know?" I search his serious blue eyes, looking for answers in the soul behind them.

He lays my hand on my lap before taking the wrist of my injured arm and resting it across the console between us. Then he leans over and reaches into the backseat, where he withdraws something from underneath my seat. A first aid kit. I say nothing as he sets it on his lap and unzips it. He rips open an alcohol swab, and I hiss when he draws it over the raw claw marks on my forearm, but he doesn't stop, holding my wrist gently but firmly in place. When the swab dries, he opens another and continues to wipe the skin until he's cleaned the entire tattoo area, and then dresses one of the deeper cuts with ointment and a bandage. He does all of this in silence, and only answers once he's zipped up the kit and replaced it under my seat.

"I saw you," he says, one hand still holding my wrist, his thumb drawing gentle circles around it. His eyes, however, study my face. "I was watching you when your halo alerted and I knew Terra had been upstairs and that I could get to her before you did."

"You were watching me?" I repeat his words, trying to make sense of them, and I'm suddenly aware of the fact I'm still wearing my clubbing outfit. The plunging neckline of my romper puts my modest cleavage on full display for him at this angle, and my shorts are pulled up to my hip bones from how I slid into the car, practically creating an arrow pointing straight to the apex of my thighs. Plus, the sparkles I'd felt so sexy in just hours earlier now seem garish against the near-tragedy of the evening, and I'm conscious of how wrong it all is—how caught up in Zircon life I already am just two weeks in that I'd failed my first—

"Yes." My destructive thoughts melt away as I lock onto the intensity in his eyes, the power of that one word. "I looked for you all evening, and when I finally found you, I couldn't look away. Just like most of the other men there." His voice is low, his words measured, and I wonder if he can feel my pulse increase beneath his hand. Okay, perhaps I have a bit of adrenaline left after all.

My soul can't help herself—she turns my skin pink at his words, which seems to delight him even as it distresses me, his lips curving up in a small teasing smile.

"Well," I manage, "I'm glad you saw me. Thank you for helping me tonight. I would have been crushed if..." I can't finish the sentence, but he knows.

I don't know when, or how, but at some point, we've both leaned forward toward each other. Our faces are closer than they need to be—not as close as I'd like. If he looks at my chest, he'll for sure be able to see my heart pounding through my skin as my breathing shallows. He's searching my gaze, the depths of his soul visible in his eyes, and I want nothing more than to fall into them. Despite my better judgment, I lean forward a hair's width more, hoping and not hoping that he'll see my invitation, that my best friend's brother will do what I've wanted him to do my entire life and finally, *finally*, kiss me.

The door of the apartment building opens and a couple walks out, laughing and holding hands. Though metres away, the intrusion breaks the tension in the car, and he releases my wrist and leans back into his seat. I swear the air in the car cools five degrees, goosebumps skittering across my skin.

He reaches for the door handle of the car, then shoots me a mischievous look, back into friend mode—if he'd ever even left it. I wouldn't doubt the heat between us to have only been one-sided, his side oblivious as he'd always been, my side inventing things that would never be. "Honestly, Forest was starting to push back on the whole, 'I have to buy my Guardian angel all of his beer' thing, so now I can use it against him as a 'you have to buy your sister's Guardian angel all of his beer' thing."

I'm not ready to leave the car, not ready to explain everything to Dayva yet, but I let him walk me into the building and up the stairs to my apartment door. Before he leaves, he gives me a quick hug and a peck on my temple, a friendship kiss that shouldn't make me feel anything but sends tingles down to my toes.

I enter the quiet apartment to find all the lights on. Dayva's bedroom light is off, but her door is open to the living room to allow the light to indirectly stream in. Neither of us are ready to commit to the dark nights of Zircon, and after the darkness

I'd just experienced in the alley, both literally and figuratively, I'm not ready to face the night alone tonight either. I slip off my romper and throw on a t-shirt and slide into Dayva's bed. I'm thankful she's asleep though, wanting to process by myself a bit more before diving into it with her.

I find her hand and hold it the rest of the night as she sleeps and I stare at the ceiling and replay the scenes of the day in my mind over, and over, and over. Including the moments in the car with Cato, where I berate myself for how quickly I pushed aside my promises to myself all because of the tiniest possibility of a kiss.

I swear to be better.

15
CATO

CHRISTMAS

There are no holidays in the Realm of Lights, but they are something I've grown to love in the Realm of Bones. Christmas is my favourite. I have vague memories of my last Assignment, where I'd taken a grandfather role and wholly poured myself into being the kindest, jolliest old man there'd ever been.

In my current Assignment, my backstory includes a single dad who lives across the country and no other close relatives. The only thing I'd been sad about in choosing a more solo role was the potential for missing out on numerous Christmas festivities. But from the very first year, Forest has refused to let me be alone on Christmas, inviting me out to the family cabin, along with all manner of other various friends. Forest's parents love being a safe home for their kids' friends and always keep an abundance of bedding and too much food at both their house and the cabin, ready at a moment's notice for a duo or a dozen of their kids' friends to show.

It's been a busy semester, and I'm looking forward to the break. Being on the senior dive team takes a lot of time, and I also volunteer on various student committees. I enjoy staying busy and being useful in the human realm beyond my role as a Guardian, because Forest so far hasn't incurred many warnings. I've only had two mild halo alerts this semester, easily headed off.

But it means I also haven't spent much more time with Lucie. I meet Dayva for lunch once a week, though we try to keep it on the down-low—the last thing we want is for our friends to think we are into each other in a romantic way. Lucie has joined us a couple of times, and I see her at dive meets, of course, but we've had no other interactions anywhere near the depth of that night at Bar Furthermore. I get the feeling she's trying to avoid me, and I don't want to make her uncomfortable, so I have kept my distance.

It doesn't keep me from thinking about her every day, though. From smiling any time I glimpse her in the university hallways, or cheering extra loud when she's on the diving boards, or asking Dayva how she is as often as I think I can get away with it. I even go on a few dates with other girls, but upon their conclusion, I end each night at their doorsteps kindly telling them I'm not interested in anything more. I try to convince myself it isn't because of Lucie but because of my busy schedule, figuring that if I tell myself something often enough, eventually I'll believe it. Because it's making me feel a little crazy, wondering why she's under my skin like this, when nothing has actually happened between us.

Last week at lunch, Dayva asked if I was going to Forest and Terra's cabin for the holidays and said Terra had invited

Lucie—and Ainsley, who'd joined us every year, and so by extension now, Dayva. Both Dayva and Lucie had done exceptional work at becoming close friends with their Assignments, and I was genuinely happy and relieved for them. According to Dayva, Lucie has headed off a few more alerts without incident so far, and Dayva has only had two—both minor, easy ones to avoid relating to Ainsley's peanut allergy.

Now, as Forest and I pull up to the cabin, my palms turn clammy as I take stock of the cars there and determine we're likely the last to arrive. It's Christmas Eve day, and I know Dayva and Lucie got here two days ago. I would have loved to have come then, but I pretended I had volunteer obligations, because Forest wrote his final semester exam last night and couldn't leave until this morning. As his Guardian, I have to remain in his vicinity, so I stewed around my house for the two days refreshing social media for the odd glimpse of the festivities at the cabin. So far, they'd done some snowshoeing, Christmas tree decorating, and a lot of reading under blankets by the roaring hearth. Hallmark shit—I couldn't wait.

We push open the door to the cabin, which is improperly titled. It is a cabin in that it's built of logs—but it's far from the small, rustic picture usually brought to mind by the word. The impressive stone fireplace rises to meet the vaulted ceiling, and the thick live-edge dining room table can easily seat 20, though we've squished in more during the summer when the cabin becomes the go-to weekend getaway for everyone and anyone in Forest and Terra's circle.

To the left of the fireplace are expansive floor-to-ceiling windows that overlook the lake, where we rip around the jet skis in the summer and play shinny on the ice in the winter. In the middle of the windows is a 30-foot Christmas tree bedecked in the sparkliest holiday decor. Various beanbag chairs and couches round out the entire space, with pillows and plaid blankets placed and draped on every other seat.

But my gaze skims over all of that and is drawn like a magnet to the enormous kitchen to the right, where everyone is currently gathered. White stone countertops sit atop jewel-green cabinets, the large island in the centre of the kitchen surrounded by women dressed in matching Christmas pyjama pants, sipping from glasses of wine in various stages of drink. The scent of fresh baking makes my mouth water.

My eyes settle on Lucie. She's leaning forward on the counter, her height forcing her feet a few steps away from the island, causing an arch in her lower back that pops out her perfect round ass. When she straightens, I notice immediately that she isn't wearing a bra under her cropped t-shirt, though just as quickly, I chastise myself for wishing that it were two inches more cropped, that I could see the soft weight of her breasts peeking out from under the hem.

"You guys are early!" Terra's perched up on the counter, her proclamation drawing all eyes toward Forest and me. "It's only 10—you said you'd be here after lunch."

Forest kicks off his boots. I lean over to straighten them before taking my own off and placing them in a neat line beside his. I stand to follow him to the kitchen, to Lucie, but she's disappeared and I pretend I don't notice, taking up the space she left at the counter instead.

"Bozo over there was banging on my door at six this morning, so I didn't really have a choice," Forest grumbles as he swipes Terra's wineglass from her hand and takes a swig. She protests against his thievery and yanks it back, but he retorts, "Really? Like you said—it's 10. That's not exactly prime wine-drinking o'clock. You have no moral ground to stand on."

Ainsley appears beside him, offering him a full glass, which he happily accepts. "It's not wine—it's sangria. So it's basically juice. And it's the holidays, so time doesn't exist," she adds. Then she steps over to pass me the glass in her other hand before returning to snuggle up beside Hailey.

"I can't help it if I have FOMO," I say with a shrug. "Besides, we all know Forest and I bring the party, so we didn't want to leave you too bored until we got here."

The front door opens, and Forest and Terra's parents walk in, their noses pink from the winter chill. "How was your walk?" asks Clementine. She's also become more of a mainstay friend since Dayva and Terra arrived, and always brings a fun energy. For a few months, she'd been quite flirty, but even before Lucie came around, I hadn't reciprocated. She's fun, but there just isn't a chemistry there. Thankfully, she seemed to catch on that I wasn't interested after a while, and we had moved past it into a comfortable friend zone.

"It was lovely. It's cold, but calm," says Forest's mom. She peers over her shoulder at us as she unbuttons her jacket. "How goes the baking? And, apparently, the alcoholic festivities?"

Ainsley once again appears with two glasses of fruit-infused wine and hands one to each of them when they approach the kitchen. "You know you can't beat 'em—so you might as well join 'em," she says.

I notice out of the corner of my eye that Lucie's coming back down the stairs that she must have darted up when I was arranging shoes. There's only one bedroom in the cabin, despite it being so large, and it's where Forest's parents sleep. Everyone else sleeps camp-style on cots in the massive upper loft, where Lucie had escaped to change her top and don a bra. The t-shirt is snug, though, and I appreciate this view just as much as the one before. Her hair's in a loose braid and bunny slippers cradle her feet, painting her the picture of Christmas cozy.

"Anyone want to go skating?" Hailey asks. Forest raises his hand right away, and Ainsley and Clementine also chime in their interest, though I hesitate, waiting to see what Lucie and Dayva will do. I don't think either of them have skates or even know how to skate.

"I don't have skates, but I'll come slide around," says Dayva with a shrug, ever open to trying new things.

Lucie nods in agreement. "Same."

But Terra shakes her head. "I've got a couple of pairs here; they'll probably be big on you, Dayva, but you can try wearing extra socks. Lucie, do you want to snowshoe with me instead? I want to hit up the lookout—it's such a clear day, it will give us a beautiful view over the lake."

My heart sinks at the idea of not getting to hang out with Lucie, help her learn to skate, hold her hand to keep her from falling. But Lucie looks excited at the prospect of snowshoeing, and I can't begrudge the joy on her face. I try to catch her eye, but she heads off to the gear room with Terra, not having ignored me, but not having exactly engaged with me either.

"Hey, why so glum?" Ainsley pulls a sheet of fresh cookies out of the oven and turns it off before laying the pan among the other half-dozen sheets on the island. "Have a cookie—you look like you need some sugar."

I swipe one from the pan and then promptly toss it back and forth between my hands as I yelp at the heat before dropping it on the counter.

Everyone laughs. "Dumbass," Dayva says, rolling her eyes, picking up a cooled cookie from her end of the counter and tossing it to me. I catch it and pop the whole thing into my mouth, the buttery soft texture melting against my tongue.

"Oh yeah, that's what I needed," I lie, pulling my happy-go-lucky mask back over my features. "Ok, let's go play some shinny!" I swipe two more cooled cookies from the countertop before following everyone to the gear room. It might not be sugar that I need, but that doesn't mean the cookies aren't amazing.

16

LUCIE

Terra and I make our way to the treeline a hundred meters from the cabin, our snowshoes sinking but holding us a few inches from the top of the soft snow. I don't see an obvious trail, but Terra knows where she's going, her footsteps straight and sure.

Our breaths crystallize around us. Her parents were right when they said it was cold but calm outside—there's not a hint of a breeze. It doesn't matter how many layers I put on, I'm not sure I'll ever enjoy the cold, but as fall turned to winter over the past few months, I've been growing to recognize the beauty that comes with a fresh snow, and how warming up with a hot drink and an oversized sweater and knit blanket after being outside creates a level of warmth in my soul I've somehow never reached before. I am pretty confident that I will always seek warmth and prefer it to the cold, but I'm accepting that it's an aspect of Canadian living that I can handle and even learn to appreciate.

The snow glitters under the clear sky and sunshine, almost blinding us, even through our sunglasses. Our snow pants make loud swishing noises, and we walk in contented silence for the first few minutes. When we hit the treeline, I fall in behind Terra as she weaves through the winter woods on an invisible-to-me-path, until finally, I have to ask. "Are we following an actual trail?"

Terra glances back at me and laughs. "Yep. You need to come back in the summer—you'll see how obvious it is then. But we grew up here and have taken this path a million times, so I could probably even find my way blindfolded."

"Mhm," I answer, skeptical of her self-proclaimed way-finding abilities as I follow her tracks between two trees whose boughs, sagging heavy with the weight of snow, I have to duck deeply under to avoid being buried by. "I've only known you a few months. For all I know, you're a serial killer luring me into the woods where they'll never find my body."

She snorts, then does an impressive slide/ski/snowshoe shuffle down a small bluff before turning to look at me. "True. I could have all kinds of nefarious plans in place."

I stand on the bluff's crown and glare at the slope, and then at her. "I think just the act of snowshoeing is nefarious enough. I'm for sure going to eat it if I follow you down this death slope."

"Oh, valid point—hold up one second." She pulls a mitten off with her teeth and reaches into her jacket pocket to pull out her Tone. She grabs the mitten from her mouth and shoots me a wicked smile as she holds up the device in recording position. "Ok, as you were."

I go to give her the finger, but in my fingerless mittens, it just looks like I'm holding my hand up to her, but she cackles, realizing what I'd intended, which makes me crack a smile, too. With a deep breath I shimmy forward, but as predicted, within 0.002 seconds, my feet have slipped out and I'm on my back sliding the entire way down, my snowshoes acting like a plow in front of me and throwing all the loose powder straight back into my face. I slide to a stop right in front of her and her camera, though I can barely see through my snow-crusted face.

"Oh, fuck you," I say, scowling in mock anger as she giggles, and then I swing my leg out to catch her behind the knees and she flips onto her back beside me, immediately becoming buried in the light powder. She pops up with a face covered in snow just like mine, and we both burst into a fit of giggles.

Once we've stopped laughing enough to be able to stand up and wipe ourselves somewhat clear from the snow now melting down our necks, we continue on, the route winding back and forth and, to my mind, endlessly upwards. With the effort it takes to slog through the increasingly deep snow, we're soon sweating and puffing, our cheeks pink from the cold but our hands red from the warmth of exertion, our mittens now carried instead of worn. We pause several times to catch our breath and peek through the teasing views of the trees as we get higher, and every time, Terra promises me that the best view is yet to come.

At one point, we stop, and at the same time, I become aware of a warm tingle on my left arm. My breath catches, and I survey my surroundings. It's not a strong burn, but it's there nonetheless, heating my arm. "Why are we stopped?" I try to keep my voice casual, but I'm on high alert.

"We have two choices. We can either go right here, which will take us straight up to the lookout, or we can go left, which will continue winding like we've been doing. What do you want to do?"

I glance both directions, but nothing obvious appears either way—no flashing green arrow that says "this is the safe way!" or flashing red "x" warning us to avoid a certain path. If only that were the system, instead of these vague, burning alerts—something I plan to take issue with when I gain a position on the High Council.

I decide to gamble on the more challenging trail being the more dangerous one and opt for the winding route. But we make it only a few steps when she follows the invisible trail around a turn and my tattoo begins to burn more intensely. I don't know if changing direction will save her or if the situation is inevitable; both dangers exist in Zircon, requiring us to make snap judgment calls and hope for the best a lot of the time—and be ready to react to either result.

"Actually..." I hedge, stopping. "Can I change my mind? Can we go the other way? If I'm out here for an adventure, then I should embrace adventure, right?" I laugh, imbuing my voice with a light-heartedness I don't feel, and force myself to stop rubbing my burning tattoo through my jacket.

Terra smirks. "Okay—hope you've been keeping up on your cardio!" She crosses in front of me to head to my right. And I mean, I have been, having taken up running every morning as part of my diving and general fitness regime, but I swear snowshoeing uses a different cardio I haven't tapped into yet.

She tromps past me to take the lead in the opposing direction and I gently shove her—not enough to do anything, but enough to come across as playful. "I don't see you running the track every morning—I'll show you what cardio is!"

She laughs, and despite the warmth on my arm, a momentary heaviness settles on my heart that is both sad and deeply joyful. I'm so thankful she's my first Assignment. We've connected so well, and it feels like we've been friends for much longer than we have. Her heart overflows with genuine kindness, and she sparkles in a way that lights up a room. I love being her friend, and that's where the joy is. But there's sadness, too, in knowing she's only a short, temporary part of my long Guardian life. In 29 years (I hope, should I be successful), she will expire, and her soul will become an eternal part of the Realm of Lights—and I'll return to the Retreat and my memories of her, my love for her, will dim 50 years to the past, and will continue to fade with each passing year. I think maybe now I understand why Dayva thinks the fade is so sad, and not a gift like I've believed it to be.

We pass the junction where we went left and continue right, and I let out a quiet sigh of relief as the heat encircling my arm disappears. At least for right now, it appears the alert was warning against an avoidable situation, and I've made the correct choice.

As we wind through the trees, we talk—about our plans for the future, about the best campus eatery, about her eagerness to finish high school and join the college dive team, about her crush on a junior team boy. It's perfect, and I realize how content I am in this moment. I'm not actively working towards something, I'm not doing anything but living in the moment, and it is a beautiful and strange realization to experience this kind of contentment for the first time in my life.

"Ready?"

I look up from my snowshoe steps as we come upon a nearly vertical 30-foot slope. I raise my brows, though they're hidden under my toque and sunglasses. "Well, what a view," I say drily, and make as if to turn back around.

Terra grabs my arm, her pink nose scrunching. "Hilarious. There are stairs under here in the summer, but we're just going to have to harness our inner mountain goat and claw our way up this drift. It will be worth it, I promise!"

"Mountain goats don't have claws," I retort, but I step up beside her and we begin using our arms to grab hold of branches from trees lining the slope, sliding back nearly as much as we gain ground for every step. "I changed my mind again," I huff after a couple minutes. "Let's go back in the other direction."

"So much for all that cardio you were boasting about," she says between her own gasps. "Almost there!"

To my chagrin, she makes headway more quickly than I do, and she crests the ridge a full minute before me, during which time she offers absolutely no assistance. Instead, she pulls out her Tone to record my struggle, which I adamantly demand she stop doing, claiming she already has too much embarrassing snowshoe footage of me—though of course that only makes her giggle harder. Finally, I pull myself over the top and flop onto my back, the snow that had fallen down my jacket and waistband in the scramble now chilling against my sweaty skin.

"Come on!" She doesn't wait for me to recover, yanking my arm to pull me up.

We are in a small clearing only a few meters in diameter, but the trees drop away on the other side. The first thing I notice is the wind. At this elevation, and without the trees to block it, a stiff breeze pulls past my cheeks. Then my eyes widen as I take in the unfettered view across the lake. For a moment, with the wind kissing my face and the dizzying drop before us, I can almost pretend that I'm flying again, can imagine feeling the wings I left behind in Celestia shift beneath my shoulders.

"Look, we can see them skating." Terra points at the tiny figures swirling around below us.

"No wonder we're tired—we climbed a lot more than I realized," I note. "If you had pointed this mountain peak out to me before we started, I probably would have changed my mind."

She laughs, slinging an arm around my shoulder, an affectionate movement I mirror. "Where would the fun be in that? Besides, I wanted to show you this place because it holds so many memories for me. There's a ring of rocks for a campfire in the middle, three feet under all this snow, and Forest and I have spent hundreds of evenings up here. We'd camp up here as kids with Mom and Dad, and then with friends, and sometimes alone. I've spent so many nights staring up at the stars here, wishing they'd give me the answer to a problem, or point me in the right direction in life. And I swear, I always leave here feeling better, a little more certain, a little more confident, so maybe they are listening."

I smile and lean my head sideways to rest my temple against hers, warmed by the idea that the Luminaries are watching over her and that she recognizes it in her own human way. I feel the ghost of a freedom I've never felt before. This is what I've been working towards, and I vow in this moment to make the most of all the lives I'll live, to not only excel in my role, but to let myself take chances, fall in love, be heartbroken, embrace everything it means to be a Guardian in Zircon, a version of human, to feel all the things I'd never let myself be distracted by in Celestia.

"Thank you for bringing me here," I say, releasing a contented sigh. "I'm so happy to have met you."

***

By the time we return, we are exhausted and hungry, and the smell of chili that assaults us the moment we step back into the warmth of the gear room makes our stomachs growl in tandem. We'd each carried small backpacks of snacks and survival gear ("just in case," Terra had said firmly, "because you never go into the wilderness, even the wilderness you know well, without being prepared"), but the frozen nuts and granola bars were a bandaid solution to the deep desire for a hot, comforting meal.

"What did you think of the lookout?" Forest swivels on a stool to face us as we make our way to the kitchen, bowl in one hand and spoon in another.

"It was stunning," I admit. "Well worth the trek—especially since I didn't know exactly what a beast of a trek it would be. Thank you very much, Terra, for keeping that not-so-small tidbit of information from me." I shoot her a mock glare, and she bats her eyelashes at me as she beelines for the pot on the stove and begins ladling two bowls full.

A moment later, everyone's Tones vibrate or chime at the same time, and we all reach for them except Terra, who innocently presents me with a bowl of chilli. I scowl at her and don't bother to pull my Tone from my pocket. I'm sure that what she sent involves damning evidence of me flopping unceremoniously through the snow.

Sure enough, Clementine is the first to press "play" on Terra's shared video and everyone crowds around to watch me bulldoze down the bluff and emerge like an abominable snowman. Though I do smirk as the camera abruptly tilts to the sky when I upend her, the video stopping mid-squeal.

"You clearly had no fun," says Clementine in mock seriousness when the laughter dies down a bit—after they freeze the video on my stunned crystallized face and howl over that for another entire minute, of course.

"Did you run into the cougar at all?" The question comes from Cato, who pushes up to sit on the kitchen counter where Clementine had sat earlier in the day. Despite having a massive dining room table a few feet away, we'd had yet to use it, the flow of the kitchen making it the gathering point both during and between meals.

I swallow a piping hot bite of chili before answering. "Damn, that's amazing," I say, distracted by the hearty chili flavours. Then I look at him and fully process what he just said. "Wait. What cougar?"

"It came onto the lake from the direction of the lookout," says Ainsley. She's stacking cookies into containers.

Cato and Dayva are both looking at me, the question on their faces going deeper than the others would ever know. I nod for their sakes, even while Terra answers that no, we didn't see a cougar. I now knew that if we had continued on the path that veered to the right, our answer might have been different. And we might not be standing here all happy and healthy, either.

I slide onto a stool and shiver at the thought, which Forest interprets as a shiver of being chilled from outside—which, now that I think about it, isn't not true, so I gratefully accept the blanket he grabs from a nearby couch and drapes over me. It's not long before the conversation moves on, so I eat my chili under my blanket and move on with it. I don't miss the meaning behind Dayva's gentle massage of my shoulders, though, and Cato's subtle press of his foot against mine. And once again, I let myself sink into the contentment of being a part of this group, experiencing these moments with humans and Guardians alike.

17

CATO

I wake up in the night with my bladder begging for relief, so I shimmy out from under my blanket and tiptoe past the others scattered about on various cots in the loft. I make my way downstairs and go to the bathroom, but as I'm about to return to bed, a flickering light outside catches my eye.

The propane fire pit on the porch is lit, the flames blazing against the otherwise dark night, and I see a person curled up on the bench beside it, a toque popping out from a pile of blankets like a cherry on a whipped ice cream cone. I study the figure for a moment, trying to determine who it is, when a hand emerges from the mountaintop of layers to itch a nose, the head turning slightly to do so, and I realize it's Lucie.

The clock above the slumbering fireplace in the living room reads three in the morning, and I wonder how long she's been out there. I grab a quilt from a nearby couch and wrap it around myself, my t-shirt and boxers an inadequate barrier to the cold beyond the doors.

She looks up from the fire in surprise when I push the doors open and slide through, closing them quietly behind me. "Cato? What are you doing up?"

I don't spare a glance at the other chairs, knowing the only place I want to sit is right beside her, even if there are a hundred layers of blankets between us. I quick-step my bare feet over the frozen porch and then squish onto the bench with her before pulling my legs up to my chest under the blanket, mimicking her position. "What are *you* doing up?" I counter, adjusting to get comfortable. It's an admittedly small space for two adults and this many blankets.

She shrugs, her head tilting back to the sky above us and the Luminaries sparkling there. "Just trying to get used to this darkness thing. It's not that bad when the Luminaries are this bright, I guess, though I far prefer the sunshine of the day."

I nod, understanding, memorizing the sight of her skin pinking with the cold while glowing with warm amber tones from the light cast from the fire. "I've been here 25 years and while I'm okay with night, I still breathe a sigh of relief when the sun rises every morning."

We sit in silence for a while, alternating our gazes from the fire in front of us, to the view of the frozen lake beyond, and the inky skies above. I wonder if I should say something, but I also don't want to ruin the tranquil vibes of the moment with meaningless small talk. I'm debating myself on the matter when she hesitantly leans over to rest her head on my shoulder.

"Cato," she whispers. Not that I'd been moving, but every nerve in my body stills at the sound of my name on her lips. There's still not a hint of a breeze outside, and her whisper carries across the frozen air as crisp as her voice would have. "I'm really glad we found you."

Despite the layers, I shiver, from a combination of the cold seeping through and the promise I'm reading into her words. She feels the movement and shifts, unwrapping the blankets from herself to drape them around me, and wordlessly, I do the same. Our bodies press close, no blanket barriers between us, only around us, guarding us together from the chill of the night air. Although the frost cools my exposed ears and cheeks, my body warms from its proximity to her, and while I hold the blankets closed around our knees with one arm, my other slips behind her, around her hips. Her shirt is slightly pulled up and my forearm presses against the bare skin of her lower back. I swear I hear her breathing shallow at my touch. I feel like a child with their first crush, my heartbeat picking up at her nearness, the way she's leaning into my side.

We don't say anything else for a long time, content to be huddled together under the Luminaries keeping watch, our breaths mingling visibly in the cold air, backlit by the orange flames in front of us. I pull her more tightly to me. I wish I could stay here forever, balancing the line of beauty and pain, of wishes and futilities, where everything is possible even when you know nothing is. When you realize your entire world is within reach and yet the moment you try to hold on to it, it will disappear like the crystal mist of our breaths mere seconds after exhaling.

But nothing lasts forever, not in the Realm of Lights, and even less so in the Realm of Bones, so much later and all too soon the cold begins to creep past our blanket shield, and she shivers against me.

"Ready to go inside?" I murmur, my face half-buried in her wool toque. She'd leaned into me again after we'd adjusted our blankets and tucked her head into my neck and hadn't moved since.

"I might be too frozen to move," she jokes, her teeth chattering at the end of the sentence.

I don't respond. Instead, I lean over and flip the switch of the propane fire pit to extinguish the flames, and then take her by surprise as I stand and scoop her up in one movement before she has a chance to react. She gasps and clutches at the blankets to keep them from falling to the snow-covered patio. "Cato!" She looks at me through her long lashes, her face the perfect mixture of shock and delight. I'm conscious of my heartbeat ticking like a bomb in my chest, knowing I'm treading a dangerous path but unable and unwilling to do anything but continue down it.

We slip back through the door. The warmth of the cabin envelops us like a familiar hug, welcoming us home from the cold. The door closes behind us with a gentle thud, and I know this is when I should set her down. But though my body is already warming, I'm now frozen in place as I stand there holding her, her bare legs draped over one arm and the soft skin of her back pressing against the other. I squeeze her closer as I stare into her wide brown eyes, relishing her weight in my arms.

She moves first, slowly releasing the blankets from one of her hands to allow them to unwind around us to the floor, revealing her pyjamas of choice for the night: little silk shorts and a matching tank top, under which her nipples are hard and straining against the thin blue fabric. My breath catches at the same time that my dick hardens, and I drag my eyes up from her tempting chest, almost desperate to study her face, to confirm that I'm not the only one of us feeling this tension. But though my intention is to find her eyes, my gaze stutters instead on her mouth, where her plump bottom lip is caught nervously between her teeth.

Her palm is hot on my chest as she slides it softly over my pec, and I'm sure she must be able to feel my heart racing beneath my shirt. I meet her eyes, and it's as though time suspends itself as we stare at each other, hesitant, the heat in her eyes matching mine, both of us pausing with the weight of uncertainty and repercussions.

I swallow hard, the sound loud in the thick tension of the moment. Her hand travels over my shoulder. I shudder—and I hate myself for it, as though I'm a teenager being touched for the first time. I don't understand how this has happened; how my little sister's best friend has re-entered my world or how she's been tugging on the thread that holds it together ever since.

Her hand wraps around the nape of my neck, and my skin torches at her touch. Then, with a gentle pull, she applies pressure to the back of my head, inviting my face to tilt closer to hers, and it's all the encouragement I need to fall for her.

I lean my head forward as I hold her closer to me and then I'm in her space, our breaths skating across each other's mouths in excruciatingly slow and delicious anticipation. The moment our lips graze, I lose conscious awareness of every-thing but the touch of her pillowy lips against mine. Tentative at first, our kiss is nervous, as though we're still giving ourselves permission to pull back. To separate and climb the stairs to the loft and pretend this moment of madness never happened.

As if either of us truly believes that's still an option.

I dip my tongue past her lips and graze it in a question against her teeth, and she eagerly opens for me. As though we're dancing a choreography we both know the steps to, our kiss intensifies, her tongue demanding and mine answering in kind. She threads her fingers through my hair, her nails scraping against my scalp and I can't help the soft groan the sensation elicits. Her other hand wends behind my back to clutch my shoulder as she draws me impossibly closer.

I kiss her like a man starved, and she reciprocates, raising our kiss to feverish and desperate levels, our hands pulling and searching and our breaths gasping until my arms can no longer hold her. I break our kiss just long enough to set her feet on the floor, intent on resuming the kiss as soon as I straighten, but she stumbles back and leans down to pick up the blankets. She rises, holding them to her chest in front of her, as though they can shield her from the emotions I know are written plainly across my face.

"Lucie. What are you doing to me?" I whisper only loud enough for her to hear, taking care not to wake the sleeping souls in the mezzanine above.

The words ache between us in a tangled mess of confusion and desire. She takes another step back, her expression unreadable, her eyes searching mine as she lifts one hand from the blanket and touches a finger to her swollen lips. The image momentarily pushes aside any questions, because all I want to do is kiss her again—to lay her on the couch behind us and strip off that tiny tank top and kiss the dips of her collarbones, lick her tender breasts, suck her hard nipples. The desire is so strong I reach for her, but she's already turning away, leaving my hand empty in the air as she slips across the floor and up the stairs, the blankets whooshing against the wooden floor as their lengths drag behind her steps.

I can do nothing but watch as I drop my hand listlessly to my side and wonder what in the Fates I'm supposed to do now.

18

LUCIE

I *kissed Cato.*

I toss and turn, unable to sleep, instead replaying the feeling of his lips pressing against mine, the eagerness with which he stole my breath and the tender way he held me to his chest.

Fucking Fates. I kissed Cato.

Despite the outside chill still deep in my bones, my skin has become uncomfortably hot. I'm too aware of the fact he's laying just over there, within pillow-tossing distance.

I don't want to think about what this kiss means, or even if it means anything at all. Prior to coming to Zircon, Cato had never so much as blinked at me. I'd been firmly planted in the "little sister's friend" domain, no matter how much I'd wish he would see me as more than that. No matter how many years or decades I harboured my secret crush.

So what is different now? Or is anything different? Perhaps I'm inventing things far beyond what they are. I start thinking about our kiss from an analytical perspective instead of an emotional one as I stare up at the wooden beams arranged in even lines across the white ceiling. I block the sounds of the peaceful breathing of my friends around me and the occasional snore that emerges from Forest at the other end of the loft as I dissect the memory.

I'd initiated the blanket sharing outside.

I'd laid my head on his shoulder and leaned into him.

I'd complained about being cold, so he'd just been kind in picking me up to keep my bare feet protected from the snow.

I'd put my hand around his neck and pulled him forward.

He'd ended the kiss first and put me down.

A thistly vine of dread winds around the sweet memory of his kiss. During the kiss, he'd seemed into it, but he had probably just been too polite to reject my advances. And maybe he enjoyed it fine for what it was—a kiss with a pretty woman. After all, my Form, inasmuch as it is me, is also not me. Not in the body he'd grown up associating me with. Perhaps for a moment he'd been able to push aside the thoughts of it being me, Dayva's-best-friend-Lucie, and pretend I was instead a random, hot-enough human girl.

The analysis is enough to cool my thoughts as well as my body. I pull the blanket up around my chin and roll over, away from the windows, where the dark pitch of night is lightening, and finally fall into a restless sleep.

The rest of Christmas break at the cabin passes as promised—with drinks, games, food, snowshoeing, skating, and general merriment-making while gathered around fires, both inside and outside. I don't leave my bed the next two nights, even when sleep eludes me. There's no way I'll tempt the Fates to see Cato just so I can torture myself with additional mental gymnastics of will-he-or-won't-he-kiss-me, does-he-or-doesn't-he-want-me, and I-care-but-I-definitely-shouldn't.

While I don't avoid him (as in the small space with only the few of us present, it would be pretty much impossible to do so), neither do I let myself be alone with him. I use everyone else as a buffer, and we engage in conversation only within the context of the group. Sometimes I catch him looking at me with a strange expression on his face, but I don't allow myself to spend any energy trying to decipher it, not wanting to delude myself any further than I already have that this man might be into me. I try to extend my energy instead into reinforcing the importance of my long-term goals. Which absolutely, one hundred percent, do not include a serious relationship with another Guardian.

I distract myself by swiping a sugar cookie every time I find him looking at me, and by the time Dayva and I get home on December 28th, I think half of my Form's composition has become cookie dough.

"I legit gained ten pounds," I groan as we step through the door to the apartment. Dropping my duffel on the ground, I spin, falling backward over the arm of the couch and flopping onto the cushions. For the most part, I'm used to the pull of Zircon gravity now, but it feels like it's stronger today with how heavily my body is dragging.

Dayva heads into her room, smacking my feet as she walks by. "Cookie fiend," she affirms. "Don't get me wrong—they were good, but I'm pretty sure every time I looked at you, you were shovelling another one into your mouth. You got a sudden sugar deficiency I'm unaware of?"

I roll my eyes, despite her being nowhere near enough to see it. Obviously I can't explain to her it was a coping mechanism after making out hot and heavy with her brother. No, that's something I'll take to the Luminaries with me. "Just really wanted to make the most of my first Christmas in the Realm of Bones."

Dayva emerges from her room naked, a towel tossed over her shoulder, en route to the shower. "I gotta say, it was a pretty great time." She hesitates when she gets to the bathroom door and turns, leaning against the doorframe and fiddling with one edge of the towel. "I wonder what some of our other Guardian friends did over the holidays. I hope they all got to experience a heart-warming and cozy holiday."

"I hear the mountains by Calgary are stunning this time of year. I'm sure Ellis got out there—wasn't his Assignment into snowboarding?"

She pulls the towel from her shoulder and whacks my dangling legs with it in mock anger. "I didn't just mean Ellis, thank you very much."

"But you did, and we both know it," I retort, grinning. But then I sober. "It's okay to miss him. It's okay to miss our friends and our family and our lives in Celestia. But we'll get back there someday, older, wiser, more experienced—" at this I waggle my eyebrows suggestively, and she smacks me with the towel again, the smirk I'd hoped for breaking across her face.

"Sure, Lucie, you of all people tell me all about how much more 'experienced' we're going to be when we Return, eh?"

We both startle at her use of the common Canadian accent tag, then burst into giggles. "Does this mean we're officially acclimated?" I ask.

She continues to chuckle, then turns to the bathroom again. "Guess we're certified Crazy Canucks."

I hear the shower start and breathe a quiet sigh of relief at the distraction it brought from her question, certain my soul would give me away if the topic suggestive of me doing anything sexual continued. Not that I'd done anything more than kiss her brother, but still. It was weird.

She starts to belt out a pop song in the shower, and I force myself to standing so I can shut the bathroom door and at least somewhat dull the screech. Perfect pitch (or really, pitch of any kind) is something Dayva had forgone in this Form, and I am beginning to wish she hadn't for how much she's taken up singing lately. ("Zircon music when on Zircon hits different," she insists.)

I lay a hand on my bloated cookie belly and sigh. I slacked on training over the days at the cabin, a few skating and snowshoe excursions the only exercise I'd gotten, so not only am I housing ten pounds of cookie dough, but I'm also sluggish from a lack of general movement. Since it's early afternoon and the sun is shining, I decide to get back into it with a run around the neighbourhoods—something I've been too afraid to do in the dark of the mornings by myself.

Because of the short days of winter, I haven't run around the area much, as my schedule usually has me on or around campus during daylight hours. But in the fall, I mapped out a nice 10K route that takes me through a variety of suburban and park terrain. While diving doesn't necessarily require us to train a lot of cardio, I've discovered in this Form that a way to combat the heaviness of Zircon is to keep my cardiovascular fitness up, and running has become an enjoyable way to do so. I enjoy the sensation of my muscles constricting and expanding as they propel me forward as the wind brushes past me—in a mere echo of a way, it reminds me of flying. I can't wait for the days to grow longer, for the sun to rise earlier and set later, so I can run around my neighbourhood before or after school instead of feeling limited to the indoor gym and track.

A half hour later, I've unpacked (read: thrown everything into the laundry basket for future me to deal with), donned a pair of shorts and a running jacket and am headed out the door with a wave to Dayva, who is now lounging, still naked, on the couch, with her hair coiled up in a towel as she watches reality TV—another thing she loves here.

The crisp air is cool on my bare legs as I exit the building, but it doesn't take long for the blood pumping through me to stave off the shivers as I begin a gentle warm-up jog. Although we had been in the snow and cold of the mountains in the distance only hours before, our return to the low ocean-side elevation of Vancouver is a welcome relief. Not that it's warm, but with 12 degrees in December and a rare afternoon of sunshine, it might as well be spring.

I pop the small bone-conducting headphones around the outer edges of my ears. They're a pretty pale blue and look like jewelry, but allow the wearer to enjoy music without becoming deaf to the outside world—an important safety consideration for women especially. As an alternative folk beat plays, I have to begrudgingly agree with Dayva; Zircon music is definitely a vibe here. We had studied it in Celestia, of course, but it had seemed somewhat dull and flat there. That isn't the case when listening to it here, because while I still hold the opinion it lacks the depth of sound that music in the Realm of Lights has, the music is suited to Zircon and I'm increasingly finding myself enjoying it.

I register the sound of my feet slapping against the ground outside the music, and I turn my legs over to the rhythm of the song, setting a comfortable, easy pace for the duration of the run. I want to enjoy the sunshine, the warmth, the company of humans who look a little less stressed than usual as they embrace the magic of the holidays.

I'm halfway through the run and wondering if I should extend it, already saddened by the idea of returning home, when I'm startled as someone falls into a running step beside me. I turn my head sharply and falter in my steps, only to see Cato's grinning face. It's not from the cardio exercise that my heart picks up speed in my chest.

"Hey!" I immediately slow to a walk, thankful I chose a chill run so I'm not pouring sweat or gasping for breath. I imagine I just look nicely exerted, with pink cheeks and a tousled ponytail.

"Hey yourself," he responds, settling into a walk beside me. "What are you listening to?"

"Honestly, no idea," I respond, lengthening my walking stride to match his longer gait. "I just hit 'play' on a chill running playlist and took off."

I glance at him again and take stock of his running outfit. He has a ball cap backward on his head, which, for some reason, I find nauseatingly attractive, and a slight sheen of sweat dampens his skin. He's wearing a pair of black athletic shorts, and I note the fitted t-shirt is from a marathon last year. "Didn't realize you were a runner," I say, nodding to the emblem across his chest.

He looks sideways at me. "Didn't realize *you* were a runner," he returns, emphasizing the "you."

I point at him. "Touché, my friend. I'm usually at the gym early to get my workouts in, since I don't like running outside in the dark."

He's still looking at me, and my stomach flip-flops. "Want to sit on the seawall for a few minutes?" he asks.

My stupid lovey-dovey soul giggles and kicks her feet, but I maintain a chill exterior. "Sure. I was out for an easy one today anyway, mostly to get outside into the warmth and feel a little less than 50% sugar cookie."

His laugh warms me, and we settle on the sea wall, our legs dangling over the edge. The tide is in, so our feet are only a few inches from the water, but it's calm, with ducks bobbing on the low swells nearby. Our shoulders brush—I hadn't meant to sit so close, but it would be awkward to move away now, so I try to ignore it despite the nervous goosebumps the touch elicits down my arm. I'm thankful we're both wearing sunglasses that hide our eyes, the barrier adding a layer of protection against my heart with our close proximity.

"Why don't you like running in the dark?"

I'm surprised at his return to the topic, as much as I'm surprised by the question. "You do realize I'm from the Realm of Lights, right?" I joke. "You know, where darkness literally doesn't exist?"

"Realm of Lights? Never heard of it," he shoots back, his words laced with sarcasm. Then, "Still sleeping with the lights on?" There's no judgment in his voice, only curiosity, knowing it's common for Guardians to keep them on during their first few months or even years on Zircon.

I swing my legs back and forth, not embarrassed to admit that I do. "Not in the bedroom, but in the living room, and I keep my bedroom door open."

He nods, looking across the sparkling blue vista in front of us. "I still use a nightlight," he admits. "I think a part of me will always yearn for the light. It's why I love days like today so much." He motions vaguely toward the sun and clear sky. "But I've found the beauty in darkness, too." He pauses, then adds, "Like the other night at the cabin."

I swallow, or try to, but my mouth has turned dry at his casual mention of the other night, brushing up against the memory of our kiss, and I focus on the paddling ducks. "There's definitely beauty in it," I agree, keeping a wide berth around that moment of insanity. "I love how the Luminaries gleam against a black backdrop, especially outside the city."

"Running in the dark under the Luminaries or even under the streetlights, when it's quiet and still and you're the only one around, is a different kind of magical." He puts his hands behind him and leans back against them.

"Maybe," I say. "But, like, I know I'm immortal here, and my fighting and self-defence skills are incredibly high by human standards. But things can still happen—I'm still susceptible to drugs, to being knocked out, to being raped, to experiencing horrible human pain in this Form. And you know as well as I do that female-presenting bodies are at a far greater risk of attacks at night. I'm just really not interested in seeking out opportunities for pain, and the darkness is full of those."

I'm aware of his eyes on me, but he's silent for a long moment. After a while, I look over my shoulder at him, wondering if he's bored and wishing he hadn't sat down with a new Arrival to talk about things he doesn't deal with as someone who primarily chooses male-presenting Forms. I open my mouth to say something about how I ought to get back to my run, but he speaks before I can.

"My first Assignment? His sister was raped. She was dating this guy when she was in her early 20s, and I never liked him, but it wasn't my place to say or do anything. I don't know who her Guardian was, but they must have taken a more hands-off approach, which is their prerogative," he says with a shrug. We both know that inserting ourselves as same-age friends isn't always the best course of action for Guardians, and sometimes we have to take positions that are less involved in the daily life—like a teacher or extended relative. Such choices can allow us to protect our Assignments from a relatively close position, but keep us from being there to help with many other things. "But honestly, most of the people we hung around with for that first decade were shady characters. It was a rough Assignment for a first one," he admits, biting the corner of his lip as he disappears into his memories—while I try not to be distracted by the memory of me biting those very lips a few days prior.

"Anyway." He pushes up and leans forward with his elbows on his knees. "I was leaving a party one night and heard screaming, so I ran down an alley and she was being gang-banged by five or six of these trash bags, including her boyfriend. I went ape-shit on them and beat them up—broke a bunch of bones in them and a few knuckles on my part." He rubs his knuckles together as if remembering the feeling. "I wanted to kill them, honestly." The admission was hushed—we couldn't, shouldn't, ever take the life of a human, no matter how much we want to, because that would position us as actively working against another Guardian doing their job. "She was never the same after that. Not only physically did it take her a long time to recover, but she never fully did mentally. She died from suicide a year later." He sighs, and it's clear he's still carrying the burden of responsibility for her life. "I obviously can't be certain, but I'm betting it was before her assigned expiration."

Grief lingers in the air between us, and I can't help but touch his arm, extending a small measure of comfort. "I'm so sorry," I say quietly.

He keeps staring out at the water, though he puts a hand on top of mine. "Thanks. It was a long time ago, both in Zircon time and in Guardian fade terms. But I'm telling you about it because I get it, at least as much as I can get it, without being practiced in a female Form. I don't blame you at all for wanting to avoid situations that might put you in harm's way, even if your chances as a Guardian are especially high for getting out of any dicey moments."

I pull my hand back to rest my elbows on my knees and lean forward as well, mirroring his position. "Thanks. I do appreciate that. I know it's less common of a thing for Guardians to fear—Dayva certainly thinks she can take on anyone or anything the dark throws at her, and I envy her that, but my soul has always been more cautious, calculated."

I see myself reflected in his sunglasses as he turns to me with a fond laugh. "Dayva's attitude is going to get her in trouble someday." He softens. "It's okay to have a careful soul. The beauty of our souls is in their differences."

I raise my eyebrows, wanting to lead us back to lighter territory. "How very philosophical of you." I hadn't expected to have a heart-to-heart with Cato by the ocean when I'd set off on my run a half hour ago.

He smiles, a wide grin that stretches across his face and melts my poor little susceptible heart. "My soul has many sides." His voice is a little too low, a little too suggestive, and just like that, my soul jumps from empathetic to horny, and I fight the blush it wants to give me. A slight breeze kicks by, giving me the edge, and I tamp the heat down before it can reach my skin.

"Well," I say, pushing myself up to standing, "I should get back to my run. Thanks for the chat."

He hops down from the wall and offers me a hand, which of course I take, not because I need the help to balance but because I can't resist an opportunity to touch him again.

"I'll see you around," he says as he starts jogging backwards. "Enjoy the beautiful, safe sunshine!" Then he spins and continues on the way I'd come, and I admit to standing there a moment longer to watch his long strides eat up the ground, his calf muscles straining and his glutes looking incredible in those shorts.

Unfortunately, he turns to look over his shoulder and catches me watching him. I hear him bark a satisfied laugh and this time, my soul wins, and I turn crimson I'm pretty sure from head to toe as I spin away and take off at a far more punishing pace than I'd begun the run with.

19
CATO

It's nine o'clock in the evening, but I'm already laying in bed—so sue me. The days at the cabin were amazing, but I didn't sleep much, so I'm feeling the need for a good, long sleep tonight. I'm scrolling social media on my Tone when a message pops up from Lucie, and I click on it faster than I would have thought my Form reflexes capable.

> It was fun "running" into you today. Thanks for the chat and sharing a bit about your last Assignment. I hope you enjoyed the rest of your run!

I realize I'm smiling like an idiot over this seemingly inno-cent, mundane message, but it's more than that to me. We've never texted for general conversation before—the only reason we even have each other's numbers is because of group chats regarding diving or our little core group of friends. And while I've been tempted many times over the months to send her a message, I've always deleted them before getting up the gumption to do so. I haven't wanted to breach a boundary I'm not welcome past. Her being Dayva's best friend, I know that line is there, and I've read her signals to keep a distance and respected it. But to my mind, she smudged that line at the cabin with her kiss, and with this message, I'm ready to help her erase it further.

I sure did—how about you?

I send it and then groan. Could I have been any more bland? That message had all the personality of a limp spaghetti strand.

But her immediate response tells me I might be able to stage a comeback.

I ended up doing 15K—five more than planned, because it was so nice outside and I wasn't ready to finish. Got that runner's high today, for sure!

That's awesome. Are you planning to run tomorrow again?

> Probably. I ate too many sugar cookies at the cabin not to.

> Pretty sure there's no such thing as "too many sugar cookies." Especially with Ainsley's recipe.

> Tell that to my hips. Dumb human bodies and their caloric math.

> Your hips could never not be perfect—eat all the sugar cookies you desire.

There's a longer pause this time, and I roll onto my back and lift the translucent, glowing screen above my face, willing her response while I hold my breath. Too flirty? Finally:

> Then I'm dragging you along with me to shop for a whole new wardrobe when I outgrow my current one.

> If that means getting to see you model tight little running shorts like the ones you were wearing today, then I'm in.

> Only if you return the favour—you were showing your legs off in your shorts today, too.

> My legs weren't all you were ogling when I jogged away.

> Ogling is a strong word. I was merely appreciating the craftsmanship in a nicely built Form.

> If you enjoy evaluating Form components, I'd be happy to let you see one that I'm particularly proud of…

Okay, that might have been too far. I'm forgetting myself, forgetting her boundaries. I can't exchange flirtatious text messages with her. Can I?

> I see you in spandex swim tights all the time. Safe to say I've already evaluated the component in question—and found it suitably impressive.

I almost choke on my tongue at that response. If my soul was the blushing type, I definitely would have been pink. I hover my nervous fingers over my Tone as I try to come up with another witty response before finally typing back.

> Coming from the master Form maker, that's high praise indeed.

> I sense sarcasm, but I'll have you know I got some of the highest marks in my Dek for my Forms—thank you very much.

> See, now that I'm surprised at. From my vantage point, your tits are way too perfect to not have had marks docked.

> They're pretty good, right? Too bad you'll never get to see the nipples—they're perfect enough that I actually did lose marks on them.

Great, I'm sporting a semi now because now I'm stuck imagining her nipples—the ones that peaked so beautifully through her silk cami when I carried her into the cabin. Scratch that—it's more than just a semi now. But before I can respond, another message comes through, telling me she's logging off for the night, but she'll see me at the New Year's Eve Party.

It's only a couple of days away, but I want to see her before then. I want to have her company to myself again, not have to share her with a house full of drunk teenagers.

> Be in your lobby at seven tomorrow morning, ready to run. It will still be dark, but I'd love to show you the beauty of dark morning runs when you don't have to be scared. I'll have your back.

> Are you offering to be my personal Guardian tomorrow, Cato?

> Not that you need one, but yes.

> Don't be late.

***

I show up five minutes to seven the next morning in grey sweatpants, a hoodie, and a toque. The clear night grips tightly to its final hour, the cold settling into the bones of the city to remind its residents that though yesterday may have felt like a spring reprieve, winter still reigns supreme. I figure we'll go for a slow jog, where we can chat and stay warm without overexerting ourselves, and I hope she's dressed in a similar fashion despite my having forgotten to tell her the plan.

I lean against the outside of the building, under the light, so she can see me—and I can see her—when she enters the lobby, which she does a minute later. A quick look tells me she's on the same page as me, sporting leggings tucked into long socks and a zipped sweater with an athletic down vest on top. Her hair is braided in two plaits, and a knitted green toque is pulled all the way over ears.

"Where are the cheeky shorts?" I ask with a smirk as she pushes through the door. Her eyes sparkle, and I want desperately to think that it's because of me.

"I don't recall any such promise," she retorts. "The only promise I remember being made is that you'll protect me from any night goblins and ghouls trying to nab me, so you better hold up to that. I don't think Dayva would ever forgive you for letting something happen to me."

We turn onto the sidewalk and break into a slow jog. "You're not wrong. She'd trade me in for you in a beat. I know where her true loyalty lies," I say, only half-joking. I may be close to my sister, but Lucie and Dayva's relationship is on a different level.

Lucie giggles, and the sound wraps around my heart, squeezing in an unfamiliar, nervous way. "You're also not wrong," she says.

We settle into a comfortable rhythm, soaking in the sounds of stillness, only our slapping footsteps giving a heartbeat to the city. The sidewalks ebb and flow with light and shadow as we flit across them, occasional cars whooshing by with gentle purrs.

We turn to head into the seaside park, and her pace picks up slightly, though I doubt she's aware of it. The lights illuminating the path are spread further apart here, and we lose the sense of security provided by passing vehicles. I match her pace, but she continues to increase it until finally, I grab her hand and tug her to a walk. "Lucie. It's ok. You're safe. You don't need to race through here, I promise."

She ducks her head, her breathing heavy, her cheeks tinged pink with cold and embarrassment. "Sorry," she says, shooting me an apologetic smile.

I chuckle. "It's fine." My voice carries on the calm morning air, and we catch our breath after our little sprint as we continue to walk, her hand still clasping mine, tighter than she needs to, but I'm certainly not about to pull away.

We're the only ones in the park, and I lead us onto a much smaller path off the right side of the main one, into the bush, where no lights line the trail. Her footsteps stutter, but I press the light on my beanie, which gives just enough illumination to make my way by, and she grips my hand with both of hers now as she follows as close behind me as she can without stepping on my heels.

"I thought you were here to be my Guardian, not my murderer," she jokes as we wind deeper into the trees. "If we were in a horror movie right now, the music would be ominous as fuck."

I know she's trying to keep the mood light, but I hear the trepidation in her voice. Thankfully, we reach the small clearing right then, with an incredible view of the lit-up harbour below us. I can tell the open space makes her feel more comfortable, and she slows to take in the vista.

There's a stiff breeze coming up from the ocean, and even in the dark, I make out how her face lights up. "I love the wind," she breathes, tilting her head back. "It's like for a moment, I can imagine I'm flying. My wings are what I miss most."

I recall the first days she and Dayva got their wings, how nervous they both were. Dayva acted confident and cocky, but her trembling legs gave her away. For all the words of bravado that came from Dayva, Lucie had no words at all, her teeth clenched as she quietly steeled her resolve. I had so much fun mentoring them in the sky, teaching them how to bank without flipping over, how to pocket their wings away and spread them to their fullest lengths. The memory opens the door for dozens more to crash through of Lucie over the years, and I realize that while I may not have recognized any attraction to her in Celestia, she'd also somehow stood apart. I'd always enjoyed her company, always been happy to help her, always watched out for her. I thought I'd done all of these things in obligation as her friend's older brother, but I hadn't done the same thing for any of my sister's other friends.

There's a large rock to one side of the clearing, and I gently tug her over to sit against it before I click off the light from my toque. Darkness closes in on us and I hear her tiny gasp, so I let go of her hands only so I can put my arm around her lower back and grab her hip to pull her closer to me. I don't miss the stutter in her breath as she molds against me, naturally seeking my warmth.

"And if this were a romance movie instead? What would the music score be like then?" I don't know where the question comes from, why I ask in such a low, husky voice. Truly, my intentions had been just to run in the dark with her, enjoy her company before dropping her back off at her apartment. But then I'd remembered that path to this clearing, and now I'm here, my lips inches from where her earlobe peeks out from her toque, begging me to nibble around the three little piercings glimmering on it.

She swallows, drawing my attention to her neck, and I see her pulse fluttering under it. She's so alive, so vibrant, so beautiful, and my cock stirs in response to her closeness.

"If this were a romance movie," she whispers, staring across the harbour at the shy promise of sunrise warming on the horizon, "the music would be suspenseful in a whole different way."

My free hand traces a finger down her flushed cheek, and I turn her face toward me. Though it's dark, she's so close that I can still discern her features, still be captured by the intensity of her gaze. She doesn't move closer, doesn't move at all, her body motionless as she watches me. In her eyes dance the emotions of both predator and prey, wanting to run from these feelings as much as she wants to pursue them. I know, because I feel the same conflicting emotions, but right now, I also know which is stronger.

"Why are you so determined to keep me at a distance?" I ask. I feel the importance of the question as it hovers between us, though I don't expect her to answer with such certainty when she finally does.

"Cato, I'm afraid I could love you so fiercely that it would lead to the extinction of who I am and who I aspire to be."

I let my hand drop from her chin, stroking down her arm until I find her hand and thread my fingers through hers, trying to understand what she means. "Can you expand on that?"

She leans her temple against the rock, studying me as she ponders my question. "I have plans to become a High Magister so I can advocate for the angels and make changes to improve the Guardianship. Every day in Dek, I sacrificed parts of my life in pursuit of the academic excellence that will form my foundation for succeeding in this goal. I'm proud of the hard work I've put in, and I plan to continue to work hard to be an incredible Guardian so I can Return with insight and wisdom." Her gaze drops to our entwined hands as the night begins to fold away above us. "I made a vow to myself a long time ago to not become distracted from my dreams. To you, I might be a fun soul to have a good time with while you're on this Assignment, but I can't risk you becoming more than that for me. I can't risk compromising my goals or being distracted with love or heartbreak. I can't risk falling alone in love and giving someone everything when I've already promised myself that I'm worthy of my life's intentions and goals, and don't deserve to compromise my identity for the sake of someone else's pride."

The words are intended to keep me at a distance, but all they do is push me off the precipice I've been standing on, the ridge I've been cautiously walking between care and love disappearing beneath my feet as I tumble headfirst into the unfamiliar abyss of the latter. I've always known she was determined and driven, but before she'd Arrived, I hadn't taken the time to understand how deep her convictions and sense of self were. A lump forms in my throat as an impossible, yet entirely possible, thought dawns on me—that this might be what it feels like to recognize that your truest soulmate has been right in front of you all along.

"I am confident you will never compromise yourself for me, or for anyone," I finally say, knowing my words won't be as eloquent as hers, but hoping they will still convey my heart. "But it seems you're also afraid that if you allow yourself to love someone, they would never love you back as much. Protect your heart, Lucie, but don't hold on so tight that you strangle it. You're worthy of all the success you will achieve in your life, but that doesn't have to come at the exclusion of making you unworthy of love. A pure love will push you to shine even brighter than you can imagine, not ask you to diminish yourself." I swallow hard, searching her eyes for hope as I lay my heart before her. "If you'd let me, I could be that love for you."

Her lips part in surprise as she studies my face, processing my words. I hadn't planned to say that last bit, and yet it had tumbled from my tongue so naturally, like an autumn leaf falling from a branch. I'm drawn to Lucie in a way I've never connected with anyone else. It's like she walked off that diving board at Terra and Ainsley's party and straight into my heart. She's in a beautiful Form, yes, but it's as though seeing her in a different body is allowing me to see her soul in an entirely new way, too. I'm captured by her fierce independence, her loyalty, her drive, her wit, and I wonder how blind I was to have never seen her soul like this before.

Then, like a love-drunk fool, I ask, "Lucie, may I kiss you?"

Her eyes flick back and forth between mine, looking for faults and insincerities in my words. For reasons to say no. "You're Dayva's brother," she finally responds, grasping to the last reason she can find to deny me.

I lean forward, pressing my forehead to hers, our breaths meeting between. "And you let her love you," I counter gently, almost holding my breath as I pray to the Fates that she'll open the door to her heart for me, too, even just a little.

Like an unspoken promise, her lips graze mine. I press forward, sinking into the feel of the lips I'd been dreaming about ever since they'd last left mine, and within moments, we fall into each other, hungry and passionate, a new level of depth and honesty shimmering beneath our desire.

Her hands wrap around my neck as she pulls me closer, but sitting beside her isn't allowing us to be close enough. I grasp both her hips and easily swing her over my legs until she's straddling me, her profile haloed by the lightening sky behind her. She gasps into my mouth at the sudden movement but doesn't pull away, pressing her chest against mine and running her hands over my shoulders as she deepens the kiss further.

I'm wedged firm between the rock and her body, and I've never enjoyed being anywhere else more.

I tug on her hips again, bringing her core to press against my sweatpants, which does little to hide my now fully erect cock. She pushes her fingers up under my toque to wend them through my hair as she lines herself up against me, lighting me on fire. My fingers dig deep into her hips, not enough to bruise but enough to keep her exactly where I want her.

"Fuck, Lucie," I groan when she bites my lip hard and then soothes it with her tongue. The words only seem to spur her on, and she wiggles in my grip, finding friction against my dick, and I can feel the heat of her centre even through the layers of clothing that separate us.

She grinds harder, a needy moan escaping her perfect lips, and then she's grinding faster, and our kisses can't keep up as our concentration focuses far lower. Our breaths pinball between us as she moves against me in an agonizing, beautiful rhythm and then, with the most exquisite gasp I've ever heard, she tilts her head back and finds her release. The picture undoes me as I pulse through my own pleasure against her, only fainting registering the thought that I'll now have to run home with cum soaking my boxers, and knowing anyway that it's a price I'd pay a hundred times over.

As we come down from our heights of pleasure, she rests her forehead against mine, our eyes closed as we steady our souls and gather ourselves again. After a minute, she slides off my lap and snuggles back up beside me, and we don't say anything else, content to sit and watch the sky as it finally erupts with the first full rays of the sunrise.

With Lucie in my arms, I think that a day has never dawned so beautiful.

20

LUCIE

We stroll home hand-in-hand, neither of us bothering to even pretend we want to run. The city's awake now, lit by the morning sun and energized by the hum of cars and commuters. We chat as we walk, laughing and teasing as if this is our daily routine, as if we're any other couple, as if we could be so much more to each other than we are.

We turn the corner to the street of my apartment and I surreptitiously tug my hand from his, tucking both hands into my vest pockets, trying to put some distance between our familiarity as we come into view of the building. I'm almost certain Dayva's not awake yet, but on the minuscule chance she's looking out the window, the last thing I want is for her to see me holding hands with her brother.

I haven't told her about our encounter yesterday. Or about our plans to go running this morning. I feel a pang of guilt about it as we step up to the apartment sidewalk, knowing I've never kept anything from her our entire life except for this, my crush on her brother. And now, all my reasoning that he hadn't wanted the kiss at the cabin doesn't hold water; all my arguments have fallen out the window and shattered into a million illogical pieces below my heart.

He'd asked me to run.

He'd pulled me to snuggle beside the rock.

He'd listened to me share my heart and heard even beyond what my words said.

He'd challenged me on my conception of love.

He'd kissed me.

He'd pulled me onto his lap.

I still don't know what this is, or if this is anything at all, or if it can truly be anything more, but I'm not ready to give it up yet without considering his words and my heart.

We reach the doors of the apartment and I turn, suddenly awkward. "Right, well, thank you for showing me that darkness doesn't have to be all bad."

His eyes glimmer, a sexy smirk curling at the corner of his mouth as he leans against the brick wall in the same pose he'd been in when I'd walked down the stairs that morning and my soul had spun cartwheels at first glimpse. "There are many fun things we can do in the dark, Lucie."

Heat curls in my core and I fold my arms over my chest, creating a physical shield against my soul and its urging for me to grind up against him again right here in front of the apartment. I glare at Cato for daring to suggest more illicit activities, despite desperately wanting the same.

He barks an amused laugh at my expression, then steps forward. I retreat a step, but he continues, until it's my back now against the opposite brick wall. His hands press against it above me, caging me in until I have to tilt my head up to meet his heated gaze. I swear I almost orgasm right then and there. "Cato," I squeak, equally turned on and panicked that Dayva will waltz down the stairs at that moment.

He dips to press a hard last kiss against my lips and then he's gone, flipping his hood up over his beanie and jogging down the sidewalk. He raises a hand without turning back as a final farewell, and I let out an enormous sigh as I fight to calm my pounding heart.

"Fucking Fates."

I climb the stairs to the apartment—or at least, I must do that, though my mind is completely unattached from the present, instead greedily settled in with a bucket of popcorn with my soul as they press replay on all the spiciest moments of the morning. I slip past Dayva's room, noting her still-sleeping Form passed out on the bed, and make my way to the shower.

I close the door to keep the steam in, wanting to build warmth in the room as quickly as possible, chilled from the winter air. I step into the shower and slowly work up the temperature until my skin pinks from the heat.

My pussy aches, tortured from just the memory of grinding against his impressive length. I'll admit it—it was my first orgasm in a human Form. I could have made myself come or bought some toys to do the job, but I had kind of wanted my first time in a human Form to result from being with someone. Never could I have imagined that someone to be Cato, or that it would happen while dry-humping him under a sunrise, but I definitely wasn't mad about it. I recall Saffi saying how Form sex is similar to angelic sex when wings are involved. Since I'd never involved my wings, I didn't have that to compare to, but seeing as how I'd come harder than I ever have, I can only assume she's right.

I close my eyes and reach a finger down to my clit, which is already sensitive and eager. My soul wants more; it wants to feel the intense build in my abdomen, feel the heat coil like a tightly wound spring in my core, feel the eruption of electricity as I pulse through my release. It's as though my nerve endings are more hypersensitive in my Form than in my angelic body, which is unfortunate in pain but mind-blowing in pleasure.

I give in to my soul's demands and grab the shower head. Cooling the temperature a fraction before bringing it between my legs, I brace one hand against the tile wall as I prop a foot on the side of the tub. I bite my lip to keep from moaning aloud as the water hits exactly where I need it to, and I torture myself in glorious fashion as I replay every second of the morning, culminating in another agonizing orgasm as I pulse with the intense desire to be with him again, to have him want me as much as I want him.

As I come down from the heights of release, I allow myself to daydream about falling in love with Cato—although if I'm being honest, I fell in love with him decades ago. So really, it's a dream of him falling in love with me. Of a future with him in both realms, and I wonder if it's so outlandish to think after all. The words he spoke before we'd lost ourselves certainly seemed to present the possibility.

But, I remind myself as I dress and plan for the remainder of the day, I've had a grand total of two make-out sessions with the man and I'm already practically planning our Divine Accordance (the Realm of Lights version of a marriage). It's ridiculous to be jumping so far ahead of myself. Maybe he isn't interested in the Accordance; some angels never are. Or maybe he would want to join in Accordance with multiple angels—we are far from a monogamous realm. I've never felt drawn to the idea of having multiple simultaneous partners myself, but I realize I don't know if Cato does.

The more I ponder it, the more it dawns on me how little I know about Cato the man. Cato, the brother of my best friend? I know him well enough: I know he loves potatoes and always drowns them in too much gravy; I know he lets Dayva beat him at competitions sometimes, but lets her think she's truly bested him (he always winks at me after); I know he liked to play wingball and was captain of a team in the most elite realm league for a decade. But Cato the man, the Guardian? I don't know his dreams and aspirations, his sexual preferences, his career goals upon Returning. I don't know if he wants to Cast future angels and raise them with anyone. I certainly know far too little to be daydreaming about melding our halos together already.

I'm saved from ruminating too intensely for too long by Dayva barging in to the bathroom yelling at me to come grocery shopping for snacks for a TV-binge day, and she and I spend the rest of the day hanging out. I push away the niggle in the back of my mind that I should say something to her about Cato, trying to tell myself that there's nothing to say yet, even though I know the justification is weak. We watch TV, cook dinner, reminisce on Celestia, and make up pretend, outlandish stories about what we think Ellis' Assignment is like, until we end up cackling so hard tears fall down our faces. It's the perfect day with my best friend, and my heart is so full of love for her that as we fall asleep beside each other on her bed watching the umpteenth episode of one of her favourite reality TV shows (okay, I'll admit, I'm getting pretty into them, too), I can't help but tell her so. In response, she reaches over and squeezes my hand. "You're my heart," she whispers back, and

I wonder how it would feel to let another person love me in the fierce, pure way that she does.

21

LUCIE

"**D**amn, Lucie, you've got one fine ass." Dayva whistles as I emerge from my bedroom, and I know she's right. The high-waisted flare jeans I'm wearing accentuate my curvy hips in just the right way, and I have a nice handful of rear end if I do say so myself. It would seem that Cato thinks so too; if his texts the other day about booty shorts is any indication of his love for curves, I can be pretty confident he'll like the outfit. I could get over my aversion to tight clothes for his sake, probably. Maybe. The twist-front crop t-shirt I'm wearing does nice things even for my little chest, the faint glitter I've dabbed across my décolletage drawing the eyes to that region.

"So, who are you kissing at midnight?" She yanks a tube top over her far bustier chest, then frowns down at herself. Before

I can answer, she jumps in with another question. "Should I tape them?"

I purse my lips and study her for a moment before I nod. "They could go for a little boost. Ugh, don't you miss our Celestia boobs so much?"

Dayva disappears into her room and re-emerges a moment later wearing a different top. "I'm too lazy to tape. How's this? And yes, I miss my Celestia boobs something fierce. I'm tempted to get implants, honestly. These mu'fuckers won't stay UP!" She pushes against them and then lets them drop, before saying, "Forget it," and whipping off that shirt too. "I should just go topless. They look best naked."

I laugh. "That would certainly give you your pick of midnight kisses."

She disappears into her room again, but this time I follow her to sit on her bed while she rummages around the closet. "I already have my pick of kisses," she claims, her voice saucy but muffled by the clothes she's burrowing through. "But," she says as she pops out, a minidress and a bra in hand, "honestly, I'll probably just grab whomever's closest when the clock strikes midnight."

I pucker up a kissing face. "I'll be right there waiting, babe."

The bra hits me across the face as she changes her mind again. "Better not be, because you really need to get some actual human action, Luce. What's taking so long?"

I raise my eyebrows at her as I twirl the bra around my finger like a helicopter. "Excuse me. Exactly how many sexual partners have you had since we Arrived?" I drop the bra and hold my fingers up in the oval of a zero. "Oh right. As many as I have. And yet I'm the one who needs to get some action?"

She squirms into a tight royal blue jumper with a halter top, and I nod in approval. "That's the one, wear that."

She checks herself out in the mirror, then agrees before jumping back to the conversation. "That's different. I've at least had some good bar make-out sessions. Just haven't had an urge that my vibrator can't scratch, you know? It's always a gamble with men whether they're even capable of scratching that particular itch. Based on rumours about humans, they're actually pretty bad at eliciting a female orgasm. So anyway, how many boys have *you* kissed since getting here?" she challenges as she pulls her hair into a sleek ponytail.

There's no way I can answer that without having her pry for more, so I just laugh nonchalantly. "Point taken. Okay, our New Year's resolutions? Get laid."

She finishes tying her hair up and reaches a hand out to me with her pinky finger extended. I frown at it and she laughs. "Wrap your pinky finger around mine—it's called a pinky promise."

I do as she asks, but shake my head. "That's a weird human custom I don't remember learning."

"Kiss your thumb," she demands, and we both lean forward and kiss our thumbs. "There. Now you have to, as you've made the most sacred of elementary school promises."

She goes back to the mirror to finish her makeup and I flop backward on her bed to wait, my stomach swirling with the thought of fulfilling the promise by sleeping with her brother, an idea that equally thrills and shames me.

I'm still feeling that way when we get to Terra and Forest's house an hour later, where the New Year's Eve party is in full swing. It's reminiscent of Terra and Ainsley's birthday party, though it's mostly confined to the inside of the house and not spilling into the backyard and pool this time of year.

Clementine waves at us from across the living room as we enter, and we wave back. She's sitting on a boy's lap and doesn't seem interested in leaving. "Who's he?" I ask Dayva, knowing she will know who I'm referring to.

"Jack? Jent? J-something," she says with a shrug as she follows me into the kitchen. "She works with him at the restaurant, but I didn't know they were a thing. She hasn't mentioned him to you?"

I shake my head. "Nope. But clearly there's some tea that needs spilling."

"Who has tea?" The question comes from behind us, and we turn to see Terra.

"Not us. What's with Clem and that guy?" Dayva asks as she grabs a couple of beer and pops the tops off them before handing one to me.

"Oh, Jet. Yeah, he seems nice enough. Don't really know him much; he works a lot, but Clem's mentioned him a couple times in the last month. Looks like she was holding out on us to not even mention him at the cabin." She snags the beer from my hand and claims it for her own, tipping it up to her mouth for a long swig. In turn, I grab Dayva's and take an equally long sip to claim it as mine. Rolling her eyes, she lets me keep it and reaches for another one as Ainsley sweeps by us to slide a massive platter of sugar cookies on the kitchen island.

I groan.

All three of the girls turn to me in surprise, and I hasten to correct myself. "Ainsley, my darling, my sweet, beautiful, incredibly talented baker friend." I put down my beer so I can grab both her shoulders with my hands to face her square-on. "Your cookies will actually be the death of me because I cannot resist them and Dayva already had to roll me home from the cabin thanks to your baking. So consider yourself warned: my death is on your hands."

She laughs, spinning from my hands to pick one up and hold it teasingly in front of me. "No one's forcing you to eat them, Lucie. You hold the power to resist."

I glare at her, then pluck it from her hands and shove it all into my mouth in one horrible, unattractive bite. "Wrong," I mumble around the mouthful of delicious, melting-in-my-mouth crumb.

Of course, it's at that moment Cato appears behind Ainsley, and he quirks a brow at my stuffed cheeks. I promptly turn pink and grab my beer to wash it down, giving myself a second to pull my dignity back together.

We hadn't texted or seen each other since he'd left me with that bruising kiss on my apartment doorstep. I'd thought about texting him, but kept chickening out. I had wondered why he didn't text me either, before admitting how hypocritical that was of me, which helped a tiny bit, but not all the way.

Damn it, if the man doesn't get more attractive every time I see him, though. Maybe it's because I now know what it's like to taste his perfect lips, to run my fingers through his thick hair, to grind against his—

I choke, the combination of beer and cookie and lewd thoughts turning out to be dangerous, and pivot to lean over the sink as I try to swallow and not spit everything out. A hand thumps against my back and after a few seconds, I regain my composure and spin, wiping my mouth with the back of my hand and using the other to point at Ainsley with wide eyes. "See, I told you. The death of me!"

Everyone laughs, especially when Ainsley innocently holds another cookie out in her palm and bats her eyelashes at me. Obviously, I take it. This one I don't devour like a goblin, however, taking small bites to savour it instead as the conversation continues on around me.

Cato rounds the island to lean against the counter beside me, a safe distance between us, but close enough for me to hear him remark slyly, "Shall we set a shopping date?"

I smirk, knowing he's referring to our chat about cookies and buying short shorts. He smiles in return, and my knees literally weaken as he looks at me like I hung the moon. I pull my gaze away before anyone can notice us giving each other googly eyes.

"Lucie!" Dayva's voice breaks through the chatter and I snap my attention over to her, afraid she noticed. But no, she's just beckoning me to the living room. "Beer pong. You and me versus Terra and Ainsley, stat." She's already dragging a groaning Terra by the hand, but Ainsley grins at the challenge and jumps up from her stool to follow.

"You'll regret this, Dayva," she warns. "You'll be begging to be my partner again."

We situate ourselves at either end of the table, and I fold my arms over my chest and snort. "Well, that's for sure, because I suck at this."

Dayva nods, serious. "She really does. And rumour has it, Terra also lacks skills in this department. So it's basically me versus Ainsley." She fills the cups on her end of the table as Ainsley does the same at the other end. "This is how we'll keep each other sharp, Ainsley, since no one else is competition."

Ainsley pulls her hair back into a ponytail, her bangs falling free around her face as she nods, and I can't help but smile at her. She's Dayva's antithesis in style—where Dayva is all hard angles and edges, Ainsley is more like me with her soft curves. Dayva's decked in her sexy royal blue one-piece with a deep V showing off her assets, while Ainsley's wearing a buttoned up pastel pink cardigan and a pair of light blue ripped jeans. And yet their competitive personalities connect them in a way even I don't relate with Dayva, and I have loved watching them become friends and discover the common ground they have beneath the surface. Between Dayva's love of cooking and Ainsley's love of baking, there is no dinner party quite like when those two team up.

Predictably, Terra and I contribute basically nothing to the game, with Ainsley managing to eke out Dayva for the win. Dayva wastes no time calling for a best out of three, and Terra and I don't even bother stepping up to pretend we need to be part of the team—this is Dayva versus Ainsley, pure and simple. When Dayva beats out Ainsley, the party goes wild, everyone crowding in to watch the spectacle as both of them taunt good-naturedly and hype up their crowd. The tie-breaker begins at ten minutes to midnight, and the pressure's on to finish before the clock strikes. The pair thrive under pressure, though, and their shots are clean, and we're all on the edge of our seats as we watch.

The TV broadcasting the countdown had just put up the timer with the two minute warning when I feel a hand on my elbow. I turn to see that it's Cato, and he's jerking his head in the direction of the kitchen, so I shrink back from the crowd and follow him. But he doesn't stop there, instead pushing through the doors to the patio outside. He closes the door beside me and pulls me down the porch a bit, away from view of the kitchen. My sock feet chill against the cold but dry wood, though I forget about them as soon as he wraps his arms around my waist and leans me against the house.

"Cato," I breathe, my heart rate increasing in both panic and heady attraction. "What are you doing?" I snake my hands up his chest, so I can push him away if Dayva sees—or pull on his shirt to bring him even closer. I haven't decided yet.

"I'm kissing you at midnight," he says, his voice low and gravelly. It shoots a thrill through me and, lo-and-behold, I pull him closer.

"How will we know it's midnight if we're not by the timer?" I ask.

He gently rubs his nose against mine. "I think we'll know."

A moment later, I realize how dumb I am—not only can I hear the eruption from inside the house, but from the entire neighbourhood as cheers of "Happy New Year!" ring out. But my foolish brain isn't a topic I have time to dwell on as his lips find mine and he kisses me with urgency and need, making the most of what we both know is limited time.

But apparently, we lose track of that of time, as a gasp interrupts us and we freeze. We spring apart: I push Cato back, or he steps back, or we both do those things.

Dayva stands there, half-in, half-out of the door, staring at us in bewilderment.

My dumb brain is back in full force as I look between Cato and Dayva, unable to find any words. My heart is at my feet as I scramble for an explanation that will make this seem like it's nothing, even though it *is* something—

"Happy New Year, baby sister," Cato says casually as he steps forward and gives her a big hug. I gape at his back, straightening my face when Dayva comes into view again after the hug. "I'm so glad the Fates brought us together in Zircon." He releases her and turns back to me with a finger gun and a wink. "Thanks for the New Year's kiss, Luce. Perhaps we'll do it again next year, eh?"

With that, he pushes the door open wider as he puts an arm around Dayva and leads her back inside. I hear him ask who won the beer pong tournament before Terra and Ainsley's giggles drown out their words as the two girls pop outside, a joint ready to be lit in their hands. They see me and skip over, but Ainsley puts an arm out to stop Terra when she sees my face.

"Whoa, whoa. Lucie, who died? Why does your face look like that?" Ainsley looks nearly panicked, and Terra follows suit with her own "Oh, shit."

I sigh, grabbing the joint and the lighter, and a moment later, take a long pull before I finally admit, "I kissed Cato."

Ainsley's eyes light up as Terra squeals beside her and grabs my arm. "You're kidding. You and Cato? I had no idea!"

"Ainsley, babe? You out here?"

I groan as Hailey pops out the door and joins us. "Nevermind, I shouldn't have said anything," I say, instantly regretting it.

"Too fuckin' late, babe, but don't worry, we won't tell," says Terra. She puts a finger up to her lips and giggles. "Shhhh."

"We won't tell who, what?" Hailey asks, wrapping her arms around Ainsley from behind.

Ainsley holds the joint to her girlfriend's lips, and she takes a drag as Terra says in a conspiratory tone, "Lucie and Cato are fucking."

I gasp, horrified, slicing my hands in a back-and-forth motion and shaking my head vigorously. "Nononononono." The last thing I need is for that to get to Dayva when it's simply not true. A dry hump one time can't be qualified as fucking. Right? "We're not fucking," I hiss. "We just kissed at midnight, but it was kinda hot and Dayva saw and she's not going to be happy."

Hailey frowns. "Why would Dayva give a shit if you're fucking—sorry, kissing—" she amends at my glare, "Cato?"

All three girls look at me expectantly, and I freeze. Dayva and Cato are not siblings in these Forms on Zircon. I definitely should not have opened my big mouth connected to my dumb brain. "Um, because she likes him," I blurt out. Then I wince. Dayva might actually have more of a problem with a rumour about her and her brother being romantically linked than she would be about us dating.

The three girls gasp. "No, seriously?" "She never told me!" "Lucie, you knew, and you kissed him anyway?"

I grimace at that last one, scrambling to flesh out a story. "Cato doesn't know—she's never told him or anything. And then it was midnight, and he kissed me and it sort of turned hot, and I know I should have stopped it, but she walked out and saw us and—fuck. I fucked up," I finish lamely.

Hailey nods, quirking an eyebrow. "Yeah, you kinda did."

Terra elbows her, but Hailey shrugs. "What? She did. She knows it."

"Yeah, but we all make mistakes. And let's be real, if Greek-god bodied Cato starts kissing you, you're not likely to push all that man away without getting a taste first."

Hailey rolls her eyes. "Well, actually, I am—dicks are not it."

Terra huffs. "You know what I mean."

Ainsley interrupts before they can continue, crossing her arms to ward off the cold, and I realize I'm covered in goosebumps thanks to the scant protection of my t-shirt against the winter evening's chill. "But realistically, it's not that big of a deal, right? You say you're not fucking, it was just a New Year's Eve kiss, so she'll get it. You guys are the best of best friends. I'm sure it's not the first time one of you made a poor decision in life and you had to work through things, yeah?"

I shiver, but nod, knowing she's right, and that Cato's casual exit helped downplay the situation. "You're right. It'll be fine. I should go talk to her though," I say, except now I'm distracted with wondering why exactly Cato had acted so casual about it. My soul tightens at the thought, nervous about the answer.

"Yeah, it's freezing out here. Let's get back inside," says Hailey. She drags Ainsley back through the door with her. Terra slings a comforting arm around my shoulders and steers me inside too, and once again I'm thankful for the Assignments my best friend and I chose, that we can live relatively genuine versions of ourselves in this life—that there exist humans who love me even when I fuck it up with my Guardian family.

***

"You and Dayva want a ride home?" Clementine appears before me as soon as I step back onto the warm floor of the kitchen. "Jet's sober and lives right by you guys, so we're headed that way anyway."

I nod, giving her a strained smile. "That'd be great, thanks—I just have to find Dayva."

"Oh, she's right there," Clem says, leaning back into the living room. "Day! You want a ride home?"

Dayva turns and sees her, and me. I can't read her expression, but she nods, jerking a finger down the hallway. "I'll grab my coat and be out in two seconds," she says.

"You have a coat?" Clem asks as she shrugs into hers. "Come on, I think Jet's already outside," she says when I shake my head.

A minute later, I'm climbing into the backseat with Dayva. She's quiet, but I keep up the conversation with Clementine, not wanting to make things more awkward than necessary. Clem realizes something's up, but she goes with it, mouthing "text me" as I slide out after Dayva in front of our apartment.

I smile, thank Jet for the ride, and hurry into the building after Dayva.

The moment I close the door to our unit, she spins. "Are you fucking my brother?" Her voice is steel, a tone she's never once taken with me but has many times with others—and I've always been so grateful not to be on the receiving end of it. Until now.

"No," I say firmly, remaining where I am in front of the door, not wanting to move and aggravate her more somehow. "I swear to you, Dayva, we are not fucking. He's not dating anyone, and I'm not dating anyone, so at the last minute, we agreed to be each other's midnight kiss. I won't be kissing him again until next New Year's Eve," I say, attempting to make light of the situation, but the joke lands flat.

I step forward into the kitchen for a glass of water, needing to do something with my nervous energy, trying to add casual movement to my body. She crosses her arms under her breasts and narrows her eyes, suspicious. "That wasn't just a kiss, though, Lucie. You guys were seriously making out."

I throw a glance over my shoulder as I fill my cup and let a mischievous smile cross my face. "Dayva. Have you seen his Form? It's not my fault it's smoking hot. So I got carried away for a second." I turn as I raise my glass to my lips, hoping she doesn't see the cup trembling in my hands, praying to the Fates that she takes my words at face value.

She fakes gagging. "Um, no. I do not and have not ever thought he was hot, because no matter what Form he's in, he's my brother, and that's disgusting."

I quirk an eyebrow. "Sure, well, then, just trust me, he is. So yeah, I got a little into it, but Dayva. This is Cato we're talking about. Your brother. He will only ever see me as his little sister's bestie, so you have nothing to worry about." I remind myself of the likely truth behind those words, but Dayva tilts her head, not ready to let it drop.

"And if he didn't?" she asks carefully.

I choose to continue with the gross-out factor. "Then I'll ride him like a fucking cowgirl, how's that?"

Her jaw drops. Before I can register what's happening, she grabs the water glass from me and dumps its contents on my head. "Girl, now I'm picturing my brother fucking and I want to DIE!" she screeches. I push my now-soaked bangs out of my eyes and find her grinning at me, perfectly annoyed and no longer at all serious, and my soul breathes a sigh of relief.

She refills the cup and takes a long sip as I slip past her to take a late-night shower and wash the stickiness of the party off my skin, but she stops me by grabbing my elbow. I brace myself, but turn back to her. "It's not that I'd be against you guys getting together, you know. It's that I'm not sure how I would handle it when he inevitably breaks your heart. You both mean the world to me, and to have to choose time between you two and tread on the glass left in the aftermath? Lucie, please don't make me do that." Her voice is pleading, sincere, and I can't make myself do anything but nod before I close myself into the bathroom so she can't see my heart break by the surety in her words that he could never love me.

***

I send Cato a message after I've crawled into bed.

I can't.

And then I let hot tears track down my cheeks when he doesn't respond, eventually falling asleep with my Tone clutched to my chest, rebuilding the walls around my heart to

protect me from the love that Dayva reminded me will only
end in pain. I had been a fool to believe his words, consider
his offer of love, wonder if maybe I could have a reciprocal,
romantic relationship that wouldn't compromise my worth.
But deep down, I know: it's time to set my feet back on the
solid ground of reality.

22

LUCIE

New Year's Eve, one year later

"Ten!"

I glance around the room, searching for him.

"Nine!"

I catch his eye, and he flashes me a wicked grin.

"Eight!"

I look away and find Dayva.

"Seven!"

She has her arm around a guy she's being seeing casually since the new semester started.

"Six!"

She sees Cato striding across the room and looks in the direction he's headed—to me.

"Five!"

She raises an eyebrow, but smiles, and gives me a nod.

"Four!"

She turns back to her guy and tilts her head up in anticipation of their kiss.

"Three!"

Cato is now just a few steps away, and I shudder at the unrestrained heat in his eyes.

"Two!"

He reaches me, his hands gripping firmly to my waist, and the feeling of his touch is molten against the thin material of my dress. My body instinctively arcs toward him, magnetic to the connection I've been yearning for the entire year.

"One!"

He's dipping me, and I'm squealing in surprise at the sudden movement, and then his mouth is crashing into mine.

"Happy New Year!"

And then it's over, and I'm standing there alone again, and I have to pretend that kiss didn't break my heart all over.

23

LUCIE

New Year's Eve, another year later

We're here again, in Forest and Terra's huge living room, and the clock is counting down. Memories of the last two years assault me—the midnight kisses with Cato both as bitter to remember as they are secretly sweet.

But it won't be him I kiss this year. Standing beside me is my date, the first human I've allowed myself to date since my Arrival. I met him in one of my classes when we sat at the same table, and we'd hit it off. A couple of weeks ago, he'd asked me out, and I'd accepted his offer of coffee and a stroll along the beach.

Then last week, we'd gone to dinner. He's funny, and he's kind, and he's a skilled conversationalist. He kissed me when he dropped me at my apartment, and it was a fine kiss.

When he asked about my plans for New Year's Eve, I'd told him, and invited him. It would be an opportunity to meet my friends, to get their gauge on him. So far, everyone seems to like him, which I'm happy about, but also kind of disappointed by, though I don't really know why. This guy is great on paper. I could fall for him, get married, have a happy life until my Assignment ends, and then move on.

I raise my glass and begin chanting the midnight countdown along with everyone else. Turning to him, I smile at his kind face and close my eyes in anticipation of the kiss as the countdown hits "two."

Then I hear, "Sorry man, it's a tradition, nothing personal—" and my lips are on someone's lips, but not his.

Cato's.

My eyes fly open as his tongue swipes past my lips and my brain stutters before frantically rebooting, screaming at me not to waste this moment—to kiss him back! And I do, but then it's over, and my date is looking at me with his eyebrows raised as everyone shouts, "Happy New Year!". I grin sheepishly and raise my glass to clink against his and give him a gentle peck on the cheek. "Sorry. Happy New Year."

And the gentleman he is, he just chuckles and pulls me in for a hug. "Happy New Year, Lucie," he says against my ear, and I shiver—not from his words skating down my neck, but from the molten gaze pinning me down from across the room.

24

CATO

THE FOLLOWING SPRING

I speed up my pace, sweat dripping into my eyes, and frown. We are running extra fast today, and she only does that when something is weighing heavily on her mind.

A few months after the...eventful...morning run I'd taken with Lucie, I'd found out in conversation with Dayva that Lucie had started that new year by running outside every morning at seven, a habit she'd kept to religiously ever since. Curious at her route but not wanting to step over the re-established firm lines of our friendship (or, more accurately, acquaintances-ship), I trailed her one morning like some kind of stalker. I'd kept well and far back so she'd never see me, guessing at her route a couple times when I had to fall back to avoid being seen and I'd lose sight of her. I had been surprised to see that she took the route I'd taken her on that memorable morning, despite how nervous she'd been at the park section.

Every day since, I've shown up in the shadows down the street at five minutes to seven and waited for her to exit her apartment. The only days I don't are when I'm out of town because of Forest, or she is because of Terra. I am confident she can take care of herself in the daylight or the darkness, but a small part of me likes the idea of being her own secret Guardian. Even if it's only a one-sided connection, it makes me feel close to her when I'm not able to do so any other way.

I hadn't responded to her text that night two years ago. "I can't," it had said. Two little words that held too much weight. I'd typed out and deleted a hundred variations of a response before deciding I needed to talk to her in person about it. But the next time I'd seen her, she'd given me a tight smile, thanked me for being a wonderful person, but firmly pushed me back across the friendship line with a request to respect her wishes. I didn't understand what had happened, having thought we could build something together, but of course I respected her. I stepped back across that boundary, but I refused to go any further than that, maintaining a presence in her life through our friends and watching out for her whenever I could.

The only difference between her jogging route and the one we'd taken together is that she never takes the side detour to the rock where we'd kissed. She jogs right by it without ever giving it a second glance. I, however, think of that morning every single time I pass it, stepping on the shards of my heart that would lie there forever.

I'll take my New Year's Eve kisses once a year, and someday (hopefully soon), I'll move on. Like she'd been trying to do with that classmate of hers that I'd stolen her most recent New Year's Eve kiss from, before they'd decided just to be friends—at least, that's what Dayva told me had happened.

And it seems the case; he's still around at some parties, but not as anything more than a platonic friend with Lucie now.

By the time Lucie turns onto her street and I continue past it, the Luminaries have disappeared, replaced by the morning sun. I slow to a walk as I wonder how I can find out what's agitating Lucie. Pulling out my Tone, I shoot Dayva message, asking if she wants to grab coffee later. She responds within seconds, and I break into a jog again to get home with enough time to shower and make it to campus to meet her there before her first class.

I order a coffee for me and a mocha for her, then pull out a chair at a table in a corner of the cafe and wait. I sit up straighter when Dayva enters—with Lucie in tow.

I raise my hand, and they wind their way toward me. "Sorry, Lucie, I didn't realize you were coming; I only bought a drink for Dayva," I apologize, quickly standing. "I'll get you one."

She looks distracted and shoots me a half-smile. "No worries." Her hair is wet, washed after her run, and it's dampening her shirt where her braid lays over her shoulder.

"No, I'll go grab another one. Here, you have this one," Dayva says, pushing Lucie's shoulder down to make her sit across from me. "Tell him—I'll be right back."

I frown, sitting down again and focusing on Lucie. "Tell me what?"

She sighs, then leans forward on the table and rubs her eyes with her palms. I push the mocha toward her and she clasps her hands around it but makes no move to drink from it. "What's the longest halo alert you've received?" she asks abruptly.

I cock my head, confusion and concern warring within me. "Are you being alerted right now?" My gaze strays to her arm, where her halo-bound tattoo hides beneath her sleeve. "Why aren't you with Terra?"

She shakes her head, frustrated. "Just answer the question."

I study her—her face free of makeup, the oversized sweater, the hollows under her eyes. My chest tightens, unease building. But finally, I answer. "Three hours? Four?"

Her eyelids close, and I push again. "Lucie. What's going on?"

I'm almost startled when her eyelids snap open and her eyes collide with mine. "We learned in Dek that the longest warning we'll ever get is six hours, and the shortest could be mere seconds, right?" It's a rhetorical question, but I nod anyway. She spins the still-full mocha in front of her, her gaze remaining locked on me. "I've mostly had minutes with Terra's so far, excepting that car accident last year where I had an hour."

"Lucie, is Terra okay?" A thread of panic winds its way through me—is this Lucie's goodbye? Did she fail her Assignment? My eyes shoot to my Tone on the table, but there's no notification from Forest about any tragedy having befallen his sister, and I know I would be his first support call, so I breathe a little easier.

Before I can push for more details, Dayva returns, grabbing a chair from the table beside us and swinging it backwards so she can straddle it. "So, what do you think?"

She directs the question at me, but I shrug, exasperated. "I don't think anything yet, because Lucie hasn't told me anything."

Dayva kicks Lucie under the table, and Lucie scowls at her but says nothing. With a sigh, my sister sets her coffee on the table and reaches over to yank up Lucie's sleeve.

I can't help the audible growl that escapes me, and before I register what I'm doing, I'm reaching out and grasping her best friend's wrist so I can pull her arm closer to me.

Lucie's forearm is swollen, her tattoo angry and red. Bloodied and scabbed scratch marks zigzag across the flowers, a harsh juxtaposition. It doesn't look like anything is currently bleeding, but a slight pull of the skin the wrong way could open any of the wounds.

"Lucie's been alerting for two weeks, Cato."

My fingers squeeze around Lucie's wrist. I pinball my gaze between the two of them, trying to process the impossible words. "That's not...that's not possible," I stammer. "That renders the system useless."

Lucie yanks her arm back from me and shoves her sleeve down before dropping her hands into her lap. She still hasn't had a sip of the drink in front of her, and for some irrational reason, it's adding to my stress.

Dayva rolls her eyes. "You think? Wow, we hadn't realized." Sarcasm drips from every word, and I kick her shin under the table, returning the favour on Lucie's account. "That's why Lucie's here and Terra's not. After the first day, we were curious. By the third, we were worried. At this point, we're beyond knowing how to feel. Is Terra in imminent danger? Is this a false alarm? After about 10 days, Lucie was going mad shadowing Terra so closely, being on such high alert, and so she took a step back. Nothing has happened to Terra yet, but we don't know what to do."

"I'm so...tired..." She trails off on the words like she meant to say more, and I can imagine additions such as being tired of worrying, tired of not knowing, tired of Guarding, tired of everything. She absentmindedly reaches her hand to her sleeve to scratch, but Dayva grabs her hand. "Don't," she says sternly. "You were supposed to bandage it before we left, but since you didn't, you're not getting blood all over your sweater."

"I'm so tired of the burn," she says, finding more words to add to the sentence, her voice coming out small and uncertain.

Dayva turns to me. "What should we do?" Her fingers intertwine with Lucie's in a gesture both supportive and firm. The action twinges at my soul—it should be my hand that Lucie's holding right now.

"First of all," I glare at my sister, "why the Fates didn't you come to me sooner?"

Dayva meets me with an equally fierce look. "Because Lucie didn't want to distract any more Guardians than necessary. But it's been so long now, we're out of options."

I scowl, understanding but also angry that she didn't come to me, that Dayva didn't tell me. But I push down those emotions, recognizing them as nothing but an irrelevant distraction right now, and slump back against the wall and try to think.

Twelve days after an Assignment expires, our Intermediary comes to escort us back to the Retreat through a Channel. On occasion, an Intermediary will appear at other times if there's need for it. Each Intermediary Oversees dozens of Guardians, but their systems are set up to monitor every Guardian and alert them of unique situations they may need to intercede on. It happens, rarely, but this is an unprecedented case that our Intermediary, Ruel, should absolutely be stepping in for, and the fact they haven't is more than concerning—it's scary.

"I honestly don't have any idea what to do," I finally respond. "Ruel should have been here days ago—within hours, if not minutes, of the alert lasting longer than six hours. That's not something that happens, so they should have been aware of it immediately."

Lucie sighs, defeated. "This isn't helpful. I have to get to class with Terra. This is my Assignment, and I'm seeing it through, even if means I have to cut this freaking thing right out of my arm and become a velcro Guardian without a halo. I'm not giving up."

We all know that's not how it works, but that's not the point she's making.

"Where's Terra now?" I ask.

"Heading to class," says Lucie, exhaustion creasing all of her features. "We've got lab for three hours."

"No, you don't. You're going to go home, and go to bed," Dayva says in a way that makes it clear it's not a request but a statement. "I'm on campus all day today, and unless I'm alerted for Ainsley, I'm sticking around Terra. Lucie—" she warns as Lucie shakes her head, "you have to sleep. Something's wrong with your halo and you can't keep pushing your Form like this. Let me help."

I stand, and I grab Lucie's mocha in one hand, my own coffee nearly empty and not worth bringing. "Let's go," I say. "I'm taking you home, and you're going to trust Dayva to look out for Terra today. I'll cover the night shift. I promise we have Terra's back, and we're not negotiating on also taking care of you." My words sound vaguely threatening, and I don't intend them to, but it's effective nonetheless; her brown eyes startle towards me and she hesitates only a second longer before she stands and pulls her hand from Dayva's. In an unconscious response to having her hand free, she moves to scratch her arm, so I intercept it and thread my own fingers through hers, satisfying my soul. "And we're bandaging your halo up so you can't keep ripping it open," I growl.

Dayva nods in approval, relieved to have brought me into the situation, no longer alone in supporting her best friend. "Thank you," she says, swinging her leg over the chair and picking up her backpack from where she'd dropped it beside the table. "I'll check in with you later."

"And you'll call me if anything happens, at any moment," Lucie demands as I drag her reluctant Form toward the front door.

"You know I will," comes Dayva's response, and then we're outside in the sun, blinking against the sudden brightness as I veer us in the direction of her apartment building.

I pass her the mocha, and finally, she takes a sip. We walk in silence, hand-in-hand, and I let myself imagine for a moment that it's a different situation. That we're together, that she's holding my hand because she wants to be close to me—not that she's tolerating my grip because she knows it's keeping her from clawing additional grooves into her skin.

By the time we get to her apartment, I estimate she's nearly finished her mocha and I feel a strange relief, like she's accepted help from me in a way she didn't know she needed.

"Where's your first aid kit?" I ask as I lead her to her couch and motion for her to sit down. It requires me to release her hand, but I do so only begrudgingly, hating the feeling of the air cooling the warmth where her palm had been.

"Bathroom cupboard." She leans back and rests her head against the back of the couch and closes her eyes.

I head to the bathroom and see the kit the moment I open the cupboard. I dump the contents on the counter and eye the gauze and alcohol swabs and decide there's enough, but I'll have to pick up more before the bandage needs changing again.

Products in hand, I head back to the living room and falter when I see she's pulled off her sweater and is sitting there in a black bra—a basic bra, not any kind of lingerie style, but it doesn't need to be to pick my heart rate up. It's not about the bra—it's never about the bra. It's about the soft slope of breasts into the cups, and I stand there a moment longer than necessary, trying to get the message to my dick that my mission is to provide attention to her halo. Not her chest.

Her eyes are closed, and she startles when I kneel on the floor beside her and gently bump against her knees. "Sorry," she says, her skin flushing as she looks down at her sweater balled up in her lap. It takes away a shade of exhaustion from her face. "I just didn't want to pull the sleeve over it once you've bandaged it, but I didn't have the energy to grab anything else to put on."

"Sweetheart, you never have to apologize for taking your top off in front of me," I say with a smirk, unable to help myself from trying to provoke her trademark blush. I'm successful, her cheeks turning a bright rosy pink, and she scoffs, but I see the small smile she tries to hide and send her a wink as I reach for her wrist.

"Flirtatious bastard," she grumbles. "Also, I can do this myself." But she doesn't make any moves to pull away, so I ignore her words and start drawing a warm cloth across her tattoo to clean it.

"We've got to stop meeting like this," I joke, thinking back on how I'd cared for her wounded halo a couple of years prior, after Terra's alert at the bar. I look up to see a soft smile on her face as she remembers, too. "Speaking of that night, on a scale of one to ten, one being the most minor alert you've felt and ten being that night at the club, where does this fall on the scale of alert urgency?"

"Like a six, I guess? It's persistent and burning and desperately difficult to ignore, but it's not agonizingly painful to the exclusion of being able to fake my way through life as needed. I can force myself to leave it alone when I'm in certain situations, you know?"

I nod, rolling her arm as I dab antibiotic ointment over the wounds. "Yeah. That kind of alert can be extremely frustrating when I have it for only a few hours. I can't imagine how you're faring after two weeks of this."

She sighs. "Well, I'm clearly not doing well."

I stroke my thumb over her wrist. "You're doing great, Lucie. This isn't something that, to my limited knowledge at least, has ever happened to a Guardian before. There's no manual for this. So trust me, you're handling it better than most Guardians would. I know that for sure."

She offers me a wan smile, her earlier blush faded, skin back to pale and tired. I force my eyes not to linger on the enticing way her chest molds into the bra in front of me and refocus on her arm. A moment later, I've wound the gauze around her forearm and obscured the tattoo from view. She thanks me, and I rock back on my heels as I gather the discarded bandage wrappers.

When I return from putting the supplies back in the bathroom, she's no longer there. From the corner of my eye, I catch movement from her darkened room, her silhouette outlined by the soft light pressing through her linen blinds. She's pulled off her pants and is standing there in her underwear—the movement that caught my eye is the motion of her pulling a large, over-sized t-shirt above her head. I should look away and afford her privacy, but the fabric is mesmerizing as it falls down her back and reaches to her thighs.

I step back before she can turn and see me, retreat another couple of steps before saying, "Lucie, can I get you anything to help you sleep?" and then walk forward again into view of her room.

She's sitting on her bed now, one hand wrapped around the bandage—not itching at it, but applying a pressure that I'd imagine lessens the pain a little, even if only psychologically. She looks up at me through her bangs and I step into the bedroom, drawn like a magnet to her. I stop abruptly two steps in and lean against her dresser, trying to portray a picture of casual friendship.

"Why hasn't Ruel come?"

My heart cracks at her despair, and I search for words to comfort her with, but she continues. "I worked so hard to get here, to be the best Guardian I could be. I sacrificed so much in Celestia so I didn't distract myself from studying. I read far and beyond what was required for Dek graduation, and I learned nothing about this kind of situation, or what to do if your Intermediary doesn't come when they're needed—because they always come." Her voice breaks and tears well in her eyes as she looks at me. "They always come, Cato. Why isn't Ruel coming?"

Despite myself, I stride forward to sit beside her on the bed and wrap my arms around her. She doesn't hesitate to melt into me, which all on its own tells me how much she's at the end of her rope. She's never strayed from her position on friendship since she sent that text and set those boundaries. It's like she had a switch on her heart that she'd been able to toggle off to cease all attraction to me—which I wished I could have done in return to lessen the hurt. Beyond the New Year's Eve kisses I stole from her, we hadn't touched in over two years.

I remind myself that there's no romance to this touch, and only friendship, but it feels so good and so right to be holding her I don't care either way. All I want to do is fix this problem for her, and yet I'm helpless to do so. If what I can offer in a hug is all I can do to help, then I'm thankful, at least, for that small option.

I stroke her back as she buries her face into my neck. "I don't know why Ruel isn't here, Lucie. But I do know none of this is your fault. You're an incredible Guardian, and your sacrifices have been—and are, and will be—worth it. If there would have been information on this kind of situation to find, you would have found it. We'll figure this out together, okay? And I swear to you that Dayva and I will do everything we can to Guard Terra as well. With three of us on high alert, she'll be fine."

Her tears dampen my t-shirt, but she doesn't sob or break into hysterics, just quietly exists in my arms as she lets the exhaustion and stress of the past two weeks flow over her. We sit there like that for a few long minutes, and I rub her back in slow circles, content to remain in this position as long as she needs. When she does pull away, I reach up to draw her bangs back from where they've caught in her wet eyelashes. And then I'm stuck, immobilized in her deep brown eyes as she stares at me and asks tentatively, "Will you stay with me for a while?"

I study the golden flakes surrounding her dark pupils, un-sure what she's asking me to do. "Of course, Lucie. I'll be in the living room and when Dayva—"

"No," she interrupts. "Stay with me here, until I fall asleep. I just don't trust myself not to lie here trying to rip my halo out with my teeth for the next few hours instead of going to sleep." She grins weakly as she blinks at me, trying to make light of the situation, and I know she's doing it for my sake. Trying to ease my stress even while she's the one enduring the brunt of it.

I swallow—of course I'll stay with her, here. In her bed. And remain focused on our friendship, on the stressful situation at hand, and not on the fact that I'm in bed with the girl I love and can't have.

I scoot back on the bed without removing my arm from her waist and pull her horizontal with me, drawing her tight against my chest with my arm now wrapped snug around her stomach, beneath her chest. I hear her let out a light gasp, as though she'd expected me to put distance between us. But she doesn't wriggle away, so I settle my head on the pillow behind hers and breathe in the fresh scent of citrus shampoo that lingers in her still-damp hair.

"Sleep, Lucie," I whisper.

Moments later, she does just that.

25

LUCIE

When I wake up, there's no more sunlight filtering through my curtains, so I must have slept through the day to the evening. I can tell right away how much that rest has reinvigorated me, my body feeling functional once again. But the realization is short-lived, the burn of my halo reminding me that all is not yet well, and that Terra may or may not still be in imminent danger.

I resist the urge to claw at my halo and roll over instead, my arm flopping to the other side of my bed before I jolt into a sitting position, remembering that I'd fallen asleep in Cato's arms.

He isn't here anymore, and from the faint humming coming from the kitchen, I could assume that Dayva is home and her brother has taken a shift watching over Terra. I have no reason to believe that's not the case, but my stomach clenches anyway at the possibility of Terra being left alone while my halo burns of a threat against her, no matter how long it has been alerting. I jump up from my bed and hurry to the door of my bedroom, which is open as it always is, to see Dayva chopping vegetables in the kitchen, her dark hair tucked behind her ears.

"Is Terra okay?"

"Ahhh!" Dayva squeals, jumping back and dropping the pepper she'd been holding onto the floor. Her now-empty hand flutters to her heart, but she uses the other hand to brandish the knife at me. "You sneaky beast. You're too quiet."

I raise my eyebrow at her and ask again. "Terra?"

"Yes, of course she's okay. You think I would have left you to keep sawing logs in there if something had happened? A little credit, Luce." She disappears from view as she bends behind the counter to pick up the pepper. "Cato's spelled me off for the night," she explains as she pops back up to rinse the escaped vegetable under the tap. "He's lurking around her apartment, true stalker-style." She looks at me standing there in my t-shirt, and whatever she sees has her putting down the knife and wiping her hands on a towel before coming over and drawing me into an enormous hug.

I sigh into her arms and wrap my own around her back. "Good hugs must run in your genetic coding," I joke when I pull away.

Dayva shoots me an overdramatic frown as she goes back into the kitchen and picks up her knife again. "My brother better not be getting handsy on you again, or I'll filet him—I swear I will! He'll have to pop to the Retreat to get a new Form cuz this one will be in pieces."

I snort, allowing myself to relax for a moment into the banter with my best friend, though I squeeze a hand over my bandaged tattoo to relieve some of the burning pressure. "Thanks, but I appreciated his hands on me today." I freeze, realizing how that sounded, and swiftly backpedal as Dayva gapes at me. "No, I just mean he gave me a big hug and laid in bed with me until I fell asleep—just laid there, to make sure I didn't scratch at my halo." I amend my sentence to make sure it doesn't sound sexual. Not that it was, so I'm not lying. I didn't need to tell her how fast my heart had beat when he'd pulled me against his chest while we laid there, or that I'd fallen asleep so quickly because being in his arms afforded me a sense of peace I hadn't experienced since my halo had begun alerting two weeks ago.

She giggles at my flustered words. I giggle too, and then we're laughing together, and my heart releases a fraction as I make my way to the kitchen stools. I pop onto one of them and steal a slice of pepper from her cutting board. Our conversation turns to Dayva's day of Guarding Terra. She'd had no alerts about Ainsley, so she'd focussed every minute on my Assignment. I am so grateful to have a friend like her—and Cato, who is doing the same right now.

We eat dinner and spend the evening watching TV, though I keep distracting myself with texts to Cato to check in about Terra, and texts to Terra to chat and hear from her myself. At some point, I drift off on the couch, rousing only to walk to my bed when Dayva tugs on my arm, before falling right back to sleep.

The next morning, I wake to voices. Dayva's, and Forest's. I scratch at my bandage, frustrated that the burn hadn't disappeared overnight. I'll need to shower and replace the bandage today. I stand and grab a towel, but hesitate as I remember the last time I emerged from the bathroom in just a towel and basically run straight into Cato. I'm not interested in a repeat performance, so I also grab underwear and a light dress to throw on in case he is also out there.

I step out and see it's not only Dayva and Forest who are making breakfast in my kitchen. Clem is straddling a barstool, Hailey is sprawled on the couch flipping through music on the TV with Ainsley sitting on the floor next to her, and Terra is emerging from the bathroom. My body sags in relief, which Dayva sees. She smiles at me, nodding knowingly. I shoot her a look that I hope portrays all the grateful feelings I'm having toward her right now before composing myself—shoving my bandaged arm under the towel I'm carrying so as to not raise questions from any of the others.

"Morning sleepyhead," Terra says teasingly as she hops up onto a barstool. Just the sight of her makes me want to tear at my burning halo, even though it's not any more painful in her presence than it has been for the past two weeks.

I glance at the clock in the kitchen and raise my eyebrows at the time displayed there. I haven't slept in this long in...well, have I ever slept this late since arriving in the Realm of Bones? But it's so good to feel even a semblance of myself again, having slept soundly knowing Dayva and Cato were in on things and would help me figure this all out. Somehow.

Speaking of Cato—he's not here, which is strange, considering our little group seems to travel as a pack. Although if he was awake all night Guarding Terra, he might be back home, catching up on sleep. I can't begrudge him for that, though I can't help but be a touch disappointed. He was my safe place yesterday, and I want to thank him for looking after me. Even so, it feels weird without him here, so I step up to the counter to pop a couple of grapes in my mouth as I ask where he is.

Dayva averts her eyes, looking cagey, and I eye her with suspicion. "He's grabbing some bagels from the bakery," Clementine offers, oblivious to the silent tension between the angels in front of her.

Dayva turns her back to me as she moves to cut a melon on the opposite counter. "Brunch will be ready in like, twenty minutes though, so if you're going to shower, do it now."

I narrow my eyes at her back, then cut my gaze to Terra, but she's swivelled on the barstool beside Clem and has her hands above her head in a "raise the roof" kind of motion as she engages with the other girls about the music playing from the TV. Sighing, I let the matter drop and scurry to the shower—the point being that although Cato isn't currently here, he will be soon.

I remove the bandage and shower, using my harsh exfoliating scrub a little too vigorously on my tattoo, causing it to turn an angry red again, though not enough to bleed this time. I re-bandage it as well as I can with one hand, noting that the first aid kit has been restocked, before braiding my bangs back and throwing my wet hair into a messy bun, swiping on some mascara and slipping the long-sleeved dress over my head.

When I open the bathroom door and glance at the kitchen clock again, I see it's been almost exactly 20 minutes. Forest is plating bacon and Dayva is sliding a dozen sunny-side-up baked eggs out of a muffin tin onto a plate, so I grab the pitcher on the counter and take it to the living room coffee table where the rest of the food is already waiting.

The front door opens, and my pulse flutters in anticipation of seeing Cato. Although nothing romantic happened yesterday between us, and despite spending two years on top of the last few decades trying to quash my feelings for him, the soul wants what the soul wants, I guess.

But as I turn, it's not Cato's warm eyes that capture me—it's a pair of sparkling green ones, which I only have a moment to register before I'm tackled by a hug and deafened by a squeal in my ear.

"Hi, stranger!" Saffi squeezes me, then turns to give Dayva an equally exuberant hug. Her grin stretches from ear to ear, mismatched dimples etching deep into her cheeks. Her long brown hair is split into two wide French braids that reach midway down her upper arms, and she's wearing black leggings with an oversized off-the-shoulder sweater in the same green shade as her eyes.

"What are you doing here?" I ask, excited to see a Guardian angel friend while on Assignment, but equally confused. We'd connected with Saffi on social media right after beginning our Assignments, but since hers was based in New York, we hadn't had any opportunities to meet up.

"I needed a change of scenery," she says, gesturing in a vague manner that tells me absolutely nothing about why she's here. "Hi, I'm Saffi!" She pushes past me and puts her hands on her hips as she surveys everyone else. "Wait, wait, let me guess!" Pursing her glossed lips, she points over her shoulder in the general direction of Forest, who's still in the kitchen. "By default, that's Forest. You must be Ainsley, because Dayva's obsessed with your baking and you have flour all over your shirt."

Ainsley gives her a crooked grin as she looks down and brushes at her chest, which, sure enough, has a smattering of flour across it. "Guilty as charged," she says, at the same time as Hailey grabs a cinnamon bun from the coffee table and proclaims, "She made these this morning and I've already eaten two."

Saffi's smile grows even bigger, and she leans down to grab one as well. "Then you must be Hailey, the girlfriend." She takes a huge bite of the cinnamon roll, cream cheese frosting sticking to her lips. Her eyes roll back into her head as she groans a very sexual-sounding groan and looks at the two girls to say around a mouthful, "Are you guys into polyamory? I'm not, but for these cinnamon buns, maybe I am."

We all laugh, knowing that the cinnamon buns really are that good, but then Saffi turns to Terra, and her face softens. She swallows her cinnamon bun bite, places the remainder on a plate in front of her, and envelops Terra in a warm embrace. "And you're Lucie's Terra."

Terra looks surprised at the hug and term, but smiles at me over Saffi's shoulder. "Sure," she says with a laugh. Still hugging Terra, Saffi points at Clem and finishes her guesses by saying, "And you're the Clementine that brought everyone together!" which brings a proud grin to our friend's face.

Cato had followed Saffi in, and leans against the closed front door with a pink backpack dangling from his arm while he takes in our reunion. I realize he must have been picking her up from the airport. He's wearing a backward-turned hat, and I swallow at the ridiculously hot picture he poses there before Saffi's bubbling personality draws my attention again.

We all settle around the living room as we catch up and swap stories, some of us on the floor, others on the couch, all of us heaping our plates with the impressive brunch spread before us. It's beautifully distracting from the burning of my arm and only once does Cato gently nudge his foot against my hip from where he sits on the couch next to my place on the floor, and I look up at him to see him looking pointedly at where I'm rubbing my arm. I mouth "oops" and grab my mug of coffee so I can have both hands wrapped around it and occupied.

If it weren't for the pain of my arm, I'd be completely, utterly content in this moment, here with my favourite humans and Guardians. Saffi slides in to the group like she's always been a part of it, and the laughter and stories swirl around us like the icing on the rapidly disappearing cinnamon buns. All too soon, though, it's early afternoon, and we've cleaned up from brunch and make plans to move on with our days. Terra and Forest are going home for dinner; Hailey and Ainsley just moved into a new apartment together and want to get started on repainting its atrocious yellow-green walls, and Clem is going to see a movie with a couple other friends, trying to keep busy to distract her from her break-up with Jet a couple of weeks prior.

Panic begins to well in me, knowing the easy Guarding for the day is over and I have to turn stalker mode back on. Having a malfunctioning halo system is one of the worst—maybe, actually, the very worst—thing I can imagine happening to a Guardian, and it's not something I ever even thought to consider before, since we're taught that the Guardianship is infallible. I force my face to stay genial, but Cato leans over and says in my ear, just loud enough for me and only me to hear, "I've got this. Talk to Saffi and text me later."

I nod, thankful but still stressed, as he makes his exit a minute after Terra and Forest. Ainsley, Hailey, and Clem follow a few minutes later, and then only Dayva, Saffi, and me remain in the apartment. The moment the door closes the three of us in, Saffi grabs each of our arms and drags us to the living room. Her face is serious, no trace of a smiling dimple left, her expression a somber reflection of Dayva's. We sit on the L-shaped couch, but Saffi doesn't let go of my wrist, instead pulling my arm to her and pushing my sleeve up.

My bandage is loose and unwinding, not nearly as secure as when Dayva or Cato bind it, my mobility limited by doing it with one hand. Saffi unwinds it the rest of the way, her touch gentle, while my attention turns sideways to Dayva. "You told her?" The words by themselves might have sounded accusing, but my tone is curious. I should have realized that's why Saffi was here, but I still didn't know exactly why. Having another Guardian with no idea how to fix this isn't going to help matters, regardless of how happy I am to see my friend.

Dayva nods, but both of us turn our attention back to Saffi as she pulls a couple of items from her pink backpack. She wriggles one hand into a rubber glove and squeezes a gel-like lotion from a small bottle onto my tattoo. "Cato and I were talking and realized that Saffi has a different Intermediary than you and Cato and I, so calling her in could alert Reed. It's worth a shot, anyway."

Saffi's gently massaging the gel into my tattoo, and I'm not sure what it is, but just the friction from her glove feels good against the agitated skin. "I hopped on the first flight here as soon as Dayva called me," she explains, peering up at me with those stark green eyes, concern etched in the dainty crows feet of her eyes. "This must be excruciating."

I give her a weak smile. "It's not exactly my idea of a good time, no."

Dayva picks up the bottle from where Saffi had placed it on the coffee table. "What is this?" She turns the container around, looking for clues, but it's unlabeled.

"It's a numbing cream," she says, her fingers continuing their circular motion on my arm. "It's like a topical anesthetic. I figured it was worth a shot to see if it would stop the burning." She raises her eyebrows at me. "Is it doing anything?"

I pause, evaluating the pain. It's still there, but now I realize it isn't only the friction of her glove against my skin that feels good—it's the lessening of the burning as well. "Yes, actually," I say in surprise, leaning back against the couch. "I'd say it's like a three out of ten instead of a six. It's more like an irritated spider bite now." I let out a relieved breath, my body relaxing with the pain alleviation.

Dayva puts the bottle back on the table and smiles at me, her own relief evident. "Saffi, you're a genius."

"Saffi."

A voice that isn't any of ours startles us. Dayva lets out a small shriek and Saffi and I gasp as we all whip our heads to where we didn't hear the front door open or close.

"What's going on?"

***

The three of us sit there gaping at the tall, muscular man standing in our kitchen. His blond hair hangs to his shoulders in gentle waves, and he wears a light blue button-up shirt that strains across his impressive biceps.

Reed.

He stares at us with glittering grey eyes, and we stare back. Silence sticks in the air between us before he places his hands on the counter and leans forward, blowing a breath out and making a curl flutter beside his face.

"Saffi." He says her name again, assessing us. His gaze stops at Saffi's still-gloved hand on my arm, and he frowns.

"Hi," breathes Saffi. I look away from Reed to her, and despite the abrupt and serious moment, I want to giggle. Her eyes are wide and fluttering, and her grip on my arm is now more painful than the burning halo itself. I kick my foot subtly against hers and she looks and me and blinks before seeming to come back to herself. "Hi," she says again, more firmly and less breathlessly. "Reed. How are you?"

"I'm fine, but that's clearly not relevant at the moment. Someone please tell me why one of my Guardians left the vicinity of their Assignment to fly across the continent with no warning." He rounds the kitchen island and leans back against it. Saffi's breathing rate increases beside me, and I can't blame her—from a purely physical point of view, he's damn near perfect, and she did say he was exceptional in the sack. I bet she's replaying a highlight reel in her mind right now. I squint my eyes a little as I make a more clinical assessment of him than I had ever bothered to before. He's still in his Retreat Form, and I wonder if there are fewer rules for Intermediary Forms than Guardian Forms, because the imperfections are far more subtle.

His attention is on my arm again, and I gently pry Saffi's hand off it. She snaps the glove off and tosses it on the table. And then all three of us begin to speak at once.

"Her halo is malfunctioning and—"

"My halo has been alerting me for two—"

"Dayva called me and said—"

He raises a hand and we all stop as abruptly as we'd begun. "Lucie."

That's all he says, but I take it as my cue to be the storyteller.

I start from the first moment of alert and walk him through the following hours, then skim the next few days. I tell him about how Dayva has been helping Guard Terra, and how we wondered why Ruel, our Intermediary, hadn't appeared. How we told Cato and how the siblings had come up with an idea to get another Intermediary's attention—enter, Saffi.

Reed stands there the whole twenty-or-so minutes it takes for us to relay the story, crossing his arms over his chest about half-way through but otherwise remaining stationary and silent. At the conclusion, his frown deepens, and he steps forward to kneel before me.

"May I?" He asks, his palm open by my arm.

I nod, and he takes my wrist in his hand and studies my tattoo, similar to how Cato had done so. Despite the handsome Form in front of me, I realize that Reed's touch does nothing to me—not in the way Cato's does. I hate thinking that, hate having another thing confirm that I'm destined to pine for a man I'll never have.

Saffi stands from the couch saying, "I'll get us all some water," but then pauses behind Reed, out of his view, and gestures in her typical vague, excitable way as she mouths "Fucking Fates," and fans herself with a hand.

Dayva giggles and Reed looks up at her, still frowning, and I realize he's worn the expression the entire time he's been here. Dayva tries to cover up her giggle by turning it into a cough, popping up from the couch to scurry into the kitchen with Saffi.

Reed releases my arm and then rocks back onto his heels before standing in one swift motion. He sits beside me on the couch, taking Saffi's place. A moment later, Dayva and Saffi return, glasses of water in each hand. Reed lets out a stressed breath as he takes a glass from Saffi and says, "Where's the best place to get takeout around here?"

"Oh, definitely Pizza-So-Pizza," I answer without hesitation. "The jalapeño garlic sauce they use on their chicken pizzas would be worth Luminescing early for." My mouth waters in anticipation, but then I shake my head. "Wait, why?"

He takes my Tone from the coffee table and hands it to me. "Order enough for all of us, and Cato. We've got some things to talk about, so we're going to be here for a while."

26
CATO

I'm sitting in Terra and Forest's childhood playhouse in the backyard of their family home. It's near the back, so it's shrouded in darkness, but gives a full view through the windows to the kitchen and the living space beyond. The family of four recently finished dinner, and are now milling around cleaning up and moving to the living room when I receive the text from Lucie.

I hate that I'm not there with the three of them, getting to be a part of puzzling all of this out together, holding Lucie's hand in support, making sure she's okay.

> Reed's here.

My eyes widen. That didn't take long. Relief washes through me, knowing he will give us the answers and help we need. I haven't responded yet when another text comes through.

> He wants to talk to all of us.

I peer through the slats of the playhouse into the cozy interior of the house I'm spying on and see Forest pulling out a board game. There aren't many families whose 20-something kids still live at home and choose to spend time with each other, but this family has always had those wholesome ideals. I figure they'll stay occupied and relatively safe for the next couple of hours at least and won't be leaving anymore for the night, so I type back the situation and that I'll be there in ten. With one last look at Terra as she curls up with a blanket on the couch and begins unfolding the board game, I shimmy my way down the tree and disappear from the yard, nothing more than a silent shadow.

Nine minutes later, I'm walking into Lucie's apartment building. I use the app on my Tone to open the door, not bothering to knock. Dayva had given me access almost immediately after our reunion in case of emergencies, though I never use it unless other friends are already visiting inside. I don't want her or Lucie to feel like I would just waltz in at any moment.

As soon as I step through the doorway, I lock eyes with Hercules. Well, that's who he looks like in my mind, anyway; the Hercules of human legend and fairytales, who has long blond hair and muscles bulging from every angle. My soul stands at attention, urging me to straighten my posture and expand my lats in an effort to appear bulkier, though my muscle is lean and no competition for his—insecurities that may also be spouting from the fact he's holding Lucie's hand.

My brain sputters, but then I realize he's bandaging up her tattoo. I'm relieved, but only for a moment as I recall how intimate it had been when I'd done that for her. My soul swings right back to jealousy—and yeah, jealous is the word I'm using. Lucie's not mine. I know that, logically. But every ounce of my soul is throwing a temper-tantrum telling me otherwise, demanding that I clock the blond god feeling up my woman.

But then Lucie looks over at me, and her face softens as she smiles. That look isn't for him. That look is just for me.

And now my heart hurts for so many other reasons.

"Hey," I say, closing the door behind me.

Reed finishes pinning the bandage before extending his hand to shake mine. "Hey, Cato. I'm Reed."

His handshake is firm, though I expected no less. I'd seen him around the Retreat once or twice—you can't miss him, as few other angels have a Retreat Form that bulky, but we've never actually been introduced.

He steps a little further into the kitchen to throw away the bandage wrappers, and I shamelessly sink into his previously occupied space on the couch beside Lucie.

"Hey," she says, her gaze capturing mine. I want to kiss her cheeks, which are the perfect pillowed bookends to her beautiful, if weary, smile. "Thanks for coming."

I put a hand on her knee and squeeze it before removing it, not tempting myself further. "Of course. Has he fixed your halo yet?"

Dayva hears my question and pipes up from the barstool. "No, but now that you're here, maybe he can explain why he hasn't yet." There's an edge to her voice, and I raise my eyebrows at Lucie.

She leans over and flicks her friend's nose. "Dayva, it's okay. Saffi's numbing cream is making a huge difference. I'm sure Reed has valid reasons to want to talk to us all together."

The mountain of a man rounds the counter to sink onto the opposite end of the sofa. Far from Lucie, I note with satisfaction. He rubs his temples, a man in crisis, which makes me uneasy. Surely, he can jump to the Retreat and flick a switch or something? I admit, I know very little about how Intermediaries do their job, but still. They're tech, and this is realm tech, so...

Before he can say anything, the doorbell rings. Saffi jumps up to get it and returns with three pizza boxes a moment later. We settle around the coffee table, not unlike how we had earlier that day for brunch, serving ourselves slices and looking expectantly at Saffi's Intermediary.

His first words are not what I expect.

"Guardians used to be able to use their wings in the Realm of Bones."

I freeze mid-chew. Dayva and Saffi wear similar expressions of shock. Lucie beside me had been taking a drink of water and sputters over it, and I pat her back. This woman always seems to be choking.

Lucie regains her breath, though I keep my hand on her back, rubbing soothing circles on it. "That can't be true," she protests. "We would have learned about that. And we didn't learn that—I didn't learn that." She looks around at each of us to confirm and we all shake our heads.

Reed's pizza remains in front him, untouched, and in turn, each of us places our own slices back on our plates too, the food not nearly as interesting as his words.

"You wouldn't have. Magisters haven't taught about it for thousands and thousands of years. Most of the texts mentioning it have been destroyed."

"What are you talking about?" Dayva's voice is demanding, and I'm thankful in this case for her take-no-shit attitude. "I'm hearing your words, but they're making no sense. Make them make sense."

Reed clenches his teeth, somehow further defining his already steel-cut jaw. I clench my own, annoyed at how distracted I am by sizing this man up all because he has the audacity to appear for his Guardian and care for my—for Lucie, when we literally called him to do just that. I'm such an idiot.

"It's a long story, and the truth is, I don't know most of it," he begins, carefully choosing his words. "And perhaps no one does. We're putting all the pieces we can find together. But the gist of it is this: Guardians are not equipped to do their job like they used to be. Imagine how helpful wings would be in saving Assignments from certain death in all kinds of situations. Alerts used to happen exactly 24 hours in advance—how amazing would it be to have that kind of advance, reliable warning? And Guardians used to work in tandem with their Intermediary, able to use their halo to summon them at any time, which would be an incredible system to have access to in a crisis. The list goes on."

We're struck speechless, struggling to grasp the things he's telling us. It's Saffi who finally breaks the silence, her voice sounding small after his commanding one had filled the room. She speaks the words we're all wondering: "What changed?"

But Hercules shakes his head and doesn't answer her, continuing with his news bombs. "Things are failing." He looks over at Lucie's arm. "Like halo alerts. Like Intermediary connections. Like Channels. But these things are being erased and covered up nearly in live time, as it happens, so it's ridiculously hard to put together any semblance of reason or logic or perpetrator." He leans forward on his elbows, his gaze intense as he looks at us. "Put simply? The Guardianship is failing, and someone—or rather, some group of someones, since the evidence goes back hundreds of thousands of years—is slowly weakening us, and biding their time to do so in a way that we don't even realize it's happening. Erasing our history, our memories. Changing and lowering the expectations of our abilities and making our jobs monumentally more difficult in the process. Guardians are failing at an unprecedented rate in comparison with dekamillenium ago, but the Magisters don't tell you that in Deks. Everything in the Realm of Lights is still presented as sunshine and roses, but our jobs are in jeopardy—which means our literal existence is under threat. We're all well aware that the Realm of Lights relies on the energy of the souls we bring successfully to their expiration. So if our failures continue to increase in frequency, we could be in real danger."

My head is simultaneously overfilled with information I can't process and strangely empty. I hear and understand his words, but grasping the magnitude of them is going to take more than a few minutes.

"Okay, wait, hold on, back up, chill out, pausepausepause." Dayva stands and begins pacing, her nervous energy bouncing off of everyone else's. She spins and points at Reed, her eyes narrowed. "First of all, who is this 'we' you keep talking about? And second of all, how can we be sure that what you're saying is true? This turns our whole lives upside down if it is. And, third of all, and arguably most important of all at this particular moment—" she leans down and grabs Lucie's wrist to raise her arm up, and turns her pointed finger to her bandage. "Can you or can you not relieve my best friend of this never-ending alert and find out if Terra is in any real current danger?"

Reed finally picks up his pizza slice and takes a large bite. He looks at Lucie, and I feel that annoying growl in my soul again. "You're right—this jalapeño garlic sauce really is incredible. And," he continues after he swallows, "I can kind of help with Lucie; for now, you'll have to take my word for it being true; and the 'we' of it is a couple dozen of us who have each stumbled across things that made us ask questions and led us together. We call ourselves Labyrinth, but only those of us involved know of its existence. We need to keep a practically invisible profile, because we don't know who's behind this and don't want them getting wind of us."

I got stuck on the "kind of" helping Lucie part, and evidently, so did she. "What do you mean you can 'kind of' help me?" she demands, sounding like Dayva.

Reed swallows another bite of pizza before answering, his tone apologetic. "You're not going to like this. I can sever the halo bind until the end of your Assignment. When you return to the Retreat, your halo should reset itself to be used in a new Form for your next Assignment, and this Form will be permanently retired. But that means you won't have an alert system for the rest of this Assignment." He looks pained as he says it, knowing, as we all do, that the likelihood of Lucie Guarding Terra successfully to her expiry just became highly unlikely.

Lucie pales, and Dayva drops to the floor and grabs her arm. I move my hand from Lucie's back to around her shoulders, pulling her into me, unable and unwilling to not provide physical support. "It's my only option then, isn't it?" Lucie asks, her voice hollow. "It's not working as an alert system now, plus I'm in pain. If it's severed, I won't have the alerts, but at least I won't be in pain."

Saffi jumps in again, asking why Luci can't return to the Retreat and come back in a different Form, but Reed shakes his head. "You know as well as I do that you can't go back to the Retreat for any reason while on Assignment or your human will drop dead—which is why Intermediaries exist, so we can go back and forth when it's needed. That's the case even with a severed halo—it still retains its bond to the human, and the human can't handle the halo travelling back through a Channel travel. We discovered that unfortunate fact a while ago with one of the first halo failures." He winces at the memory. "And before you can ask, there's no way to reassign a human to another Guardian. Their souls will only bind once. So yes, Lucie, this is your one and only option."

"Hold on, hold on." Saffi rubs at her eyes, as if it's physically paining her to put the pieces of this chaos together—which I can understand, based on my way my own head is aching. "Where's Ruel in all this? Why didn't they come as soon as Lucie's halo began malfunctioning?"

Despite the solemnity of the moment, Reed can't seem to help himself. A small smirk creases his face as he looks sideways at her. "Why, Saffi," he says as he makes a sweeping gesture down his annoyingly muscled body, "surely you aren't telling me you're disappointed to have me show up?"

If looks could kill, Dayva would be arrested for attempted murder right now. I take note of Saffi biting her lip and it dawns on me how enamoured with him she looks. My soul settles a little at that—if Saffi looks like she wants to take a bite out of Hercules' biceps, then she's welcome to do so if it keeps him from looking any type of way at Lucie.

Reed pulls his gaze from Saffi's lips and realizes we're all still strung tight as a wire and pivots back. "I mentioned things in the Guardianship were fracturing, yeah? Like halo alerts—from what we've been able to figure out, it's happened about a couple dozen times across Zircon in the past half-century or so."

Lucie gasps. "Then we should have learned that before we ever Arrived!"

Reed nods and spreads his hands, helpless. "That's what I'm telling you—this shit is getting locked up and burned as fast as it happens. My best guess is that Ruel's connection to you has also been severed somehow. I'm going to check in with them as soon as I get back to the Retreat, because if they've lost connection with all three of you, I think its likely that all the Guardians Ruel was Overlooking might be running around solo."

Saffi is chewing on the end of her braid, but drops it as she asks, her voice concerned, "Do you think they're okay?"

"Ruel? Honestly, I'm not sure. I haven't seen them around lately, but that doesn't mean much. We're not really friends, so I wouldn't much notice their absence."

"This kind of mass Intermediary Overlooking severance has happened before as well?" I ask, finally adding my voice to the conversation.

Reed nods. "Once, at least as far as we in Labyrinth have discerned. About a decade ago. The connection was severed to all 106 Guardians. It was realized pretty quickly, because a Guardian was waiting for their Intermediary to jump them back to the Retreat and they never came. He managed to find another Guardian under a different Intermediary. All the Guardians were quietly reassigned to other Intermediaries, because the one in question had disappeared. The official word is that they were transferred to a different Retreat, but the records don't corroborate that, and no one seems to know what actually happened to them."

"Angels can't disappear," Dayva argues. She's standing again, pacing. "We're Cast. We Arrive. We Return. We Luminesce. It's an iron-clad, A-to-Z system. We don't just disappear," she repeats.

Reed nods gravely. "And yet…"

Lucie glances at the clock on the wall, and I'm certain her thoughts are returning to a very un-Guarded Terra, if they ever left. "I'll go to Terra," I say, moving to stand, stretching out my back as I do so. "Keep me informed, and get that halo severed." I direct all of this to Lucie, but Dayva shakes her head, already pulling her jacket from the hook by the front door.

"Nah, bro, I got this. I'm too amped up to stay here. Lucie, spell me off in the morning, yeah?"

And then she's gone, the door slamming with a fierce finality behind her, so I turn back to Lucie as she says to Reed, "Do it. Please."

He stands and grabs another piece of pizza. Saffi and Lucie stand too, each of us a pair facing the other. "I've gotta jump to the Retreat to do so, but it will be done within minutes of me leaving here, I promise."

Saffi touches his shoulder, her fingers looking tiny when splayed against his large delts. She looks up at him, a worried expression on her face. "What if Ruel's gone? You're going to reassign Dayva and Cato and Lucie to you, right?"

Reed seems to soften a bit at the question, or maybe it's because of her, but he puts a hand on top of hers. "Of course, Saffi. I'm reassigning all three of them as my cases, and we're going to find out what's going on with Ruel, and I'll ensure all their Guardians are taken care of. I promise."

A promise by an angel is a guarantee, and all three of us breathe a little easier at his words. He drops Saffi's hand and says to me and Lucie, "I'll be around. Watch out for each other and keep your eyes and ears open." On that cryptic note, he takes a bite of the pizza in his hand as a shimmering white wall appears beside him and he steps through a Channel that disappears the moment he does.

Saffi and Lucie and I are all left standing there, blinking at one another, and it's almost comical the way we all look like lost owls.

Saffi's the first to break the silence when she flops back onto the couch and shoots us both a little smile. "Okay, but at least our world-shattering news was delivered by a smoking hot package, amiright?"

27

LUCIE

We're cleaning up the pizza boxes when I gasp and nearly drop the plate I'm carrying to the kitchen. I shove it onto the counter and yank up my sleeve.

"Is it gone?" Saffi whispers, as if scared to know. I understand the trepidation in her voice, because my body is tumbling with the same fear—a severed halo is beyond the worst-case scenario I could have ever dreamed.

I say nothing, but nod as I tug at the end of the bandage Saffi had dressed my arm with and unwind it from my arm. Of course, it's still swollen and red; just because the connection has been severed doesn't mean my Form can magically heal the trauma I'd induced to the human skin. But yes—the burning pain is gone, and I slump into a kitchen barstool, relief warring with trepidation, showered with a sprinkle of shame for feeling any relief at all.

Cato stands beside me and puts his arm around my shoulders, pulling me in for a hug, knowing how conflicting and devastating the situation is. I bury my face in his chest and allow myself to cry. Before I know it, I'm sobbing into his t-shirt, and he's lifting me up and carrying me to the couch. I register these things as if through a haze, allowing my emotions to course through me as I consider the new chapter of Guardianship I'm about to enter, what it means for my life here, and what it means for Terra.

Saffi curls up on the couch beside me and draws me into her arms as Cato strokes my back, both of them offering silent support, giving me the space to grieve, aware that no words can better the situation. Knowing they'd be feeling the same in my position—and indeed, likely are feeling many of these emotions themselves anyway, as we all process our new knowledge about the faults in our system and the risk to our realm. Fear, uncertainty, and anxiety beckon us into our future, pushing aside the certainties that had once been—consistency, stability, and safety. The matters of control that I thrived on, that I had planned my entire future on.

I'm not sure how long we stay like that, but at some point, Cato and Saffi start talking, catching up on the details of their current Assignments, setting away the stress of tomorrow for one last glimpse of today. Eventually, I gather myself enough to pull my sleeve past my tattoo and wipe my eyes, and I join in their conversations. I listen to Saffi talk about her Assignment and how much she's loving Zircon. I let Cato's rhythmic, deep voice bring a modicum of peace back to my soul, and we sit there for hours, even video calling Dayva in so she can be part of the socializing while she sits in the dark keeping an eye on Terra's darkened bedroom window while she sleeps. Guilt badgers me for not sleeping myself and taking advantage of Dayva watching over Terra, but she will hear none of my protests of spelling her off.

After some time, Saffi glances at the clock and looks at me in apology. "I know I just got here, but I left my Assignment vulnerable, too, so I had to book my return flight right back, as I didn't want to be gone over 24 hours."

I realize how selfish I've been and shake my head. "Of course. I'm so sorry you came all this way, but I'm beyond thankful."

She stands and pulls me into another long hug. "I'm not sorry at all—the risk was worth. I needed to be here. And it worked, didn't it? Leaving my Assignment behind triggered Reed's presence, and this is obviously so much bigger than we even realized—bigger than any one Assignment. But I do need to get back to the airport..." She releases me from the hug and shoots Cato a pleading look. "Please, please drive me? I hate taking self-driving taxis."

He looks at me, and I nod. "Of course he'll take you—I promise I'm fine, now that my tattoo has stopped burning."

We all look at my arm, despite the tattoo being covered by my sleeve, a somber veil of silence drifting over us once again. Then Saffi grabs her bag and gives me one last fierce hug before making her way out the door.

Cato moves to follow but before he closes the door I ask, "You're coming back here after, right?"

My voice sounds needy and I hate it, wondering where my independent nature is vacationing, but he doesn't look annoyed. He smiles instead, his eyes sparkling as he says, "I wouldn't go anywhere else, Luce," before closing the door and following Saffi into the hall.

A wave of exhaustion washes over me the moment I'm left standing in the apartment alone. I head straight into my bedroom, where I whip off my dress and crawl under the covers in just my sports bra and underwear, lacking the energy to bother removing them, a clear tell to how exhausted I am. With one last text to Dayva to confirm all is still quiet with Terra, I tell her I'll spell her off by ten, set my Tone alarm, and within minutes, fall asleep.

I stir when I feel a gentle touch on my temple, the soft brush of my hair being swept across my forehead rousing me. I peer up through drooping eyelashes to see Cato standing over me. He freezes, then scrunches his nose.

"Shit, sorry," he mumbles. "I didn't mean to wake you up. Go back to sleep."

"Where are you going?" I ask, groggy. I estimate I've only been asleep about an hour, if I assume he came straight back from the airport. Which means it's around two in the morning.

"I'll sleep in Dayva's bed." He leans down and places a warm, lingering kiss on my temple, but I snake a hand out from under the blankets to grab his shoulder before he can pull away.

"No," I whisper, the sound seeming too loud for the dead of night. "Sleep beside me again? I just want to feel safe." I feel my soul blushing at the admission as she wakes within me, and I'm thankful he likely can't see the tint of my skin in the pale, leaking light of the kitchen into the bedroom.

He searches my gaze, then nods and rounds the bed. I hear something fall to the floor, and I suspect it's his jeans, because no one wants to sleep in jeans.

I expect him to climb atop the blankets. But when he lifts the covers just enough to slide under them and a draft of cool air brushes over my bare skin, I realize what a terrible mistake I've made—I'd gone to bed in only underwear and invited my forbidden love to cuddle in with me.

Like a fool.

Like a damn fool.

All traces of exhaustion flee from my body.

I hold my breath as the mattress shifts under his weight, and I wonder if he'll stay to the opposite side or if he'll mean to curl up with me in his arms like he did the other night—when we were clothed, and on top of the blankets, and strictly, purely, friends.

I don't have to wonder for long.

His large palm finds the curve of my waist and freezes there as he realizes I'm not wearing a shirt. For a stiff moment, neither of us move.

Then I decide that, in light of the catastrophic news of the evening, I deserve a little cuddle, half-naked or not, and I lock away the part of my brain that has been running the show for the past two years. The part that has kept us friends and nothing more. That has kept me safe and focused and in control.

And lonely.

I shift an inch back toward him, signalling that I'm okay with this. More than that, that I want this, I want him close, I want his touch.

He doesn't hesitate to respond and snakes his hand around my waist, spreading his palm against my stomach as he simultaneously pulls me back toward himself and shifts his body forward. My back meets his t-shirted chest, and I bite my lip, telling myself it was too much to hope for that he'd lost his pants *and* his shirt. Of course, he'd kept his shirt on—he's respectful like that.

But I'm not feeling myself right now, because I don't want respectful in this moment. I want to cross the lines I've drawn in the sand, to smudge them out as if they'd never been there at all, the way other lines of certainty in my life have been erased tonight. A panic has lodged itself deep in my chest knowing the odds are against my success in this Assignment, and I will likely have to leave so much earlier than I planned. I don't want to leave him. Not later. But definitely not now. And while either of us could fail our Assignments at any time, the knowledge of my halo severance seems to augment that reality.

I am tired of refusing myself, of decades of resistance, when apparently life isn't as in my control as I thought it was. So I wriggle back further, pressing my ass against him.

He jolts as if I've electrocuted him, and I can't help it—a giggle escapes me.

"Lucie," he growls. My name on his lips is a warning, a temptation, a question, an answer.

I arch and feel the hard length of him through the soft fabric of his boxers, positioned between my cheeks. I don't blush, though—I'm not embarrassed that he is hard for me, and all I've done is invite him to sleep next to me. If anything, my cheeky soul is a little proud, a little sassy.

His hand is still firm against my stomach, but his thumb strays, and begins drawing gentle lines against the bottom hem of my bra. My breathing shallows as I will his fingers to explore my body, every place he touches left tingling in the wake.

We're both silent, as if should either of us speak, we might break the spell, douse the cold water of reality over the desire curling around us, neither of us willing to take that chance.

His hand torturously slowly—but in the most agonizingly wonderful way—creeps up my body until he splays his fingers across my décolletage. His fingers only graze the edges of my breasts, not touching anything more than I'd display in a shirt to go grocery shopping, but it's a possessive, heady grip as the weight of his hand presses against the very heart he doesn't know he owns.

And then his fingers dip below the cups of my bra and he's palming a breast beneath the fabric; and the spell is not broken, though it's shifted into even more dangerous territory. He lets out a ragged breath against my neck and I shudder as he weighs my breast in his palm, squeezes the soft flesh, finds my nipple with two fingers and gently rolls it between them.

Gasping, I arch further into his touch, desire coiling in my low stomach. I've never been so turned on, so breathlessly desperate for someone from a simple touch of my breast. Not in Celestia. Not on Zircon. But I'd never been touched by the man I'd been in love with most of my life, either. Just like that, I could Luminesce happy, knowing that Cato, the man of my dreams, has fondled my breast. I'd think it pathetic if I weren't so hopelessly in love.

His hand pulls from my bra, and I open my mouth to protest, to assure him I want this. But before I can say anything, his hand is against me again—but this time, much, much lower. Slipping into the band of my underwear, sliding down the smooth skin of my mound.

I don't miss how heavily he's breathing behind me, and I bite the inside of my cheek, almost dizzy with the knowledge he wants this as much as I do. Well, maybe not as much—I know he hasn't loved me as long as I've loved him. In fact, it's likely a reach to think he might be in love with me at all, but it doesn't matter. What matters is this moment, this reciprocal desire, and we've come too far to care about stopping now. I rest my leg on his to give him easier access, and I whimper as a finger creases my folds.

A low hum vibrates across my shoulders. "Lucie." His throaty voice sends a thrill through my veins. "You're so wet for me."

I don't respond—I can't respond. My brain is short-circuiting, so I merely nod, and he strokes through me, spreading my arousal as he finds my clit. Electricity sparks in my blood as I breathe his name in a plea for more.

"Say my name again," he growls in my ear, his fingers circling my sensitive nerves. His breath skates across my neck like a touch itself, and I whimper again, hating this new pathetic sound he seems to elicit from me while also too consumed by the feelings he's evoking in me to care.

"Cato, please," I gasp. I don't know what I'm asking for, even while I also know I'm asking for everything.

I buck against him as he pushes a finger inside me, and he groans. "Fuck, Lucie. One finger and you're so tight."

His thumb strums my clit as he grinds me from behind and fucks me with his finger. The heat of an impending orgasm coils within me, and this time I know exactly what I'm begging for when I plead with him for more.

I feel myself tighten, but just before I come, he pulls his finger from me and withdraws his hand from my now-soaked underwear. Before I can comprehend what's happening, he's flipping me onto my back and disappearing under the covers with a mischievous smirk on his face. I swear I almost come just from that picture—of him whipping the blanket over his head, the light from the moon outside gleaming against his blue eyes the last thing I see before I feel my underwear being pulled down my legs.

His palms push against my thighs. I hesitate only a moment before I open, succumbing to the gentle pressure. He rewards me by drawing a long, languid lick up my core to my clit, making me squeal as I arch upward. His hands keep me in that declined position, finding handfuls of my ass and squeezing as he begins expertly working me with his hot, eager tongue.

Regrettably, as I'd been on the precipice of orgasming with his fingers, it takes too little time before the coil in my centre is unsprung and my body spasms with the force of the most intense orgasm of my life, in any realm. I pulse against his tongue and he laps me up through the entire release until my body goes weak and he pulls his hands from their supporting position beneath me, laying me back down on the mattress.

He emerges from the blankets sporting the cockiest grin I've ever seen, his wavy dark hair wild and askew. Despite him having never looked so handsome, I giggle. And he chuckles. He collapses beside me and we lay there beside each other on our backs, laughing so hard we can't breathe, wheezing as we set each other off into giggle fits that make our abs ache.

When we calm down enough to regain our breath, he rolls onto his side and props himself up on an elbow, so I do the same from my position a few inches away. We stare at each other as time stands still between us, all smiles and ease as we study the curves and angles of the other's face, soaking in the closeness we've finally allowed ourselves and ignoring the pressure and stress from the rest of our lives that looms nearby.

My breath regained, my body recovered from both the orgasm and the laughing fit, I'm eager for more. I bite my lower lip and note how his gaze drops to it. I reach under the covers to lay my palm against his still-hard shaft. Before I can do anything more, he's taking my wrist and somehow spinning me around, so once again my back presses against his chest, my hand interwoven with his fingers across my hip.

"Hey," I protest, squirming in his grip but getting nowhere. "Let me return the favour." I grind back against his dick and heat courses through me again—I might pose it as a favour to him, but I want to get my hands and my tongue on him to satisfy my own nefarious desires.

His dark chuckle in my ear sends new shivers down my spine as he shifts back from my wriggling ass enough to relieve the pressure against his cock. "Sweetheart," he says, burying his face in my neck, "I would love nothing more than to have your perfect lips sucking me down, but what you need right now is sleep. I promise I'll come collecting another time."

I let out an unattractive "harrumph," which he chuckles at. "We finally get frisky after decades of being in love with you and all I get is a teaser?"

He stiffens, and I realize what I just said. He probably thought this attraction started only when I arrived on Zircon. I never let on otherwise. And now he's going to think me obsessive and psychopathic. So I bumble on, scrambling for words to move us past the moment. "I'm not tired. I just had the best orgasm of my life—" I cringe, cursing my soul for the apparent word vomit of honesty she's determined to pour out. "And surely you're not comfortable like that. Let me help. I want to." My voice drops to a whisper, to what I hope is an enticing and sexy tone. "I want to taste you, too. Let me have you, Cato."

His breath stutters behind me, and for a moment, I think I've got him. But his hand only squeezes mine as he keeps me locked in the straitjacket position he twisted me into. "Lucie, if you keep talking like that, I'll have to do more than fuck your mouth." His voice sounds like it's being raked over gravel, and I shudder against him.

"Yes, please," I say, not too proud to beg. "Have me."

"I will have you." My heart stops beating at his words, and I think for a moment that I must be dreaming to have my best friend's brother, the love of my life, be growling these words to me in the middle of the night. "And when I do, you'll come screaming my name and you'll never fuck another man, human or Guardian, ever again. Because you'll be mine, and I will ruin you for anyone else."

I squeak, the words enough to push me to the brink of another orgasm. I wouldn't have expected this sweet, gentle man to have it in him to say such dirty, possessive words, but turns out it's everything I didn't know I needed.

"But for the rest of tonight, sweetheart, you need to sleep. Just promise that you'll dream of me."

I swallow hard, and I nod and—to my horror—yawn. His chuckle skates over my neck once more as he finally loosens his grip to curl his body in a tender embrace around me, a juxtaposition to the threatening words said moments before, the difference between the two making my head twirl in sweet, delicious circles like the spinning creation of pink cotton candy.

"I will," I whisper.

And then I do.

28

CATO

When I fell asleep with my little sister's best friend curled up almost naked in my arms, the last thing I expected was to wake up and stare straight into said little sister's face.

She's sitting rigid in the chair across the room looking at us, her eyes meeting mine above Lucie's head. Her face resembles a storm cloud, and internally, I curse. This is not how Dayva was supposed to find out about Lucie and me. I shutter closed my eyelids, hoping maybe I'm dreaming, that when I reopen them, she won't be there. But my wishes are in vain; she's still there when I peek my eyes open again, leaning on her elbows, her eyes drilling into me as she jerks her head to the bedroom door, motioning for me to get up. Then she stands, her movements stiff, as though she's bearing the weight of the world, and I've no choice but to follow. With a resigned sigh, I brace myself as I extricate my arms from around Lucie and tuck the blankets back in around her.

I pull my pants on, not keen to face an angry sister who just found me sleeping beside her best friend without having my pants on—and free my Tone from my pocket. It's dead, so I shove it back in my pocket with a mental note to put it on a charge once I've finished being castrated, as I'm sure that's the best-case scenario I'm about to walk into.

Dayva had texted me last night while I'd been driving back from the airport to tell me the plan of Lucie spelling her off at ten this morning, so I wonder what could have pulled Dayva from Terra early, when I know Dayva would never break Lucie's trust. A deeper worry sinks into my chest, and I hurry out of the bedroom to find Dayva standing on the balcony, the door ajar.

I bypass the conversation about being caught in bed with her best friend for now. "Is Ainsley okay?" I ask, knowing that an alert about Ainsley would be the only thing to pull Dayva from Guarding Terra.

She's stands there, tense, staring out over the morning bustle of the street below, taking too long to answer. I grab her shoulders and spin her until she's facing me. "Dayva. Ainsley?" My panic increases when, now that I'm standing close to her in the bright morning sunlight, I see her cheeks are puffy, her eyes strained with shot blood vessels.

"Ainsley is fine."

The robotic tone she uses to say the three words I thought would release my anxiety (at least, about her Assignment, not about the ball-kicking I'm bracing myself for) does nothing to quell my stress. But before I can demand further answers, her knees buckle, and I scramble to catch her as she crumples toward the rain-stained tile floor.

I realize I'm wrong. There are two reasons Dayva would leave her Guard over Terra.

Ainsley is one of those reasons.

But Terra herself is the other.

My own knees fold as though someone just kicked them out, and I sink to the floor with Dayva, not trying to hold her up anymore, succumbing to the wave of emotion I know she's also experiencing. I want to ask what happened, but before I can, I hear Lucie's pure, sweet heart shatter behind me as she says, "What's going on?" at the same time as she realizes what must be going on.

And then she's on her knees beside us, shoving me aside, replacing my hands on Dayva's arms and shaking her violently, as if to pull her from her trance as she wails, begging her friend to tell her what happened. I'm sick to my stomach as Dayva finally chokes out the story, of how Terra had left her house at five and hopped into a car to head to the pool for an early swim workout, when someone had run a red light and smashed into Terra's car directly where she had been sitting. Dayva couldn't have known it was coming, not having had an alert for a human who wasn't her Assignment. And despite having been in a taxi behind her, despite being on the scene within seconds and an ambulance appearing in mere minutes, despite doing everything she could—none of it could have ever been enough. Terra had died on impact.

With a jolt, I'm reminded of my own Assignment and fumble with my Tone in my pocket, cursing when I remember its dead battery. I scramble up and into the apartment to lay it on a charging surface. Within seconds, it boots up, and I see countless notifications from Forest and Dayva—missed calls and texts. I hit redial and Forest answers before the first ring finishes. Or rather, he connects the call, but all I hear is his sob.

The sound of a grown man sobbing in agonizing, unadulterated grief pierces my heart in a way unlike anything else ever has.

"Are you at the hospital?" I ask, not bothering to wait for him to say anything. I tell him I'm on my way before hanging up and running to the balcony, where I drag Dayva and Lucie to their feet. They're sobbing, tears coursing down all our faces, and I know we're dealing with grief over a failed Assignment, over a broken halo, over the plans of the next few decades yanked out from under all of us, but we're also grieving Terra—the sparkly little spitfire with a heart of gold who deserved a long life, deserved a Guardian with a working halo. And in this moment, that was the grief that needed to take priority.

"Dayva, get some clothes on Lucie," I order, knowing I have to take control of the situation despite my own grief. Lucie had pulled a long t-shirt over her head before emerging to the balcony, but she needed to change before we went to the hospital. "We're going to the hospital, now. Forest needs me. Needs us," I clarify. Lucie and Dayva are close with Forest as a result of being close with Terra, and it will both break him and be a comfort to him to have the girls there.

Twenty minutes later, we're rushing down the sterile halls of the hospital hallway. The moment Forest sees me, he stands from his chair to reach for me, but the burden of emotion is too much to handle, and once again, I break the fall of someone I love as we sink to the floor together. I allow myself to cry with him, my heart breaking in tandem with his. No one could ever claim that being a Guardian angel wouldn't break your heart a hundred times over if you invested in your Assignments. It's a double-edged sword; to invest and care and live a full life through each Assignment, but hurt and break in times like these, or keep your distance and spare the pain but also spare the joy and experience. In the moments of pain like these, though, I sometimes wonder why I choose the former.

I'm aware of Lucie and Dayva crowding around us, of both his parents crying—of everyone crying, and holding each other. Ainsley and Hailey and then Clementine show up at some point, too, but when Lucie ends up in my arms, I refuse to let her go, clutching her to me as if it's the last time I'll ever hold her.

Because it might just be.

29

LUCIE

I'm sitting on the balcony, the breeze cool against my heated cheeks. They're stained with fresh, hot tears that slide unbidden down my face, practically a permanent water feature at this point. I don't bother to wipe them away as I stare one last time over the view I've come to love from my first home on Zircon.

Today is Day 12. Today, Reed, as my new Intermediary, will fetch me. We'll jump back to the Retreat, and in the space of time it will take to travel the Channel, my memories will fade into decades past and become like a dream. My grief will dull like an old wound that only aches when the humidity is too high. I crave the distance in equal measure as I dread it, both yearning for the pain relief as much as I want to hold on to the life I've built here.

Five days ago, we laid Terra's body in the ground, but what hurt the most was knowing I'd failed her soul. Gehenna had won this round. A devil had played a strong hand and taken a soul before its expiry, which damned it to wander for eternity, its anguish the fuel that would keep the Realm of Shadows stable in the same way that souls who reach their expiration date rest in peace and uphold the Realm of Lights. I'd failed the angels, and I'd failed Terra's soul, and I've realized, to my surprise, that it is the latter I don't know how to reconcile with the idea of moving on to another Assignment.

I've tied up my loose ends, having said goodbye to friends here, and handed in my diving cap, quoting a fresh start with a transfer to a university in the eastern United States. I've cried with Forest, with Ainsley and Hailey and Clem and Cato, with Terra's parents, with everyone, wondering if my well of tears will ever run dry. It hasn't yet.

I'll return to the Retreat and move on. Reed will manage the last threads of my life here for the next couple of years before submitting my death qualifier into existence to close my story here once and for all. By then I'll be long gone, invested into another story somewhere else, as someone else. People here and now will grieve me, but I'll have long blurred the memory of their faces beneath the forging of a new life, or new lives.

Legs appear in my periphery, and then Dayva is sliding down the wall next to me. She's held me together, despite her own pain, and I will be eternally grateful to have had her with me for this first Assignment.

"Cato's coming for dinner. I expect Reed will show up around then. I'm ordering the same pizza we had last time he was here, because he seemed to be a big fan."

I nod, drawing my legs to my chest and encircling them with my arms. She drapes an arm around me and rests her head on my shoulder. "I'm sorry we don't get all the time here together that we planned," she says, regret lacing her words.

"We knew nothing was guaranteed," I say, knowing the truth of the words but hating them all the same. "I'm thankful to have had this time with you at all. I think this is so much more devastating because while we expected one of us could exit early, we didn't expect it to be under these kinds of wild circumstances, with infallible systems fracturing, with questions we weren't aware even existed. Of course I'm sad, but Dayva, I'm also scared. I spent my whole life knowing what to expect and knowing the challenges I'd be facing. And suddenly, that's not the case anymore."

Her head weighs even heavier on my shoulder as she sags against me, bearing the same pressure and fear. She squeezes me, and when she speaks, I'm surprised to find her voice strong and resolute. "We have always faced hard things head-on, haven't we? Me from a place of competition and you from a place of perfectionism. This is an unexpected challenge, sure, but you and me, babe, we can do this. And now that we know a little more from Reed, we can join the investigations with Labyrinth. You can use that brilliant brain of yours to help them, to find answers."

I pull away and she raises her head to meet my eyes. She reaches up to brush the lingering wetness of my cheeks. "We'll put the realm back together, Lucie. Just watch."

I gaze into the soul I know as well as my own, and a glimmer of life ignites in my heart. It's just a spark, but it illuminates a string of hope that was previously invisible in the despair. My soul cradles it with care, cautious but optimistic, and I lean my head forward to touch my forehead to Dayva's.

"You're right—because you're always right. You're my other half, Day."

She surprises me when replies coyly, "Are you sure that's not my brother?"

I snap my head back, eyes wide. "What?"

She settles back against the wall, a small smile toying with her lips as she rests her head against the wall, her gaze still turned toward me. "What do you mean, what?"

I swallow, turning out of her arm, too guilty to allow myself to be comforted by her. "First of all, how dare you insinuate Cato is my other half when you know—Dayva, you *know*—that you're my ride or die till the end. Right?" I need her not to doubt my love for her, that I would do anything for her—that I've in fact done everything for her, our entire lives.

She turns too, and now we're sitting cross-legged across from each other, our knees touching. She takes my hands as she says, "Lucie, you are my soul's sister, of that I am confident. I will never question that."

My shoulders slump forward in relief, before tensing up again as she begins her next sentence with the word "but," and I can't bear to hold her gaze. I drop my eyes to where she's holding my hands, and I dig my nervous thumbs into her palms. "But," she continues, "are you in love with my brother?"

I think I stop breathing. I try to puzzle out her tone—is she angry? confused? hurt? I can't leave tonight if we're on bad terms. I'll fight Reed and the laws of the realm to stay here as long as I need to to make sure Dayva and I are going to be okay.

I force through the chaos in my head and I nod, ever-so-slightly, before making myself look up at her again, bracing myself for Hurricane Dayva. Instead, I find her studying me, a thoughtful expression on her face. The calm before the storm, I wonder?

I owe her words. "Dayva, I have loved Cato since I was a girl and he would wink at me across the dinner table. I have loved Cato since I was an awkward teenager learning to fly, and he graciously gave us extra flying lessons. I have loved Cato since I was in Dek 4 and struggling with physics, and he gave me his old notes. I have loved Cato since the first time I had sex, when I wondered what it would be like to have sex with him. And I have loved Cato here on Zircon more than I've ever loved him, where he has finally seen me not just as a little sister, and where he has cared for me and cherished me and desired me." I take a deep breath, the words spilling out of me now whether or not I want them to, but Dayva's face is still unreadable as she listens. "I have loved him my entire life, but I have pushed the idea of him away for just as long, because I need to be the perfect Guardian, and I can't be distracted. You know how seriously I take my goals, how fiercely I value my independence. The flings I've had were never distracting, but I've always known Cato would take everything of me—that I'd willingly offer everything. And I don't want to do that. I deserve to be the best for me, and me alone. And until coming to Zircon, I had no regrets about it. Not that it was hard to keep him at a distance," I huff a sarcastic laugh, "since he never saw me as anything more than his younger sister's bestie. Except, I think that changed here, somehow."

"The New Year's Eve kiss," Dayva guesses, cocking her head to the side. "Is that when it started?"

I nod, then I shake my head. "Yes, but also no. Yes, but you reminded me I would get hurt. And you're right, and even if I could have chanced it for me, you and Cato are so close, I couldn't imagine hurting you at the end of it all, too. So I've kept him away ever since, I swear, until..."

She scrunches up her nose. "Until I came home to you guys naked in bed the other night, huh?"

I can't blame my soul for turning us fiery pink at that comment. "For the record," I protest, "we haven't had sex. And we weren't naked. He was just...comforting me, with orgasms?"

Dayva chokes, releasing my hands to cover her face. "Ew. Stop. That's my brother."

I'm not sure where to go from here, but when she laughs, I chance a small smile, treading in uncertain territory. All at once, she sobers and grabs my hands again as she leans forward. Her voice is serious and sincere when she says, "Don't sidestep your happiness because of me, because of some dumb thing I said. I don't know anything, Luce." Her dark eyes search mine, making sure I take her words to heart. "Is it weird? Fuck yes. Am I mad you didn't tell me for a friggin' century that you had the hots for my brother? Yes again. But mostly, I'm sad that you didn't think that I'd support you in this, for better or worse." Her eyes begin to shimmer, and my throat thickens with emotion when a tear slides down her cheek. I reach up to wipe it away, but she leans further forward and wraps me in a bear hug. "I love you so fiercely, Lucie, however that looks through any situation. I'll cheer you on if you want to bang my brother, I'll welcome you as my sister in yet another way, and I'll beat his ass through every realm if he dares to not treat you with the respect and love you deserve. I know I asked you not to make me balance between you both if things go awry, but Lucie, you should never have borne the burden of my position like that and let my pessimism become your truth."

There's only one thing left to say. "I love you, Day."

"I love you, Luce."

We hold each other for a long time, until a throat clears behind us.

"Go get your man," my best friend whispers in my ear before she releases me and stands, and we smile, giant, beautiful, understanding smiles at each other, and my soul lets out a sigh of relief in knowing we can return to the Retreat tonight after all.

There's just one thing left to address, and he's sliding down the wall to take Dayva's place on the balcony beside me.

We haven't talked about that night. That night where I experienced both the highest highs of my life and the lowest lows. They're both twisted together now in a complicated web of earth and fire, and I haven't had the emotional energy to address them. We've been focussed on Terra's funeral, and Cato's been spending most of his time with Forest, which I've been thankful for. But the clock is ticking its final seconds of our time together, and I can't avoid this conversation any longer.

"Hi," he says, smiling that vulnerable smile he only gives me, those deep blue eyes capturing my soul. His wavy hair is the longest I've seen on this Form, flopping across his forehead. I memorize his face in that moment—my Cato of Zircon. A face I'll never see again, for the next time I see him could be in a Retreat Form, though most likely back in his Celestia body. But I'll always have a special place in my heart for this face.

"Hi," I say, smiling back. "Thank you for coming see me off."

He threads a hand through my fingers. "I wish I didn't have to."

He didn't need to say the words for me to know it, but I nod. "Me too."

"Lucie, I—"

I put a finger on his lips, then wish I hadn't. They're too soft, they're too tempting, so I drop my hand as quickly as I'd raised it.

"Wait." I steel myself, fortifying the wall I'd been building all week. While I appreciate the conversation I'd had with Dayva, it doesn't change anything. Not really. "Cato," I begin, "thank you for everything you've done over the past few weeks. You've been incredible. You've been the safe space I needed and the solid rock I could count on. Even beyond the past couple of weeks, you were always there for Dayva and I, and I'm so thankful we found ourselves connected to you in this realm." Confusion flits across his handsome face, and cracks appear in the wall as my soul desperately tries to push through. She doesn't want this, but I know it's for the best. So I forge ahead. "As Dayva's best friend, I've always had a love for you, and I always will." I hope that in stating it like this, he forgets the more intimate way I'd told him I'd loved him before. "But if the last few weeks have taught me anything, it's that I have to focus on my job as a Guardian, because there is so much more at stake than we could have imagined. We both have roles to play in helping to save our realms, so we can't afford to be distracted by each other."

My soul bangs on the wall harder, and it begins to bow, but I can't stop now, not even with the hurt that's beginning to shine in my beloved's eyes. I'm certain I'll never love another like him. But I'm equally certain he can't reciprocate that same depth of care, leaving me unwilling to meld myself or my future around him. I've waited a century for him—I can wait a few more, until we Return, and maybe then I will allow myself to give my soul over to love. I hope I do—whether it's with him, or with someone else.

I hear Reed's voice in the living room, and I'm ready.

I stand, pulling him up as I do.

"Lucie, wait, you can't leave like this." He pulls me into his arms, and I want to resist, but for my soul, I let myself be held once more. "I don't know what this is, but we deserve the time to figure it out together. Lucie, maybe this sounds crazy, but I think I—"

I'll never know if he was about to tell me he loves me, and that will haunt me forever. But what will haunt me more is those words following me around for the rest of my life. I refuse to hear them, so I push up on my tiptoes and press my lips against his, smothering the words before they can be given life. He draws me even closer and we kiss with the fire that burns in passion, love, and goodbyes. I pull away first, gasping for air as his chest heaves in front of me, and I press my hands against his shoulders as I step back and stare into those deep, pained eyes.

"Take care of Dayva," I say. Then I walk into the living room and pull Dayva from the kitchen barstool for one last fierce hug before I turn to grasp Reed's hand. "Let's go."

Reed looks like a child whose puppy was taken away as he looks longingly at the two pizza boxes on the counter. "But I thought we could eat dinner first."

I roll my eyes and grab one of the boxes. "We'll take it to go."

Mollified, Reed shrugs as he addresses Dayva and Cato. "The woman wants to go, so go we shall." With a flick of his wrist, a Channel opens in front of us.

Dayva's looking at me, confused, and Cato's looking at me, hurt, and it's selfish of me, but they'll have each other and I'm leaving things with both of them exactly how I need to.

"Last one to the Retreat," I say, employing my lifelong inside joke with Dayva as a farewell before stepping into the Channel behind Reed, pizza box secured.

The white of the Channel blinds me, and I can't see my own arm in front of me where it holds onto Reed. It's like being in pitch darkness on Zircon, but in a white version instead. The silence of the haze assaults me, though I strain to pick up the threads of sounds that exist beyond the silence, as I have every time I've jumped. Something of a touch whispers against my cheek and I freeze—not that I'd really been moving before, but now it's as if even the blood within me has been startled into stillness. But as quickly as it came, it leaves again.

A moment later, I step into the Retreat, the grief and pain of my first Assignment just an echo behind me.

30
CATO

23 YEARS LATER

I envelop the middle-aged woman in front of me in a fierce hug, burying my face in her thick dark hair that would be peppered with greys if she weren't so diligent with her dye appointments. She'd kept herself fit and strong, and had been the reason our core group had remained close ever since college: we'd vacationed together over the years, become godparents to each others' children, grieved with them during loss and celebrated during gain. We added to the group over the years, but our core group remained the same.

Forest, and then his wife.

Hailey and Ainsley, who'd gotten married.

Me—celibate and single ever since *she'd* left.

Clementine, until she'd died in a boating accident fifteen years ago.

And of course, the dark-haired woman standing with me, my sister Dayva.

"I'll miss you," Dayva says as she pulls back from the hug to stare up at me. My heart breaks at the tears falling down her face, knowing that in a way, we stole time together that never should have been ours in the first place, time that I'll be eternally grateful for.

"I'll miss you too," I say, emotion clogging my voice. "I'll miss all of this. This has definitely been the wildest, most challenging and yet most beautiful Assignment."

I know she knows I'm referring to so much in those words—to Lucie, to her broken halo, to Terra's death, to all the moments between then and three weeks ago, when my fit and healthy Assignment became sick and died within a week. Although it wasn't a surprise—I'd brought Forest to his expiration at age 45—it doesn't diminish the sorrow I feel for losing my best friend on Zircon. He is resting in peace for eternity, but my heart grieves in the memories he left behind.

Dayva and I are standing in the graveyard alone as dusk settles between the headstones. We're waiting for Reed to arrive to ferry me back to the Retreat. I had wanted to say goodbye to Forest one more time. Though there's nothing left of his soul in the grave beneath my feet, the human custom of having a place to remember loved ones is a practice I find comfort in.

His grave is beside Terra's. I've visited every week since we laid her body to rest there—sometimes with Dayva or Forest, or one of the other girls, but usually alone. I kept the grave clean and stocked with fresh flowers in front of it. As much as I did it for Terra, for Forest, I was really doing it for Lucie.

Dayva steps out of my arms to kneel down and fuss with the flowers decorating Forest's headstone. "He was lucky to have you."

I huff. "Everyone gets a Guardian angel. There's not anything lucky about it."

When she straightens and smooths her skirts, she shoots me a classic Dayva glare. "You know what I mean. You were so much more than a Guardian to him. I'm so proud of you." Her voice cracks, and I swing an arm around her shoulders. "I'm proud of you too, little sister."

Reed appears then beside us, and for a split second, I'm irrationally annoyed—the man who looked like Hercules 20-ish years ago looks the same now as he had then, while my Form, though I've kept it in good shape, has developed wrinkles and sunspots, thinning hair and aches and pains. He smirks at me when he sees me looking him over, like he knows what I'm thinking, and I roll my eyes. In a matter of moments, I'll return to the Retreat in my refreshed Retreat Form and leave this battle-worn one behind—and I'll look every bit as impressive as Hercules over there, I promise myself, having made my Retreat Form more muscular than this Assignment's Form—thankfully.

"Hi, Reed." Dayva greets the Intermediary by sticking out a hand, as if they're about to do a business transaction, and I raise an eyebrow. She scowls at me even as he shakes it and greets her politely in return.

"Hi, Dayva. No pizza waiting for me this time?"

Her jaw drops at the casual tone with which he references one of the most traumatic times in Dayva's—our—life, which is strangely effective in breaking the weird tension as Reed and I both laugh.

"Yeah, okay, yuck it up, you two," she scoffs, but a smile crosses her face. "Ready for you to take this one off my hands," she adds, pointing a thumb toward me. "Oh, and..." she hesitates and suddenly looks uncomfortable, her weight shifting awkwardly from side to side. "If either of you see Ellis, would you...pass along my greetings?"

I don't know what had happened with her and Ellis over the years of her Assignment, as she'd kept quiet about the details—at least to me. All I know is that at this moment, the former lovers are at some kind of strange and awkward impasse.

I nod, not needing the details in order to be willing to pass on my sister's greeting. I reach out and squeeze her hand. "Of course. If I see him around the Retreat, I'll do that."

"All right, Cato. Shall we?" With a small flick of his wrist, a Channel opens beside Reed, the pearlescent swirl seeming to match the mystical vibes of the graveyard at dusk. After hugging my sister one last time, I turn away and grab Reed's hand, and he steps forward. Just before I follow him through the Channel, I hear Dayva's last words.

"Go get your woman."

***

I'm sitting in a small room with Reed and several other Intermediaries and Guardians, none of whom I'd known before today. I'd arrived at the Retreat with Reed yesterday, and the first thing I'd done was ask if Lucie was here. When Guardians end an Assignment and return to the Retreat, their names go back into the Intermediary pool, so I knew he wasn't necessarily her Intermediary anymore. But I figured they'd kept connected since the halo fiasco, knowing her intention had been to work with Labyrinth. My heart sank when he'd said that no, she wasn't, and that also no, he was not permitted to tell me when she would be returning.

Frustrated, I had taken the night to grab some food, take a long shower, and a toss and turn in a restless sleep before I set out the next day to find Reed. I wasn't sure what wing he lived in, but it wasn't hard to find people who could point me in the right direction; it would seem that Reed is quite popular with the ladies. They all gave me directions with various levels of scorn and lust lacing their responses, which is why I chuckle when I eventually do find Reed leaning up against a counter with his biceps bulging. Clearly, he sticks to a set of moves—and just as clearly, they all work, based on the three women circled around him, hanging on to every word he said.

I'd interrupted his little ensemble and pulled him aside to inform him I wanted to meet with Labyrinth. If I couldn't connect with Lucie yet, I'd work as closely as I could with the group she'd joined to work on solving the problem that had taken her away from me.

He said he had called for a meeting this afternoon—and of course he had planned to invite me. I trusted that was true, but I felt we had a mutual dislike of each other, so I was quite certain he had only planned to do so out of obligation. Which was fine. An invitation was an invitation regardless of the motivation behind it.

That's how I ended up here, listening to updates from half a dozen other angels—which I am disappointed to discover are underwhelming at best. I have to remind myself that in human years, twenty years is a long time—but for angels, it's the equivalent of mere months. Any investigation would take time, especially when doing so under the radar and while working as full-time Guardians and Intermediaries. The cracks had begun millenniums prior, so it would be unreasonable to expect patches to be created in a fraction of that time.

But then the door opens and a woman enters, sliding into an empty seat. She motions for the Intermediary currently speaking—Arden, I think he said his name is—to continue with his updates on the research he's been conducting about when we used to be able to use our wings on Zircon. Though the subject is interesting enough, I find my attention straying to the newcomer. She's freckled and sun-kissed, her long hair damp and darkening her blue shirt with water where the braid falls over her shoulder. Something about her feels familiar, and when she looks over and catches me studying her, she smiles shyly before returning her attention to Arden.

He wraps up his report, and we all look to Reed, who's been leading the meeting—and I'll admit, he's good at it. He makes a note in his Tone, then glances at me with a strange, apologetic expression on his face before he turns to the woman who was late and says, "Lucie, welcome back."

31

CATO

I swear my heart stops beating when I hear her name. When I realize the woman across from me is Lucie—my Lucie. "My woman," as Dayva aptly put it yesterday.

Everything else in the room ceases to exist except for her, as my brain does acrobatics to reconcile this new Form with the Lucie I'd fallen in love with so many years ago in Vancouver. The Lucie I'd kissed, the Lucie I'd tasted, the Lucie I'd thought about every day since she'd left.

When she speaks, it's not with her voice—or rather, it is, but not with the voice I associate her with, either in Celestia or Vancouver. This is her Retreat Form—a Form unique to the Retreat that she will always return to. But it doesn't take long for me to pick up on the mannerisms that are, without question, Lucie's, as I'm glued to every word she says even while hearing none of them.

I don't know how long she talks, or what she talks about, even though I'll fall asleep tonight to the sound of her new voice playing through my mind. Although I'm not retaining any of her words, it's clear that Lucie is doing some heavy lifting of the research and has become a leader of Labyrinth in the time since she'd left me.

When she's concluded her update, Reed adjourns the meeting. He stands and claps me on the shoulder. "Good luck, mate," he murmurs as he crosses behind me, and I waffle between wanting to knock his lights out for leading me in unaware like that and thanking him for calling this meeting when he knew we'd both have just arrived. He'd have had no reason to lie to me about her not being here when I'd asked yesterday, so I suspected she'd arrived even more recently than I had—maybe Reed had ferried her back just before the meeting, and she'd been late because she'd grabbed a quick shower, hence the wet hair.

Everyone filters out of the room, the next meeting set for three weeks ahead, when another Guardian of Labyrinth would be returning. I move more slowly than the others, as it seems Lucie's making annotations on her Tone and trying to catch up on the notes she missed from the meeting. When she notices me lingering, she raises her head and shoots me a bright smile, and my stomach drops to my feet, more emotions than I can explain boiling through me.

"I'm Lucie," she says, her grey eyes taking me in. She stands and extends her hand, and like a magnet, I'm drawn to it. I place my palm against hers and step closer.

"Hi, Lucie. I'm Cato."

32

LUCIE

I freeze.

I stare at the face of the man standing too close to me, our hands clasped between us in a handshake that never began but also hasn't ended.

"Cato?" I breathe his name like it's the oxygen I'd been searching for underwater.

He says nothing, just studies my face as intensely as I study his.

He wears his hair cropped close to his head in his Retreat Form, a dark brown that extends through a trimmed beard—though the red highlights in it that aren't visible on his head speak to the inconsistent imperfection of the Form. His eyes are hazel, with gold flecks, set beneath a low brow bone that gives this Form a more serious look than the one I'd known in Vancouver. His voice is deeper here, too, and a touch raspier—and I'm desperate to hear it again.

Coming back to myself, I yank my hand from his and take a step back, stumbling over my chair as I do so. I clumsily grab at it to keep it from falling over, then move behind it like it's a shield. My soul is in shock, and I know I should say something—anything, but instead I fear I resemble a dying fish gasping for air.

He takes my cue and adjusts a subtle step backward as well, a smile spreading across his handsome but unfamiliar face. "It's so good to see you, Lucie."

I clear my throat, buying myself another second. "Welcome back to the Retreat," I say, and then, quickly doing the math, I realize his most likely timeline and gasp. "Oh, Cato. Forest?"

He sits down in his seat again and leans forward on the table. I maneuver around my chair to sit in it as well, keeping the table as a solid barrier between us.

"I got him to his expiration," he says, but I see the pain that lingers between the words. His grief may have been dulled by the 50 years that the Channels fade our memories by, but it's still grief. "We had a beautiful life, all of us—Forest, Ainsley, Hailey, Dayva and me." One side of his mouth quirks back as he adds, "We sure missed you and Terra, though."

I tilt my head. "What about Clem?" A latent sadness fills me as I hear of her death, and I can only hope she's resting in peace.

I briefly tell him how I've filled the years since Terra with only short-term Assignments, none longer than six months, but I don't tell him it's because I'm afraid to connect too emotionally to an Assignment and have my halo fail again. Instead, I emphasize how it allows me to spend a lot of time at the Retreat to conduct research for Labyrinth. I keep myself busy and occupied and unattached, and I have been happy to do so.

I knew Cato would return someday. But I'd not let myself keep track of when, leaving him to become my past as I focused on my future. There'd been no guarantees I'd see him when Forest expired, anyway—I could have been on Assignment, and we could have gone back and forth like that for the rest of our time in the Realm of Bones.

But now, here he is, so soon. All the energy I'd spent damning up the feelings I'd had for him had helped me survive and move on—and yet, it would seem, has done nothing in the face of seeing him again. I curse my soul, and I swear she has the audacity to dance a happy jig in response.

I refocus. "Dayva—she good?"

He leans back, a broad grin stretching across his face at the mention of his sister. "Dayva is great. She's had her ups and downs on this Assignment, but she's still a firecracker." My heart melts at the fond way he speaks of her, but then it hurts when I think about how much I miss her.

"How have you been?" He gestures around the room, raising his eyebrows. "Looks like you've been connected with Labyrinth for a while."

I blink and glance down at the Tone screen full of notes before returning my attention to him—as if I have a choice, his eyes so intense they beg to be stared into. "Oh, yeah. Since that first Assignment," I say, unable to voice her name. The memories might have faded, but knowing I damned her soul to a state of unrest for eternity keeps the pain near the surface of my heart. "I don't know if we've truly made any progress yet, but we're finding out more about the missing histories of the Guardianship, so that has to have value at some point. At least, that's what we tell ourselves so we don't give up when there's another fault in the system and it feels like we're doing nothing. Someday, it will be something." My voice is resolute, and it's not a put-on. I believe in the work we are doing, and I won't rest until we figure it out—or until I Luminesce and the quest continues with the following generations of angels.

"Put me to work, Coach," he responds, spreading his arms wide. "I'm in this. Tell me where to go and what to do."

My chest tights at the sight of those muscled arms flexing against the sleeves of his long t-shirt, and I imagine being wrapped up in them. Instead of giving in to that desire, I give him a tight smile. "As long as you understand that working together will change nothing about...us."

He folds his hands on the table in front of him, a faint smile ghosting his lips. "I hear you."

I swallow, not sure if I'm disappointed or relieved or both by his simple response. "Good. Right." Clearing my throat, I switch back into business mode. "I'll send the database to your Tone. There's a lot in there—you won't get through it all in depth during one Retreat stay, but skimming it should give you a rudimentary grasp on where we're at. Then next time you finish an Assignment, you won't have to catch up on centuries of adjusted history—whether your next Assignment is a few months, years, or decades."

The last sentence comes out a bit too much like a question, so I hurry on. "If you've got questions, Reed knows almost everything—he's been living and breathing this shit for five hundred years now. There are a few Guardians here older than him that are also involved, but of course, they have to come and go on Assignments. Just remember to keep mum about everything—we believe this is involves those with positions of power, so we can't trust anyone outside Labyrinth. That's a hard line you cannot, under any circumstance, cross."

I know I'm sounding cold and severe, but it's because I am. This is bigger than us, and I've devoted myself to the cause.

But he's looking at me in a way that suggests he's not taking this seriously at all, and I scowl. "Cato. I'm not kidding. "

He raises his hands. "Oh, I know, Lucie. I promise you I'll be secretive and subtle in my investigations and will never do anything to jeopardize Labyrinth."

I narrow my eyes. "Your words sound sincere. So why are they being spoken through that cheeky grin?"

Now, his face turns serious, and he leans forward, the table barrier not standing a chance of keeping his powerful presence from invading my space. His eyes search mine, his voice low when he finally says, "Because no matter what limitations you put on us, sweetheart, regardless of the rules and boundaries, my soul is always at its most joyful when in the company of yours."

33

LUCIE

One year later

I want to scream.

Cato is always around. I sense his eyes on me in the cafe, feel his fingers brush my arm whenever he sits next to me, hear his voice in my mind drawing tingles through my body as I go to sleep.

More to the problem: I want to scream just as much when he isn't around.

When our Assignments differ by a few days (even though I act annoyed that he always finds out my Assignment length and promptly picks one in similar length), I suffer the lack of his soul's presence like a darkness in mine.

It's been a year since Cato dropped in to the first Labyrinth meeting. I—or I guess, we—have taken multiple short Assignments in that time, ranging from a couple days to a few weeks. I've held my stance on my friendship with him, getting through the sexual tension by the grace of my vibrator, my dirty thoughts of him witnessed only by the four walls of my bedroom.

He said he'd prove he wasn't a compromise to my life, but based on my constant awareness of both his presence and lack of presence, I'd argue he was doing a shit job of it. Even though my soul tries to convince me he is investing just as much as I am into Labyrinth, that he is doing nothing to overtly distract me, and that any distractions or compromises are all of my doing, it's like that's also the point—he's not asking me for anything, but even so, I'm willing to give him everything.

It's why I'm marching over to his wing now—section six, or, ridiculously enough, SEX, as is written in Latin over the arch to his wing in the same way OCTO refers to "eight" for my wing. As if I want sex literally shoved into my awareness every time I visit his living space.

I know he got back to the Retreat earlier today. I've been here since yesterday, anxiously awaiting his return since. Hating every moment of anticipation. I appreciate his valuable insights to Labyrinth; he is a definite asset, with mad research skills. But he has to stop arranging his Assignments like this. I need space.

I reach his door and bang my fist on it, refusing to bow to this anymore.

He opens it just a few seconds later, surprise creasing the features of his Retreat Form's face, which I've come to be too familiar with this year. "Luce, hi. I was just going to come find you."

I push against him to move him out of the way so I can slip into his room, slamming the door behind me as I do. I don't need the entire wing to hear me berate the poor guy. Turning to face him head-on, my hands square on my hips, I let him have it. "That's actually what I came to talk to you about. You've got to stop. You've got to stop finding me and arranging your life around me. I told you I'm unwilling to compromise my life for you, or for anyone. Labyrinth and the Guardianship are my life, and I don't have the time or energy to share it with anyone else."

He's leaning back against the door, arms folded across his chest, pulling the fabric taut around his carved delts. One ankle crosses over the other as he studies me, and he's wearing snug shorts that show off his ridiculously muscular quad muscles. But I don't look at any of that, registering his physique only in my periphery, keeping my eyes locked on his.

"Lucie." I hate how I love the way my name sounds on his lips. "I have not asked you for anything beyond time relating to Labyrinth since I arrived here. You made it clear, and I respect you for that. Everything I do with you relates to Labyrinth. Every conversation we have, is related to the topic. I've devoted myself to this cause in equal measure to you." Concern creases his forehead as he shakes his head. "I genuinely thought I was respecting your wishes, keeping you at arm's length, as much as I'd rather pull you into them instead. But if you feel like I'm crossing boundaries, then I'm doing something wrong still."

My hands explode from my hips as I punch my fists into the air. "Fucking Fates, Cato!" I cry out. "You're doing everything right, and that's exactly the problem!" Energy courses through me I don't know where to direct, or how to direct, so I pace the short width of his room, running my fingers through my hair. "I need you to not be here, at the Retreat with me, so much. I can't think when you're here, Cato! Because all I think about is you!" I stop my manic pacing in front of him and jab a finger hard against his sternum. "You're in my fucking head and I need you to get out, because I can't do it on my own."

He grabs my wrist and yanks on my arm to hold my hand to his chest, my body now just a whisper away from his. His hazel eyes glimmer as he leans down. "I love you, Lucie."

His declaration reverberates through me, the words I'd stopped him from saying over two decades ago finding their way to me now, and I did nothing to stop them. But didn't I do everything to stop them?

"Let me love you, Lucie." My breaths stall as I stare into his eyes, the bottomless depths of his soul calling to mine. "I'm not asking you to compromise your life for me, or to sacrifice any part of yourself. I want to enhance your life, not take away any part of it. It's the entirety of you that I love, Lucie—all the parts that come together to make you the beautiful, intelligent, capable, irresistible angel that you are."

My lip quivers, the angry energy that had coiled around me just moments ago replaced by my good old friends, Fear and Uncertainty. He must sense the war within me, because when I pull away, he lets me.

When I leave, he lets me.

When I close the door, he lets me.

But that night, he doesn't let me sleep alone, slipping through my bedroom door and curling his body around mine as I cry into the semi-darkness of my room.

"Let me hold your fear," he whispers into my ear before I finally succumb to sleep, safe in his arms—the most dangerous place I can be.

34

CATO

I awake the next morning before Lucie, taking care not to disturb her as I untangle my limbs from around her. I sit beside her on the bed for a long moment before I leave, reverently pulling her hair back from her face where it had stuck to her tear-sodden cheeks in the night.

I hadn't meant to stay the night. I'd just wanted to talk more. But when I reached her door and heard her muffled crying, I moved before I knew I was, crawling into bed and tucking her into my chest. She hadn't argued, hadn't fought against it—she'd melted into me, gripping my arms like her life depended on it. And then she'd slept, and I'd spent most of the night praying to the Fates that she'd finally let me love her. Because I knew she loved me—I knew it in Vancouver, but then I really knew it when I arrived at her and Dayva's apartment the day she left, when I'd overheard her tell Dayva how long and how much she loved me. It had both broken my heart and brought life to my soul.

I'm confident she still loves me, because I had abided by her wishes (despite her complaints to the opposite yesterday). I'd arranged my Assignments around hers, but only because we made an exceptional research team, and Labyrinth was benefitting from us working together. But when it wasn't about Labyrinth, I kept my distance. I ate meals with other angels. I socialized at evening dances with unfamiliar faces. I didn't touch her unless it happened purely by accident, like if I sat down beside her and brushed against her arm—and I cringed every time, because I did not want her to take it as me pushing boundaries in any manner. And yet, despite all of that, she confessed that I am all she can think about.

That is not on me. That is on her. That is her soul pining for mine, the same way mine aches for hers.

But I love her too much to push her. To pressure her. Either she will find her way to me, or I'll spend my life loving her from a distance.

Last night, she found her way to me.

I stand from the bed and I'm almost at the door when I hear her soft morning voice squeak out, "Okay." When I turn, I find her sitting in the middle of the bed, blanket clutched in her lap as she stares at me with those grey eyes that seem to hold entire universes in them. "Okay," she repeats softly. "You can take my fear. One piece at a time."

I hold her gaze and nod. "One piece at a time."

When I leave, I nearly give in to the impulse of checking to see if my wings have miraculously appeared, for how light I feel on my feet. But it's not my wings; it's my soul relieved of the weight it's been carrying since I'd watched her walk into a Channel with a pizza comically tucked under her arm, leaving me to deal with an equally confused Dayva, who had also thought we'd just begun our happily-ever-after.

But maybe now we finally are.

***

I take her words "one piece at a time" to mean "slowly." So during the rest of our four weeks at the Retreat, I carefully diminish the space between us. I put my arm on the back of her chair. I eat some meals in the dining hall beside her and press the side of my thigh against hers. I invite her to the Retreat's movie theatre, where I hold her hand. And every night, I kiss her soundly before tucking her into bed and pulling myself away to sleep in my own room.

I wait for her to ask me to stay, but every night, she watches me leave.

We take Assignments that depart the same day. These are two-week ones—13 days for her, 14 for me. I admit that while the short Assignments make sense for allowing us the most time at the Retreat for research, this isn't something I can do long term for more than a few decades. While I grieved for Forest after Guarding him so close for so many years, there is a different kind of agony involved with knowing the 17-year-old you bind yourself to has no future at all. Even when you're successful in bringing them to their expiration, it somehow still seems like a failure.

I take background roles for these short Assignments, not bothering to insert myself into their lives in any obvious manner. It's easier that way, too.

After bringing my 14-day Assignment to his expiration, I travel back through the Channels with Reed with a heavier heart than normal. I'm thankful for the dulling of memories that the Channel brings, but even still, I'm ready to see Lucie. I need to hold her, to ground myself in her. I don't bother heading for my room first, beelining it to hers the moment Reed and I enter the Retreat. The door is closed, so I knock, but it's not Lucie's voice that beckons me in.

"Hi, stranger!" A woman with a bobbling blonde bun perched atop her head and deep dimples engraving her cheeks stands up and engulfs me in a hug. Lucie laughs at the confusion on my face as she informs me who it is.

"Oh, Saffi!" I reciprocate her embrace. I'd barely known her in Celestia and only really interacted with her that one day in Vancouver, but we are connected by the trauma of that short past, making it feel natural to have a familiarity with each other.

Lucie pushes up from the floor to give me her own hug right after, and I hold her for a moment longer than I hugged Saffi. While I had hoped to spend some time decompressing alone with Lucie, the contagious smiles on both their faces as they jump back into catching up is its own kind of balm for my soul. Lucie grabs my hand and drags me to sit on the floor with her, and I sprawl out in a half-reclined position against the beanbag chair.

"Are you done your New York Assignment?" I ask, using my last point of reference for her.

She nods, nostalgia flitting across her face. "It was such a beautiful Assignment. I loved her, and I loved the fashion work I did, and I loved the grit and hustle of the city. I couldn't have asked for a better first Assignment."

I smile, genuinely happy for her, but conscious of that pang of desire to take on another longer Assignment. It's a conversation I'll need to have with Lucie before I find myself doing the same kind of compromising that I promised I'd never make her do in life. I know she wouldn't stand for me doing that either—and I don't want to. I don't subscribe to the idea of finding your other half; I believe in two wholes overlapping, like a Venn diagram of sorts.

"Saffi got back the day after we left," Lucie informs me. "But she's been keeping in touch with Reed ever since my halo malfunctioned, and she's been trying to do some research from there."

I raise my eyebrows. "You kept in touch with Reed?" I recall how Dayva had eventually filled me on her and Reeds' "situationship."

She blushes, but waves a hand as if to wave away my insinuations. "Yeah, yeah, but also, no. Okay, we had a bit of a fling for a minute and a half there—but literally, that was it. I realized that while he's hella hunky and I love the effort he puts into Labyrinth, our actual personalities are not a good match. We can work together with some distance, but after we'd banged a few times, well, we were out of each other's systems." She shrugs. "We're good though. That was a long time ago already. No hard feelings or anything."

"Fair enough," I say. "So what have you been finding out during your research while on Assignment?"

She purses her lips, looking frustrated. "Honestly, not much. I've kept up on all the research in the database as it comes in, but I've realized that our biggest blind spot in knowledge has to do with the Realm of Shadows. There's really not much more Labyrinth has found than what Dek teaches us. And that seems awfully suspicious to me. If our realms are sworn mortal enemies, shouldn't we have all kinds of intel on them?"

I sit up, my interest piqued and attention square on Saffi, putting the puzzle together before she can explain further. "You think the Realm of Shadows is sabotaging the Guardianship system?" I ask, seeking clarification.

She shrugs again, and I see Lucie nodding beside me out of the corner of my eye. I shift so I can see them both from my sitting position. "It's a possibility," she says.

"Imagine what would happen if the Realm of Shadows diminishing our capacity to bring humans to their expiration," Lucie adds, worrying her bottom lip. "The universe needs balance, and if they overthrow that balance..."

Saffi shivers, looking a little pale, and a somber weight settles into the room. The idea of the four Realms of Almega being at risk is already serious enough—but to consider that the thousands of other realms beyond our existence and timeline could be negatively affected because of an imbalance in our little realm quad brings the situation to an even more horrifying level.

"Or maybe their systems are cracking, too..." Saffi trails off, a curious look on her face. But then she jumps up from the bed, apparently done with the doom-and-gloom conversation. "I've got an idea I'm going to pitch at the Labyrinth meeting tomorrow." Something mischievous glints in her eyes, but before we can press her for more details, she skips by us and opens the bedroom door. "I'm going to go grab an evening snack and hit the proverbial haystack. Catch you lovebirds later!"

She closes the door behind her and leaves Lucie and me sitting there on the floor, her departure causing the air in the room to thicken. I clear my throat. "Lovebirds? What did you tell her, exactly?"

Lucie blushes, then pops to her feet and changes the subject. "Want to go for a walk? It looks like the beginning of a beautiful sunset out there."

I rock to my feet and extend my hand, but not before taking a moment to appreciate the gorgeous woman in front of me. She's wearing a cropped, loose-fitting pink t-shirt with a low, torn-style neckline that exposes the gentle angles of her collarbones. A light, flowy blue mini skirt cinches in at her waist, a bellybutton piercing sparkling above it, not dissimilar in style to the one she'd worn in the last Form I'd known her in. It's a casual, ridiculously sexy look, and she ducks her head shyly under my perusal before grabbing my hand and yanking me out of the room and toward the door at the end of the hall that leads outside.

We leave behind all thoughts of Labyrinth and Gehenna and the balance of our very existence. All I can think about is her; I'm heady with the soft citrus scent of shampoo drifting from the bouncing, loose waves of her rich brown hair, and I want to lose myself in her, bury myself in her—mind, body, and soul.

We walk outside and head down the path to the ridge, and I reach my arm, the one not already holding her hand, across my body so I can run my fingers up and down her arm. I need to touch her, her soft skin slipping like silk beneath my touch. She leans into me as we wander toward the sunset, both lost to our own thoughts, reverent in the space of natural beauty around us and building desire between us.

I tug us off the path when we reach the ridge, away from where other angels gather along the hillside to watch the sunset. We weave around a few trees before I pivot without warning, pressing her up against a wide tree with smooth bark.

She gasps lightly, her lips parting. I crowd her space, bracing myself with one arm above her head against the tree, my other hand capturing that pouty bottom lip with my thumb, drawing it down. Her eyes are wide as she stares up at me, but she makes no move to pull away—in fact, she makes no moves at all, her chest hardly even rising with how shallow her breathing has become.

I draw my thumb down to her chin and tilt her head up even further. Despite having barely touched the woman, my cock shifts painfully against my jeans, already hard. I search her gaze—for what, exactly, I'm unsure, but for something that tells me she's mine.

"Cato."

Her breath skates across my lips, which are only inches from hers as I lean my head forward in a simple question. We've kissed lots as of late—every night for four weeks straight until our most recent Assignments. But I've kept those kisses in check—my hands staying on her hips, arms, or head, holding back from devouring her like I've wanted to. But something is different tonight, and I wait to kiss her. Until she says it.

"I love you."

I stare at the beautiful, crystal grey eyes that stare at me with a peace and trust I've never seen in any version of them, and I know: that's all of it—every piece of her fear. With those three words, she gave it all to me. My heart thuds with the new weight of this precious responsibility, and I'm consumed with the relief of having centuries ahead of me to care for this woman. To make up for the years she loved me and I was oblivious. To love my deepest soulmate.

35

LUCIE

I've never understood the phrase "my heart feels like it might burst." But I get it now, having shared my heart with Cato; my chest physically aches in response, my soul fuller than it's ever been before.

I could linger in this moment forever, just staring at him and revelling in the intensity between us. I think about the almost poetic nature of finding ourselves here and now with the sun setting behind us, the last time I'd been vulnerable with him in such a way also beneath the open sky as the sun rose in Vancouver.

His head dips to mine and his lips meet my ready ones, and I change my mind: I don't want to stay in this moment forever. I want to experience everything the future holds for us together. His tongue presses forward, and I answer with my own. We devour each other, as if we've never wanted something this much in our entire lives—and for me, that's true.

My arms wind up around his neck, and he steps closer, pressing our bodies together. Arching into him in the scant space left between us, I let out a little gasp as his hard length presses against my abdomen, and I'm filled with the need to touch him, to taste him. I never had the chance to do so years ago when he gave me the most earth-shattering orgasm I'd ever had, our time cut short and my resolutions reset as I'd lost control of everything I'd been certain of in life.

Slowly, I draw my hands from behind his neck, running my palms over his impressive pecs, feeling his heartbeat thrumming beneath, the pace a twin to my own pulse. Down over his chiseled abdomen, defined even with a shirt on, I reach the button of his jeans. His hands fall to my waist, skin to scorching skin below the hem of my shirt, as I unzip the zipper of his jeans and slide my hand into his pants, on top of his underwear, to cup him. He lets out a strangled moan at my touch but doesn't break the kiss—instead, deepens it even further, somehow.

I bite his lip in a gentle tug between my teeth and then pull back. Our panting breaths disappear into the tranquil stillness of dusk, soft sounds belying the intensity of the moment as I draw my hands to his hips and slip my fingers under the waistband of his underwear. Almost reverent in my actions, I lower to my knees as I tug his pants to his ankles. Despite my desperate desire to look upon what I'm certain is the most impressive dick I've ever encountered, I stare up into his fiery gaze. His eyes might melt me, the heat of his emotions scorching straight through to my core, and I squeeze my legs together, my pussy throbbing and begging not to be denied. But I have more important things to attend to first. Grabbing a handful of his ass in each hand, I lean forward and lick a torturously slow path from his root to his tip, where I taste the salty bead of pre-cum already there.

He can't hold my gaze anymore, his eyes closing and his head tilting back as he lets out the most delicious groan I've ever heard. One hand shoots forward to brace himself against the tree above my head, while the fingers of his other hand weave into my hair. I finally drop my gaze to his cock, glad he can't see how my eyes widen as I fully take in his girth for the first time. A thread of nerves entangles itself with my anticipation, not knowing if I can fit him inside me when the time comes, but both terrified and eager to try.

I pop the head into my mouth. His grip tightens on my scalp in response, the pull of my hair threaded between his fingers sending heady tingles through my body. Taking him as deeply as I can, I'm dismayed to find it's barely half his length, and quickly reassign my hands to work on the remaining span. I bob and suck and lick, his velvet skin an addicting texture against my tongue.

With a gentle squeeze, I tug on his balls, and that seems to unlock a different level of pleasure in him. He presses down on my head, pushing me to take him further, to gag on him as I take him to my throat. "Lucie," he growls from somewhere above me, his voice strained and low. "You look so beautiful taking me like this." I let him set the pace, the depth, tears streaming down my face as I choke on him, but loving that he's using me, using my mouth, to satisfy his desires. Which is why I'm surprised when he abruptly yanks my head off him and takes a step back, leaving me gasping for air as I try to orient myself in space again, my hands mourning at their sudden emptiness.

"I want to come in you," he says, bringing his hands to my face and wiping my tears from my heated cheeks with both of his thumbs. "The first time I come with you, I want to come in you," he repeats, searching my gaze almost nervously, seeking my response.

I do nothing but nod, incapable of forming words, knowing this moment and the moments to come are more than I had imagined possible—and I'd imagined it so, so many times in private moments of night, in both Celestia and Zircon, my fingers and vibrator taking the place of his hands and tongue. But nothing I'd dreamed of could ever come close to the reality of him against me, touching me, kissing me, desiring me with a desperation that rivals my own. I startle as I realize the difference is in the depth of mutual desire, a factor I'd never considered or allowed into my daydreams. I hadn't believed that he could love me with an intensity reciprocal of my feelings for him, that I could trust him to be wholly mine in body, soul, and spirit.

He kneels and then gently shifts me until I'm laying on the soft moss beneath the tree, looking up at him in the faint remaining light of day before night cloaks us. I register the irony of two Guardian angels who prefer basking in the light making love for the first time in the strange beauty of the night, and I let slip a small smile as I stare up at him. It's a testament to my growth, to my future—one where I don't control everything and instead allow life to happen to me as well.

He's propped up on an elbow beside me, one leg between mine, having kicked off his pants the rest of the way. The thin material of my skirt is all that separates my core from his muscular, hard quad muscle, and I squeeze my thighs around his leg, seeking pressure to satisfy my body's ache. But he seems to want to hold us in the moment between, tracing circles on my chest and asking me what I'm smiling about.

"I didn't know I could feel freedom in being loved like this," I whisper in return. "I always thought that giving in to love would be equivalent to giving up autonomy. That I would lose a part of myself. But this isn't like that at all."

He dips his head, kissing my throat, his soft tongue licking the curve of my collarbones as his hand drops lower, across my breasts, past my exposed stomach, to the outside of my thighs. "When you're loved right, you shouldn't be giving anything up—you should only become an even more authentic version of yourself." His hand draws up the side of my thigh, and I squeeze his leg between mine harder. When he reaches the top waistband of the skirt and realizes he encountered no fabric from underwear the entire way up, he lifts his head from where he was nibbling at my ear and raises an eyebrow at me. "Well, this is a surprise."

I wriggle, nervous, and let out a small giggle. "Oops?"

He pushes up from his elbow so he can sit on his knees between my legs, which splay out on either side of his hips. Both of his hands find the hem of my skirt, and he pushes it up so it pools around my waist, leaving my core glistening in full view. His cock is still rock-hard, jutting up in front of him, and I wriggle again, nervous and excited and eager.

His eyes gleam as he draws a finger through me, and I grab at his wrist. "Please," I gasp. "Just, please." He has to be in pain now from how long his dick has been erect, and at this point I might come simply as a result of him looking at me that way, like I'm the most incredible sight he's ever seen.

Leaning forward, he braces his forearms on the ground around my head as he guides the tip of his cock to my entrance. I grapple for purchase on his back, finding fistfuls of t-shirt as he slowly pushes the head in. I shake my head, starting to panic.

"I think you're too big," I squeak, writhing as he drives further into me.

"You can take me, Lucie. You were made for me, in all your Forms."

He shifts his weight to one arm, the other snaking out to wrap around my thigh and pull it up near my shoulder, widening me for him as he pushes deeper, until finally his hip bones press against me, telling me he's fully seated. I stare at him, eyes not quite focussing as I try to breathe and adjust myself to him.

He watches my face as gently, carefully, he begins rocking back and forth, relaxing my body's fight-or-flight mode into realizing this is a good thing. A great thing. A huge, thick, beautiful—

"Ooooh," I cry out as he adjusts the angle and hits the spot inside me that lights up with his movement. He takes that to mean I'm adjusted and pulls nearly out before shoving back in, the friction of the movement giving me everything I had been aching for. I claw at his shoulders, desperate for more—and I beg him for it, to which he lets out a dark chuckle before acquiescing. He pulls my leg even higher and sets a punishing pace, and I writhe in agony and ecstasy beneath him. His breathing is laboured and heavy, both of our bodies wound tense in anticipation as darkness slips in around us. The hushed sounds of the forest tucking itself in for the night fade from awareness as our focus narrows solely to the presence of the other.

I let out a strangled scream as I come, my core barely having the room to pulse around his thick shaft, which seems to make the orgasm last ten times longer than normal. The moment he feels me throb around him, he utters a guttural cry of my name, and he pulses his release in tandem with mine.

After a few long moments, he pulls from me and lays a chaste kiss on my lips before falling to lie beside me, twining our fingers together. We lay there, our bottom halves exposed to nature, our chests heaving as we catch our breaths and our souls process the moment. Through the canopy of leaves above, I catch glimpses of Luminaries, watching with sightless eyes as our souls blend, sparkling in response.

The brush of evening chill skitters across my skin. Cato must feel it too, because he pushes up to a sit and turns to—regrettably, by the look on his face—pull my skirt down and then pull me up as he stands. He slips his jeans and shoes back on before hauling me in for one last fierce, breathless kiss, promising that the night's only just begun—a promise he fulfills twenty minutes later in my bed, and then thirty minutes after that, and then again in the middle of the night when I wake to him kissing my thighs, and then in the faint light of dawn after I greet his morning hard-on with my tongue.

I lose track of the number of times he tells me he loves me, and I know nothing will ever be the same in my life again when he refers to my soul as his soul's mate. We'll hold each other until we Luminesce, and even then, our souls will sparkle in the sky together.

36

CATO

We arrive at the Labyrinth meeting just as Reed calls it to order, slipping in to the seats closest to the door. I glance around to see the usual faces, and an old familiar one. She shoots us a friendly smile and then turns her attention back to Reed.

Our hair is still wet, and Reed looks sideways at me and wiggles his eyebrows knowingly, like a damn annoying teenager, to which I just roll my eyes. He then begins recapping the minutes from the last meeting, but all I can pay attention to is the sexy woman beside me, still flushed from the orgasm I gave her not ten minutes ago before she finally dragged me out of the shower. We chased each other down the halls on our way to the meeting, giggling and kissing, drawing looks and gossip, but I don't care. Lucie is mine, and I'll let the entire world—no, the entire realm—no, all Realms of Almega—know it.

The updates begin, but my hands won't stay off the woman beside me. Even sitting next to her, my right hand draws designs on her soft thigh, slowly working its way north beneath another of her short skirts, which I'm quickly becoming a big fan of—even more than the tiny running shorts I'd loved her in in Vancouver. She keeps grabbing my wrist and sending me death glares, but I pay her no mind. I won't let her compromise her work with Labyrinth, but I also know we're not hearing anything new from the updates right now.

Until Arden speaks, and then even I have to still my hand and lean forward in attention.

"I found something that could be huge," he admits, running his hand through his hair. The guy looks stressed, and he's usually unflappable. He's an Intermediary with tech skills unparalleled to anyone else I've met, and from what I've learned over the months, it seems bringing him into Labyrinth was one of the best moves the group has made. He finds dusty old digital files with hints of a different history than we've known, but that's all they've ever been—hints. Until, it sounds like, now.

A glance around the table reveals everyone focussing their attention on Arden, something the normally introverted tech tries to avoid. Whatever he has to say is big enough to agitate his quiet, straightforward demeanour, but he's struggling with how to say it.

"What is it, Arden?" Lucie coaxes from beside me.

He takes a deep breath, dropping his hand from his hair, leaving it ruffled and sticking out in all directions like a classic human photograph of a mad scientist.

"I found an old database," he begins, looking at Lucie. "No one has opened it in dekamillenium—it's old, really old. You don't need to know the nitty-gritty of how I found it, but basically, I've discovered evidence since joining Labyrinth that multiple databases have been scrubbed and erased. This one was different in that it was just all alone, like someone forgot it existed. I only found it because I followed a corrupted chain in a current database that normally we wouldn't blink at—there are all kinds of software ghosts that get abandoned for any number of regular reasons. I've spent the last few months hacking it and yesterday, I had a breakthrough." His words are coming out quicker now as he talks about the topic he knows best. His eyes bounce around the table, as though he can't quite focus on one place while his brain whirs.

"And? Well? What did you find?" The question comes from Saffi, on Lucie's right, who had exchanged a knowing glance and giggle with Lucie when we'd entered. She is intensely serious now though, leaning forward in her seat as if she might reach out and yank the info right out of Arden's head.

But he shakes his head and leans back, frustrated. "And, well," he echoes her, "I'm not sure. It's like I finally gained access to the apartment lobby, but all the apartments are still locked. Everything is encrypted with a security program I've never encountered before—it's incredibly intricate, super impressive, and anything I try bounces right back at me." His hands return to his head, driving through his hair again. "I've only been at it a day, so obviously I'll work on it as long as it takes, but this is unlike anything I've come across before, angels. I can feel it—there are a lot of answers just waiting for us in there."

We're all silent for a moment as we take in the news. This is the biggest development Labyrinth has had in years—maybe ever. My palm us sweating on Lucie's thigh, the tension in the room high, and I pull my hand away to wipe it on my jeans and then lean my arm across the back of her chair instead.

Reed's the first to speak. And I have to give the guy cred-it—we're standing on the edge of a potential cliff, and he re-alizes that what Arden needs right now is some serious kudos. "Arden, you fucking genius!" he crows. He's sitting beside Ar-den, and he leans over and grabs his arm, a wide grin splitting his face. "You are the lynchpin of this whole operation. You're about to blow this whole thing wide open. I can feel it!"

Reed's enthusiasm is contagious, and an excited buzz rushes around the room. Lucie jumps up from her chair and runs around to give Arden a hug from behind his neck, nearly chok-ing him out as she squeezes him. "Arden, you're amazing," she says, genuine awe in her voice.

Around the room, the mood lifts—now it's a celebration, and we're all talking at once, eager, asking if we can help Arden even while knowing there's absolutely nothing none of us tech-dense fools can do, except for maybe Reed as the other Intermediary in the room, and even he's in a tech league well below Arden. After Arden assures us there's nothing we can do but that he'll let us know as soon as he gets any further information, Reed calls us all back to attention. "Anyone else got anything worth sharing this meeting?" he asks. None of us expects anyone to say anything, and so we all look with surprise as Saffi pipes up.

"Actually, I do."

It's comical how all our heads bounce like a synchronized choreography to her as we wonder what she could possibly add of value after having only just returned from her first Assignment, and this being her first Labyrinth meeting. She stands, rounds her chair and grips the back of it as she leans forward and surveys us. Lucie reclines into me to get a better view of her friend, and so I pull her into my lap. She lets out a small squeak but no one bats an eye, everyone having done the obvious math on us.

Saffi takes a deep breath. She tells us how she's been researching on her own ever since Lucie's halo severance, that Reed has been providing her access to databases even while off Retreat grounds. Lucie and some of the others inhale sharply at that revelation—we all know how strictly forbidden that is. I honestly didn't even realize it was possible to access databases on Zircon outside of our Retreats. But Saffi barges past the topic and says she's noticed how little information we have about the Realm of Shadows, how little we know about Gehenna, and how embarrassingly little we know of how devils work.

"Why does this matter?" asks another Guardian, the one who'd smiled at us when we'd entered—Mello. She and I had fooled around a bit when we'd first Arrived, but it hadn't been anything more than a bit of fun. Lucie stiffens in my arms when she speaks, and I wonder if she knows—and if she does, I'll have to assure her it had been a long time ago, and nothing more than a physical arrangement. I hadn't seen Mello since we had each taken our first Assignments, but the way she had just given me a friendly smile and nothing more when Lucie and I had walked in hand-in-hand told me she didn't have any hang-ups about us either.

"Well, it got me wondering," Saffi says. "If they're literally our bound enemies, shouldn't we have more information about them? Wouldn't we do a better job if we knew the intricacies about how they work? What systems they have? What their realm is like?"

"It's the opposite of ours—it's cold, always dark. They have 666 year terms and don't have specific Assignments like we do. What more information would help?" Reed asks, his tone curious, not disparaging.

Crossing her arms, she looks at him in disbelief. "Reed, that's literally all we know about them. We spend a century learning about humans, learning about angels, learning about the systems they each use and how they work together and against each other. You're telling me you don't find it strange that we don't study the Realm of Shadows as more than a footnote in Dek?"

Mello and the other Guardians are nodding thoughtfully, but Saffi's not done. "Also, these cracks that are happening with Guardianship systems; what if that's not exclusive to our realm? We keep talking about how we're experiencing these faults and malfunctions, how we're responsible for solving it and maintaining the balance of all the realms—and Gehenna might even be behind it all. But what if this is even bigger than that? What if the Realm of Shadows is cracking, too? We know nothing about them, which means we know nothing about how their realm functions or if their systems aren't operating as they should be, either."

"Ooooh," says Mello, leaning forward and tenting her hands like an evil villain from human movies. "You're right. It's hard to solve a puzzle with only half the pieces."

I nod along with everyone else, but wonder how we could possibly hope to change the situation, to magically find the knowledge we seem to have never had about our antithesis realm. But I don't have to wonder for long, as Saffi puts her hands on the back of her chair and leans forward again, her eyes sparking with intensity. "Exactly. So I intend to find the rest of the pieces."

"How?" asks Lucie as she stares up at her friend.

Saffi's face breaks into a massive grin as she looks at each of us in turn before revealing her master plan.

"I'm going to catch a devil."

EPILOGUE

TERRA

I exist, and yet I don't exist.

I am everything, and yet I am nothing.
I feel every emotion, and yet I am numb.
I reach, with the arms that aren't there, and I feel nothing. With the eyes I don't have, I am blinded by white, by a lack of anything, by pure, complete emptiness. I scream, with the mouth that isn't there, and it makes no sound—but I hear something in return, with ears that don't exist. A faint echo of a life lived, and I strain toward it. The silence is whole and encompassing, but it has an edge, and with the body I don't have, I try to move toward it.

I go nowhere.
I am nowhere.

Connect

Sign up for Dani Avelle's newsletter for exclusive access to exciting book news, special offers, and bonus content!

daniavelle.com

ACKNOWLEDGMENTS

I loved writing and designing this book—so much so that I can't count the number of times I'd immerse myself in the process to the point of forgetting to eat or drink or unfurl my body from its cramped position under my laptop. Or rather, I would have, were it not for the plates of food and glasses of diet soda and water that would appear as if by magic on my desk at intermittent points throughout the day. Turns out, my Guardian angel takes the form of my husband, who takes his job very seriously, always ensuring I'm fueled, hydrated, and taking time to move. David, thank you for always believing in me.

Thank you to my first readers David, Merle ("who dis again?"), and Laura for your invaluable feedback on book one. Your genuine enthusiasm, support, and thoughtful critiques and notes gave me the perspective I needed to adjust pacing, fill in plot holes, maintain consistency, and just generally make this book so much better than I could have on my own.

To all the friends who have supported me along the way and continue to push me forward—thank you a million times over.

And to you, the reader—my eternal gratitude for picking up this book. As an indie author, I'm beyond appreciative that you chose to spend time in the Realms of Almega, and I hope you'll join me there again as the series continues!